Making

The

List

Vee Tuohy

ISBN: 978-1-7361213-0-6 (E Book)
ISBN: 978-1-7361213-1-3 (Paperback)
ISBN: 978-1-7361213-2-0 (Audio Book)

Any references to historical events, real people, or real places are used fictitiously. Names, characters, and places are products of the author's imagination.

First printing edition 2020.

Kilbarron West
401 E 8th Street #214209
Sioux Falls, SD, 57103

To the Marines

Thank You.

Thank you for raising me into who I have become.

Thank You for being the blood thirsty Animals, Grass growing Lunatics, Cold blooded Savages, And the cold hearted War Machines that you are.

Chapter 1

Cloudy days were Sherman's favorite days. But not overcast cloudy days—big, fluffy sunny day cloudy days. He looked up at the blue sky, flat on his back atop the playground jungle gym behind the local elementary school. The playground jungle gym was shaped like a giant pirate ship, with crows' nests to climb and slides protruding from the many platforms and levels of the ship. It even had a rope bridge that swayed and bounced when run across.

Today he laid on the top platform in front of the highest slide, looking up at the slowly moving clouds and tricking his mind into seeing different shapes as the cumulus clouds slowly morphed and moved across the sky. He liked to come here when school was out because it was usually quiet and had great views of the sky. The breeze was slight, the air clean and crisp, and the warmth from the sun was just right. This was his thinking place, and today he was thinking about life. How good life was, how bad life was, and how tough life was.

Sherman was the youngest of six from what was once a middle-class family. Dad was a career police officer and Mom was a loving and caring stay-at-home mother, but they had divorced when he was less than a year old. Now, he was the youngest of six children from a single-parent home. He'd been so young when the divorce happened that he didn't have any memories of a family life before it. The only memories were those of a broken home, some siblings living on their own, some living with friends, some living with Dad, and a few at home with Mom.

Everyone came and went as they wanted. As a child, Sherman didn't hold any responsibility; often taken care of by older siblings, his opportunities to learn and grow were stunted by siblings slapping his hands away and doing it for him. There were weekend visitations of fake family times that consisted of trips to the beach and walks to get ice cream. The feeling was that this was being done almost out of requirement and less out of the desire to take someone to the beach or get ice cream. The questions were always, "What's Mom up to, how's she doing? She treating you well?" "Is Dad still dating that girl? Does he ask about me?" These were asked in a manner closer to detective work rather than casual conversation. Sherman always had to be on his toes, calculating his answers to ensure the sandbox remained cordial. "Dad's great, he asked how you are doing, he hopes all is well." "Mom's good, I'm not sure who she's dating, but she told me to tell you she said 'Hi' and hopes all is well."

He was roundaboutly raised with a sense of unimportance and a level of unsureness about his own goals or abilities. Everyone made decisions for him and did things for him. He never had an opportunity to learn from his own mistakes or try to do things on his own. He loved challenges and to be challenged, he yearned for responsibility and a sense of leadership. It seemed that he was always jealous of leaders and those above him that had the opportunities to make decisions and feel powerful.

Sherman's childhood was a troubled one, yet it was also one that didn't take much effort on his part. Being the youngest child, he was content in his upbringing and always felt love from his family, neighbors, friends, and educators. He smiled often and was known as a class clown or someone who always had the ability to make others laugh. But there was something missing; the desire to be important, understood, or appreciated? Sherman never truly liked himself. Not in the sense that he would ever harm himself; it was more a feeling of jealousy of others—or maybe not others, but more what others had, or who they were. There was always something that he just couldn't put his finger on. It seemed like every detail about himself was just one more thing not to like.

Take his name, for instance—*Sherman.* What kind of name is Sherman? He knew it had family history, but it was always a name he felt he had to defend. No one really cared that he got the name from his grandfather, who was a very influential man in the community. He quite honestly was tired of telling the story to try and explain the name. What most bothered him about the name was that his siblings had these great, interchangeable names, ones that could be used differently in different scenarios to complete the person they were at any given time. Names like William, Kimberly, Jennifer, Victoria or Christine. These names can take many forms. As a kid you can be known as Billy, Kimmy, Jenny, Vicky or Chrissy. As an adult, Jen, Kim, Bill, or Chris; and of course, as an adult in a professional setting, you could also be known by your extended birth name. "Ladies and gentlemen, please give a warm round of applause for our CEO Victoria, or William, Jennifer, Christine, or Kimberly."

"Sherman" wasn't the name of a CEO, a kid, an adolescent, nor could it be used as a catchy nickname, but it sure did rhyme with a lot of things, like Sherman the Vermin and Squirmin' Sherman. He actually didn't mind the name calling and the teasing. He knew he was better than that and he usually wasn't the butt of jokes or torment from other kids. Every kid has their turn to be picked on, but for some reason, his was usually short-lived and consisted of a few rhyming names. Maybe he'd have his hat stolen off his head and be forced to play monkey in the middle to get it back, but for the most part it was harmless, childish fun.

As a teenager in high school, Sherman was always a dirty kid with long hair and a sheepish charm about him.

Very good-looking, almost handsome, but in a dirty kind of outsiders/greasers type of way. He wasn't this way to be fashionable, or to make a statement; it was more out of necessity, a product of his environment. Without having a washing machine or a clothes dryer in his house, the hassle of dragging all of his clothes to the laundromat blocks away from his mother's house seemed to be more annoying and troublesome than just wearing dirty clothes. At the time, no one seemed to care—it was almost acceptable or cool. So it worked. Showers in themselves were an ordeal; often pipes would freeze during the cold New York winters and cause the water lines to be capped or repaired. The oil burner with no oil didn't make warm water, so cold water was the only option. Showers were more frequent during the summer, as the natural temperature of the water was more bearable than in the dead of winter. When showers needed to be taken, they were taken, but they weren't an activity taken out of leisure or to unwind. Showers were strictly business, and often needed to be taken within ninety seconds before the fear of freezing to death or getting hypothermia started to set in. (Probably those things weren't actually likely to happen, but the mind is a very powerful thing when cold water is being doused on it.)

Sherman grew up in poor surroundings, but never felt any less than his friends who were also relatively poor, as they all had the same struggles. He also never felt any less than his friends who were better off. They too had their own struggles and issues to be dealt with, as kids growing up in the same neighborhoods he did. Sherman would categorize his childhood as challenging, but rewarding in the ways of building character and obtaining tools to better his ability to adapt to most situations.

Sherman was very intelligent, smarter than many expected. His intelligence surprised people because it didn't match his appearance. He was an extremely smart kid, but fought against anyone knowing it. Cool kids weren't smart, and his desire to be known as "cool" was far greater than his desire to be known as smart. Cool kids were dirtbags, jerks, tough, unforgiving. Knowing this, Sherman often acted out to get attention or to prove to others that he was just as badass as his siblings or friends and not to be messed with.

Sherman had a stature and build that often drew comments of, "Are you okay?" "You need to eat more," and "You poor thing, your parents must be starving you." Deathly skinny most of his life, he never saw himself in the same light and often took peoples' comments as insults or reminders that maybe there was something more wrong with him than he knew. He knew he was thin, but was he really THAT thin? He started to realize from all the comments that he was.

Despite being deathly skinny, as some would categorize him, Sherman had an affinity for sports. He always loved to play any sport, and was good at them. He didn't recall ever being taught how to play any sport, just started going out there and playing. There was never anyone to tell him "This is how you hold and throw a football," or "Make sure you snap your wrist when you release the basketball." Sports were always something he just did. Sherman would mimic what everyone else was doing, and picked up what to do rather quickly. Basketball was his favorite. He could often be found by himself at the outside basketball court down by the elementary school, taking shots for hours and pretending to be different professional players in his head as he darted around the court, recreating shots he had watched on television. Scottie Pippen #33 of the Chicago Bulls was always his favorite. "He was the real reason Michael Jordan was so successful. Without Scottie, there is no Michael," he would argue, often debating the point with anyone who thought different. Handball was the other sport he loved. Although he was strangely good in football, soccer, baseball, and many other sports, he enjoyed ones he was able to play by himself or in a one-on-one scenario against others.

Basketball and handball were sports he was able to play and get better at on his own when no one else was watching. At the same time, he wanted to be able to play against others to prove his ability, his strength, and his power, to understand how well all of his preparation went into the strongest of desires to show this single person that he is as strong, as talented, or just better than they are in this one little aspect of his life. It wasn't being competitive, it was much more than that. It was a need for validation, validation that he belonged on the same court as others, or validation of something he didn't understand. It wasn't enough to be good—he had to be strong, he had to be powerful, he had to win. At all times, at all costs. Losing was just proving to him and all those around him what he already knew—that he wasn't good enough, he wasn't strong enough, he was just a weak, skinny kid who couldn't win.

Luckily, with his build and prowess for challenging sports, he also maintained a very strong will and had a witty, sharp ability to quickly come back in any verbal altercation, often making points with his mouth before he was able to realize with his brain that he made them. It was a valuable defensive mechanism that he used to deflect people from asking questions about him, his family, his education, or his life that he didn't want to answer. He believed that being in command of the conversation, all conversations, at all times, gave him the power to decide what would and would not be discussed, and often he would cut people off mid-sentence or talk over them to make his point, assuring that the conversation continued in the direction or on the topic he desired.

As the days of summer passed, Sherman often found himself at one of his favorite places—on the basketball court.

He practiced there alone, not in hopes to one day make the high school team, or in hopes to earn a college scholarship, but out of pure desire and love for the game and to just get better. It wasn't unusual for strangers to approach him while taking shots on the basketball court. Some just wanted to shoot around and get better just like him, while others would often ask if he wanted to play a game of one-on-one. Sherman often accepted the challenges, and the challengers were often out of their league.

One particular challenger would change everything. He strolled onto the court in a matching pants-and-long-sleeves warm-up outfit. He seemed to be fit, but not overly. He asked Sherman to play one-on-one, and the game started. It was a hard-fought game, one that was a great deal more physical than it needed to be for a random pick-up game of one-on-one. The need to win was evident on both sides. The battle of strengths and the point to prove who would leave the court the victor and who would leave the court a defeated competitor were on the line. There were places on the court where Sherman knew he could not miss; they were his "sweet spots." The challenger wasn't letting him get to these spots, as if he already knew the outcome if allowed. The game was close, but Sherman ultimately beat his challenger by the slimmest of margins.

As they sat after the game, the challenger stated, "I have a wager for you. If I beat you in this next game, you come down to my office and hear what I have to say about the United States Marine Corps."

"And if I win?" Sherman replied.

"You will have earned the opportunity to come down to my office and hear what I have to say about the United States Marine Corps."

"How about if I win, the big bad Marine is banished from my court forever and you vow never to step foot or play on this court again." With a handshake, a smirk, and a piercing look in his eyes, the Marine said, "Deal."

The second game was just as much of a battle as the first; still a great deal more physical than it needed to be, and ultimately the skill and will of the Marine proved to be too much to overcome. Sherman knew there was no reason to feel ashamed in this defeat. It truly could have gone either way.

"So, when is best for you to come down and talk?" the Marine asked.

"I have no desire to join the military, but I lost, so I will be a man of my word and come down to your office to hear what you have to say—but I am not joining," Sherman replied.

"Sounds fair. How about next week? At ten? Okay, see you then." And with that, he jumped in his car and drove off. Not much thought was made about the pending meeting after that. Days went by, and the memory of the appointment that he was supposed to attend never crossed Sherman's mind. The week came and went, then two weeks, three weeks, and four.

Sherman was at the basketball court again when the car with the Marine pulled up. The Marine jumped out of his car and made his way towards Sherman like he was shot out of a cannon. "So I guess you're not a man of your word! What happened?" the Marine barked. Sherman had honestly forgotten all about the meeting. He'd had every intention to go since he lost the bet, but somehow it just slipped his mind. Few seventeen-year-olds had appointments or meetings that they needed to attend on any given day or week, so to miss an appointment booked an entire week away was not out of the realm of possibility.

"I told you I wasn't joining anything."

"Yes, you did say that, but you also said that since you lost you would hear what I had to say."

"Okay, fine, I will hear what you have to say, so say it . . . I'm all ears."

"It's not that easy. Jump in, and we can go to my office now."

"Okay, fine, whatever . . . " Sherman quipped. And with that, he jumped in to the Marine's car and they drove off.

The meeting was exactly what he thought it was going to be—a lot of sales pushes, a lot of questions like "What are you going to do with your life?" and a whole lot of, "Are you ready to be a Marine?" The recruiter placed a handful of colorful plastic cards on the table, each not much bigger than a credit card. Each card had a distinct color, and they were engraved in large, white letters with words and phrases such as "Travel and Adventure", "Pride of Belonging", "Challenge", and "Leadership and Management Skills." There were a dozen or so tags in total, and Sherman was asked to choose the three that meant the most to him and which he would most like to achieve in life. After choosing the cards that read "Courage, Poise, and Self-Confidence", "Self-Reliance, Self-Direction, and Self-Discipline", and "Pride of Belonging", the recruiter modeled his sales pitch to these specific points to ensure the topics that were most important to Sherman were discussed.

After what seemed like an eternity, with many points made to which Sherman could agree, each inquiry still ended with the same response: "No." The recruiter continued the sales pitch as if he didn't hear the many times Sherman had told him he wasn't interested, that he didn't desire to be a Marine, and that he had no interest in the information the recruiter was providing Sherman. The meeting finished with Sherman watching a few videos of Marines storming beaches with patriotic music playing in the background, as well as a video of past senators, celebrities, and influential people in the country who were once Marines. Sherman didn't recognize any of them other than

Captain Kangaroo, which gave him quite the chuckle when he saw him pop up onto the screen. After the meeting was over, he was given some stickers, brochures, and a firm handshake with a promise to stay in touch.

Life went on. The rest of the summer consisted of a lot of hanging out in front of the convenience store, playing basketball and handball, and getting involved with a great deal of things Sherman had no business getting involved in. The days, nights, and dates all seemed to blend into each other, with nothing productive or positive being accomplished. There was always a desire to be successful in the back of Sherman's mind, but also a realization that if he continued to let the days slip away as they were, things were not going to change. Sherman and his friends spoke often about future plans, but they all seemed to be far-fetched ideas that they didn't have any means or abilities to achieve. They would talk about opening businesses together, driving fast cars, and buying boats. All sounded like good ideas at the time, and they all spoke in a convincing enough way that the others somewhat believed and bought into these ideas.

Sherman bounced from job to job. Landscaping was one of the first, and it involved long hard days, lots of sweating in the heat and riding in the back of an open truck. Manual labor was not something Sherman enjoyed doing, but there weren't many opportunities to do much else. The summer days were spent riding in a truck, sweating and landscaping, and the nights loitering and hanging out with friends in front of the convenience store. He hung out so often in front of convenience store that one day he decided to apply for a job. At least he would be in air conditioning and able to escape the brutal summer heat. Much to his surprise, and the surprise of his friends, he got the job. His days now consisted of making coffee, sweeping floors, and restocking shelves. He didn't mind this job as much, as he was out of the heat and not sweating.

It was towards the end of the summer one day when he went into work and there was a long line of customers. He walked over the empty register and said to one of the customers, "I can help who's next." Sherman had never used the register before, but was pretty sure he could figure it out. After all, he was just trying to ensure the customers didn't wait too long. He had good intentions. The co-worker on the other register did not see it that way. He quickly turned to Sherman and said, "What are you doing?" and in front of what seemed like an entire store full of customers, he began to berate Sherman as if he was breaking some cardinal rule. "You are not a cashier, you are a coffee bitch. You make coffee, sweep floors, and clean. Get away from the cash register and go stand in the corner or something."

Sherman felt humiliated. He could see customers putting their heads down as if they felt awkward making eye contact with him. Some snickered as he just stood there with what he could only imagine was a look of embarrassment and shame. He could have walked right out and quit that minute, but didn't. He walked from behind the counter and through the door that led him behind the huge cooler that housed all the beer and drinks. He was fuming, but knew there wasn't much he could do. One thing he did know was that he wasn't going to be here much longer, but where he would go from here, he wasn't entirely sure.

As the days went by, he started looking at his surroundings and wonder, *Why not? Why not be a Marine? What do I have going on for me here? I could use a good swift kick in my ass to straighten me out. It would get me out of here and give me a clean slate to start over. If nothing else, it is an opportunity. How many opportunities do I have? At least if I was to join, I would be a Marine, and how crazy does that sound, that I have the opportunity to become a Marine? As the recruiter said, I can earn something that less than 1% of the population has ever earned—the title of a United States Marine. I kind of like the sound of that.* With that, his mind was made up. He was going to be a Marine.

He went into the recruiter's office, and before he could even cross the plane of the door the recruiter said, "I knew you would be back. What can I do for you?" Sherman explained his situation and how he was ready to make the leap to become a Marine. The recruiter explained to him that it wasn't as easy as getting on a bus, and he wasn't even sure if Sherman had the ability to become a Marine. Sherman wasn't sure if the recruiter was using reverse psychology or if he really meant it. During the first meeting, he was almost begging Sherman to become a Marine. In this meeting it almost seemed like he was trying to convince him not to be a Marine.

Whatever the recruiter was doing, it worked. Sherman went in there to take the steps to one day be sent to Marine Corps boot camp, and by the time the second meeting with the recruiter was over, Sherman had a date to leave. It was the upcoming Thursday morning. Being that today was Monday, Sherman left the office a little dazed and confused. "I will be at your house at 0330," the recruiter had said. "Be ready to leave with the list of stuff I gave you and the documents on the paper I provided you." Sherman wasn't sure what time 0330 was, but assumed it was early in the morning.

Sherman was wrong—it turned out that 0330 wasn't in the morning at all, it was in the middle of the night. He awoke to his recruiter standing over his bed. "Let's go. Time to change your life," he said. The travel was a blur. He vaguely remembered a car ride, a few plane flights, and then ending up on a bus. In between all of this he occasionally ran into someone who yelled and screamed and asked for forms of ID or documents, or some combination of both. Each time, he wasn't sure if this was where the boot camp part of the adventure would start. The recruiter started yelling at him that morning while he was in bed. Then there were more Marines yelling at him at the airport, on the bus, in the plane, in a car, and then the yelling didn't stop for about   four   months.

Chapter 2

When he left his house that morning, it was dark; when the bus finally came to a halt at the front gates of Parris Island South Carolina, it was also dark, but about 20 hours later. The bus had arrived on gravel road in the middle of nowhere lined with trees. The gate and Marine guards seemed to show up out of nowhere. The bus door opened and one of the guards entered. He barked some orders, walked up and down the aisle of the bus, and quickly disembarked. All thirty or so of us on the bus were confused as to what was said, or if there was something we should do. The bus door closed and the driver said, "Bend down and put your head between your legs, place your hands on the back of your head with your fingers interlaced, and stay there until you are told to move from that position."

I later found out that all entrants onto the island were required to do that so they wouldn't have an idea of what direction or type of terrain there was, preventing any attempt to escape. The drive was long—or maybe not *long*, but it seemed like forever. Probably around twenty minutes or so, in reality. When the bus stopped and the air brakes let out a release of air, it was almost like the bus was making a sigh of relief for all of its occupants.

We are finally here, Sherman thought. Then bus doors opened and all hell broke loose. Two Marines entered the bus, both dressed in the most neat and orderly uniforms that could have been constructed for a human body. Their bodies looked toned and their jaws were chiseled, their drill instructor hats (the ones that looked like what Smokey Bear wears in the "only you can prevent forest fires" commercials) sat sloped forward on their heads, the brims just low enough to nearly cover their eyes and brows, but with enough showing to scare the soul out of any human being. One was more verbal than the other, and he stated clearly, as if he was talking to a preschool or kindergarten class: "Get off of my bus and get your little nasty civilian feet on the yellow foot prints."

Sherman and everyone else departed the bus like a herd of wildebeests trying to avoid being the lone weak animal in the herd as the hungry lions lunge at their heels, moving with sheer panic and the fear of the unknown in their actions. The bus bottlenecked at the entrance, and it seemed as if the bus participants were willing to trample and injure those in front of them to please the now yelling and screaming drill instructors. The yellow footprints were painted on the ground four in a row and twelve deep. As the bus participants started taking their positions on the footprints, a platoon of individuals began to form in what seemed like a somewhat organized group. They lined up the group by height order, the tallest in the front and the shortest in the rear. Sherman found himself in the front row, one of the head recruits in the group. He had a feeling of being first in line, a position of importance. It was the first time he could remember feeling that those behind him were somewhat jealous of the position he was in. He liked that feeling; he liked having what others wanted. This would be a common theme in the coming thirteen weeks, as this would be the way the platoon would get into a formation whenever they had to travel somewhere in a marching formation or when accountability was going to be taken. Sherman being in front would become a common theme, and he liked it.

The drill instructors—seven of them he vaguely remembered—were buzzing around the platoon, knocking baseball caps off of recruits' heads, screaming and yelling, bumping chest with some and demanding that they didn't look at them by barking, "Get your nasty little eyeballs off of me." It seemed that the drill instructors always spoke in a manner that made you actually have to think about what they just said. Sherman had to make a conscious effort to decipher the directions before responding to actually ensure he understood what was said. He often thought, *Why didn't the drill instructor just say, don't look at me?*

Everything had a special Marine name or term: a pen was an ink stick, a flashlight was a moonbeam, the bathroom was the head, upstairs was top side, left was port, right was starboard, and everything belonged to the drill instructors. EVERYTHING. "Get off of MY bus, get on MY yellow footprints, and get into MY building." It was as if a second language had to be learned. And of course, every sentence, question, statement, or response had to begin and end with the word "Sir."

The platoon went from the yellow footprints down an outside hallway to a room that was the only one open this late at night and had a glow that lay from the room onto the outside concrete of the hallway they were currently marching down. The platoon was eerily silent as the drill instructors continued to ensure the recruits stayed in place, in line, and quiet.

At times you could hear the drill instructors cracking jokes about a recruit that might have something out of the ordinary about them. One recruit had long hair, and the drill instructor commented, "Excuse me sweetheart, you might be in the wrong place, the female battalion is down the street." While forming a single file line down the concrete hallway, recruits were heading through the light and into the room at the head of the line. It seemed the recruits were going into the room as fast as they were coming out. They would be coming out confused, unsure where to go next, and looking rather shocked. Some came out with their hands on their newly bald head, almost in disbelief that they were currently without their hair. As Sherman came closer to the doorway, his anxiety started to build. He knew he was going to have his longer-than-normal hair cut off, and he was okay with it; he was just a little apprehensive about how it was happening so fast. When his time came, he entered through the light of the door to find about six barber chairs in a row, manned by men that all must have been in their sixties. These men were barber shop experts. As Sherman waited for the next available chair, one of the drill instructors grabbed his arm and screamed, "Yoo-hoo, how about getting in the chair behind you? HELLO, hurry the hell up." As Sherman tried to process the direction, the drill instructor pulled him closer and raised his voice at a rate that seemed to make his veins in his neck want to burst and his eyes on the verge of popping out of his skull. "What the hell is your name, boy?" the drill instructor asked. "Sherman," was the response. It was as if the drill instructor just got slapped in the face by Sherman. The theatrics jumped to a level that Sherman had never seen before; it was like this grown man was throwing a temper tantrum, but in full control of his body and mind at the same time. The drill instructor started clinching his teeth, biting his lip, and seemed to be dancing or skipping in place as if he was about to blast off into orbit. "Hello Sherman, how about you address me as Sir, how about the first word and the last word out of your mouth is Sir. Let's try this, again Sherman." His voice remained low and calm, almost in a whisper, an eerie and creepy whisper that was actually scarier than when he was yelling and screaming. Sherman didn't like the whisper, he was definitely afraid of the whisper.

"Sir, my name is Sherman, Sir," he replied.

"No, louder!" the drill instructor demanded.

"SIR, MY NAME IS SHERMAN, SIR."

"Hell no, louder Sherman!"

Sherman responded as loud as he could. He could feel the back of his throat instantly start to go dry; blood seemed to rush to his temples, and immediately he got lightheaded and feared he might pass out. The drill instructor's voice returned to the shrill shriek that it once was. "What are you, 6'0" Sherman? Eighty pounds soaking wet with bricks in your pockets, Sherman? Where did you get your name Sherman? Are you a tank Sherman? Yeah Sherman, you are a God damned Sherman tank, Sherman. We are going to turn you into a killing machine. The Sherman Tank." The drill instructor turned to the other drill instructors and barked, "Hey drill instructors, meet Recruit Tank, from now on, this is recruit Tank." The other drill instructors attempted to hide their desire to laugh at the joke but it was obvious they got quite the kick out of the idea to give a wiry skinny kid with what seems to be no strength the nickname of one of the greatest war machines that have ever been created, the Sherman Tank. It was like the guys at the gym who find the biggest muscle bound guy and nickname him

Tiny because they believe it to be a witty and ironic nickname. The drill instructor turned to the platoon and demanded, "Everyone say hello Recruit Tank." The platoon screamed at the top of their lungs almost in unison, and at a level that seemed to echo throughout the damp night sky: "Hello Recruit Tank!"

The minute the buzzing blade touched his scalp, Sherman knew he would be changed forever. He had always had long hair, or longer than a most boys his age; he drew some sort of strength from having long hair. It was a way to hide his face, hide his personality, and hide him. People often commented on the length of his hair or the fact that he looked like a girl before they took the time to actually look at his face or understand who he was, and he liked that, he didn't mind that at all. If he was able to grow a beard at a young age to hide himself even more, he would have. His transformation was at the beginning stages, and it started with the hair.

As the weeks of boot camp went on, Sherman found that he was not as strong as most but held his own in many departments. He was good at obstacle courses, learning the policies and procedures, and stayed relatively in the good graces of the drill instructors. He particularly enjoyed the two weeks he spent at the rifle range. He wasn't much of a gun enthusiast and had never been hunting growing up. He could think of only a few times he had actually ever handled a gun before and couldn't recollect actually ever firing one. But for some reason when he aimed this rifle, the M16 A2 service rifle, it was very easy for him, and the ability to shoot well came naturally to him. Many of the other recruits had difficulty aiming the rifle or having issues with the recoil of the rifle once it was fired, but Sherman didn't have any of those issues. He seemed to basically zone out, become one with his breathing, the rifle, and put the projectile rounds on the target where he was aiming them. It was almost second-nature; when it came to firing a rifle, he was good at it.

The firing requirements were from 200, 300, and 500 yards away from a target. He particularly enjoyed shooting from the furthest distance, which gave him a greater sense of accomplishment because it was so far away. There were three levels of qualified shooters. The lowest was a marksmanship shooter, then was sharpshooter, and finally an expert. After qualification day, Sherman walked away an expert. Only eleven of the seventy-two recruits in his platoon were able to shoot on the expert level, and he was very proud that he was one of them.

Graduation day was here, and up until this moment in his life, he couldn't have thought about being so proud of something he had accomplished: the thirteen weeks of what he considered hell, death, and destruction. His old self was put to rest and a new man was born, a new warrior with a new outlook on life. A positive outlook, one that would give him the opportunity to make the life and be the person he wanted to be. It was a feeling of wiping the slate clean, as though all that had been done up to this point, the good, the bad, and the ugly, had been erased, and he was reborn.

The platoon marched across the parade deck just like the many platoons that came before them. All of the pomp and circumstance came with the event. There were speeches from retired Generals, reiterating the importance in the decisions they had made as young men and women and discussions about how they would continue to protect this nation. After a relatively short goodbye following the ceremony, a quick trip back to the barracks to pick up his belongings, and a collection of a few phone numbers from those in the platoon he wanted to keep in contact with, Tank was ready to get off the island and start the next evolution of this journey. He made his way to the bus station and boarded a bus that would take him to the airport and across the country to attend his military occupational school. He was sent to 29 Palms California to attend the communications school to learn how to be a field wireman. He wasn't exactly sure what this entailed, but knew that he would be better off being whatever this was rather than staying back home and working odd jobs at convenience stores or landscaping during the summer months.

As an eighteen-year-old fresh out of boot camp and his military occupational school, Sherman became a field wireman. The job basically consisted of running wires and cables long distances so the communications department could connect radios and other forms of communications to outposts and office spaces. It wasn't an overly exciting job, and was one that was labor intensive the first few days, then relatively boring for the duration of the exercise or operation unless something broke or needed to be re-run. Sherman enjoyed the job. He found it valuable for what it was, but also found it to be boring. The wireman were often loaned out to other units to do jobs that the other Marines in those units were too busy to do. Once the initial infrastructure was set up, the wireman's job was basically done, so instead of sitting around they were given to the other units to go on patrols, help with the mess duty, or perform maintenance around the camp. This was usually the life of a wireman unless a cable line was accidentally run over by a passing tracked vehicle and got chewed up, or the cable wasn't weatherproofed properly and water got into one of the connections.

Many wiremen prayed for a line to go down while they were performing other tasks with other units. There were few happier moments than when someone would enter the mess tent and state, "We need a wireman to track down a line, we can't get in contact with post three." The wiremen would fall over each other to volunteer; tracking lines and running cables is what they preferred to do, and everyone hated mess duty.

It was 0630 in the morning, and the Marines were just completing the daily physical training session of a long run. Some were in front of the communications shop, hands on their knees, bent over, attempting to get as much air back into their lungs as possible. Others stood gasping for air, hands on the back of their heads, hoping this would work. The Marines slowly started to return to the formation so accountability could be had and the Marines could return to the barracks to shower, change, and get ready for the work day. But today, the Sergeant stood in front of the platoon and said, "Marines, we never know when we will be called to defend the constitution of the United States and take on tasks for this great country. We will be getting deployed to Somalia on a humanitarian mission to protect the interest of this great country and her allies. Ensure you have what you need to be successful in our mission and there will be more to follow." With that, the formation was dismissed and they were sent off to get ready for work.

Sherman was relatively new to the platoon and knew some but not all in the unit. A Marine walking back to the barracks next to Sherman within the hundred or so Marines who were just dismissed out of the formation stated, "What's Somalia?" Some Marines overheard the young Marine's inquiry and it started an uneducated debate. "It's in South

America," one stated. "No it isn't, it's an island off of Egypt," one responded. "Wouldn't Egypt have to be on the water to have an island?" another said. "Egypt isn't one the water?" "Wait, where is Egypt, isn't it in the Arabian gulf next to Iran and Saudi Arabia?" No one seemed to know where Somalia was, or for that matter, where Egypt was either. The mood Sherman gathered was that no one seemed to care. Maybe except for him; Sherman cared, and his insides were churning with the thought of going to Somalia.

After showering and getting ready for work, Sherman walked to the mess hall to have breakfast. Sherman often ate by himself, not because he didn't have any friends or because he was not liked, but more because he didn't like having to be social when he just wanted to go to the mess hall, eat, and leave. Many of the Marines in his unit were on the same schedule, and he would often run into them as he went from place to place. Today was no different. Sherman entered the mess hall to a packed house. The line for food was long and almost every table was taken. Sherman got his food and looked for some Marines about to leave so he could take their table.

He sat and started to eat when another Marine said, "Can I sit here?"

"Sure," Sherman responded. The Marine sat across from him, Sherman recognized him from the shop, but was not sure who he was. The Marine introduced himself as

Mikey and Sherman introduced himself as Tank. The name had started to stick through boot camp and communications school, almost to the point that it was second nature to hear someone say the name and he would respond. No one ever questioned why that was his name, that is just what people continued to call him. Mikey was no different. The other Marine had earned his name because he was one of the Marines people would dare to eat things. He would drink an entire bottle of Tabasco sauce for the money the Marines around him could scrape together, five bucks from one guy, three from another. Depending on the crowd, Mikey could pull fifty or sixty bucks for an eating stunt. After a few food stunts, the Marines would say "Mikey likes it!" It was a phrase from an old Life cereal commercial that pitted three brothers together, where two of them would put a bowl of cereal in front of the youngest brother Mikey to see if he would eat it. Seeing that "Mikey liked it", the brothers would then partake in eating the cereal. The real name of the Mikey that was sitting with Tank at the chow hall was Thomas, but Sherman was unaware of this information; he always knew him just as Mikey.

The Marines all stood in a formation, their combat gear laid out in front of them, everything exactly in the same spot on the outlaid field blanket. The Gunnery Sergeant stood on the one story building's roof and barked out commands. "Everyone hold up your canteens!" He would then scan the formation, ensuring everyone was holding two canteens. "Okay, put them down, everyone pick up your sleeping bag." The same drill; he scanned the area to ensure everyone was holding up a sleeping bag and sic'd the Sergeants on anyone who did not have the item and took note that they would have it before the end of the day. Marines were directed to go out in town after the formation and purchase any items they were missing, and to report back to the Sergeants that they received the items. The inspection continued, ensuring the Marines had every item they were going to need to be successful on the upcoming deployment. "Hold up five green tee shirts in your left hand and five sets of boot socks in your right" the Gunny continued to shout. The reality of what was happening was starting to sink in, not only to Sherman but to the Marines around him. It was being labeled as a humanitarian operation, some handing out of soccer balls, ensuring deliveries of rice and grain got to their intended recipients without warlords intercepting the aid workers' convoys and stealing all of the supplies. Although on paper it sounded like it was going to be a walk in the park, Sherman maintained a certain level of apprehension and fear that it couldn't be that easy.

Chapter 3

The Marines spent a few days in travel. First, they arrived at a local Air Force base and waited around for a few days for their flight. They spent those days sleeping in the hangar bay in sleeping bags, on cots, or on the concrete floor, depending on where in the hangar the unit was sleeping. The flight was long and grueling; it seemed as though the Marines would fly for ten hours and then land somewhere, wait five hours, and then get back on the plane to fly for another ten hours. By the time the plane landed in Somalia, the Marines were tired, hungry, and pissed off. Just the combination of feelings you wanted for a plane load of Marines to be handing out soccer balls to children.

From the moment Sherman stepped out of the plane, he knew he was somewhere different. The air was extremely dry, and the heat seemed to punch him right in the chest. The back of his throat instantly became dry and he found it hard to blink his eyes as it seemed that the fluids in his eyes were drying up. Within minutes, Sherman went from a scorching heat to being covered from head to toe in sweat. There was a line of huge military vehicles waiting to take the Marines to their bases. Some vehicles were going to a secure base just outside of Mogadishu, others to the port of

Kismayo, and a few others that Sherman did not concern himself with because he knew he was going to the base outside of Mogadishu, so where the others were going was not overly important to him. His senses were at a heightened and alert status. He feared and distrusted everyone in this country he seemed to come across, unfairly and without cause. There were many Somali people working at the airport, helping to load and unload planes, driving vehicles, directing planes. Sherman was very uncomfortable and wasn't sure if any of these people could be trusted. Did they want the Marines here? Were they plotting against them? Were they looking for their opportunity to attack Marines when they were least suspecting it? If so, they weren't going to catch Sherman unprepared. He kept his eye on everyone he came across and surveyed everything and everyone. Every detail was important. Was there someone wearing a long-sleeved shirt? And if so, why? Why in 115 degree weather would someone be wearing a long-sleeved shirt? That was an instant reason for Sherman to be skeptical and watch with a closer eye. Every detail had to be analyzed, every detail had to be mentally logged and stored, every detail had to be understood for what it was. It was a mentally exhausting ritual, but one Sherman believed needed to be done.

The Marines loaded the vehicles. They had their weapons, their packs, and a few odds and ends that they took possession of that the Gunny told them to carry: a wooden box with all of the commanding officers' office supplies, a box with recreational equipment for the Marines, a few golf clubs, a football, frisbees, anything the First Sergeant could bring to break up the monotony of what the Marines would be doing. These boxes were heavy, and often took a few Marines to carry them.

The drive from the airport to the camp was about an hour. The vehicles traveled down mostly dirt roads that were lined with makeshift shacks that sold odds and ends. Some sold what seemed to be fresh picked fruits, others sold meats that were hung from the front of the shack, covered in flies that were often shooed away by a storekeeper with a makeshift fly swatter made from a palm tree branch. The poverty was rampant; the children were dirty and had protruding bellies brought on from malnutrition. Every time the vehicles stopped, either for traffic reasons or because Marines who would be stationed at other camps were at their final destination, the mood shifted, and it shifted quickly. All conversation stopped, Marines held their weapons a little tighter, and paid a little closer attention as to what was going on. The fear was obvious, but what they feared was not. There were a few sporadic rifles being carried by locals, old, rusty beat-up rifles, nothing that the Marines feared on any level. But they were still rifles being carried by civilians that made Sherman once again uncomfortable. He was unsure who the good guys were and who the bad guys were. He had always assumed from the movies that there would be a clear indication as to who the bad guys were, and someone toting around a weapon in a civilian setting was usually a pretty good indication of that.

They arrived at the base camp and immediately the mindset shifted to setting up the camp. Marines ran in every direction, some pulling giant tents off of trucks, others starting to unload boxes, and the officers all gathered and made their way to the base commander's tent to get briefed on their unit's individual mission. The heat was intense and the work was tough. There was a lot of digging, pounding in huge metal tent stakes, and lifting of heavy cross beams to construct the large 30-40 man tents that would house the unit. The heat made these tasks greatly more difficult, every movement or effort feeling like it was doubled from the heat. The sun felt like it was just overhead, and it was unrelenting.

The Marines worked for hours, and soon the camp was coming along nicely. The tents were set and the Marines finally had the opportunity to set up their individual spots within them. Each Marine had about four feet of space that consisted of a foldout cot. There wasn't much room, but it was enough. The Marines didn't spend much time in the tent other than to sleep. Sherman was one of the lucky ones and had the first cot on the left side of the tent. He only had a bunk mate on one side of his cot, instead of both. This gave him a few feet more room on the other side of his cot because he didn't have to share it with another Marine. However, he later found that because he was also right next to the entrance of the tent, he was constantly being woken up by Marines coming in at all hours of the night from patrols. He would have preferred having a spot in the middle of the tent away from the entrance, even if it meant having another bunk mate.

The Marine next to him was in the Battalion with him, but was someone he didn't know. He introduced himself as Bean and Sherman introduced himself as Tank. Bean was from Jersey, Philly, or somewhere in Pennsylvania. He remembered having the conversation about them both being from the Northeast, he just wasn't sure where. They saw each other often, but were always busy and didn't have a lot of time to converse and get to know each other well. There wasn't a great deal of time that was not being used by filling sandbags to make bunkers, or on patrol.

Sherman spent most of his time on patrol; he was a wireman, and knew how to run cables throughout the camp, but he was also categorized as a communicator. Communicators were also radio operators and data collectors. Sherman couldn't use a radio and didn't have to gather data, but since he fell under the umbrella of communicator, he was often tasked with being a radio operator on patrols. He learned the job relatively quickly, and the parts of the job he did not know, he learned on the fly.

Sherman would run into Bean occasionally when walking through the camp, but usually missed him in the tent because while one was out patrolling the other was sleeping. Bean worked the day shift and Sherman was often patrolling at night, so their sleeping patterns were opposite. When they did get together, they spent most of the time discussing how they lived back home, things they missed, and plans for what they'd do when they left the Marine Corps—of becoming firemen, police officers, or going back to school. The two Marines got along relatively well and enjoyed each other's company; they spent time with small talk when they did cross paths and discussed their patrols and the misery of their situations. A bond was forming, but it wasn't a strong bond—just a bond that was stronger than some others in the tent because they were bunk mates.

Patrols consisted of vehicles driving throughout the town and ensuring that the locals weren't being harassed by the warlords. The Marines kept the warlords out of the populated areas the best they could, and the focus of the Marines was to show that they were there to help the local community. Every convoy departed the camp with children's toys, small packets of food, and pamphlets written in the local language of Swahili, informing the locals that the

Marines were there to help them. Sherman always had a strange feeling, a feeling he thought was like impending death. He didn't fear dying, but he feared the process of dying, the time frame between getting shot and actually dying. He didn't like to fly, but it wasn't because he was afraid of dying in a plane, it was because he was afraid of the time frame in between the plane no longer working and the plane hitting the ground. He had the continuous feeling that something bad was going to happen and it sat in the pit of his stomach twenty-four hours a day.

Sherman was making his way across the camp one day, coming from the chow tent, when he ran into Bean. "Hey Tank, we need a communicator for a patrol later, want to take a ride?"

Sherman didn't want to, but didn't want to come across as weak. "Sure, what time?" he responded.

"In about an hour, meet us at the patrol departure site at let's say 1300." And with that, they parted ways. Sherman made his way to the tent and started to grab the stuff he needed for the patrol, a few snacks, a change of clothes just in case, and some extra water. He also grabbed the patrol essential items, extra ammunition, spare batteries for the radio, a makeshift long-range antenna, and a few handheld radios. He swung his patrol pack onto his back, hung the radio pack over his shoulder, and made his way to the departure point.

Before every patrol, the patrol participants all gathered in front of the vehicle convoy and were provided with the relevant information about the patrol. The brief usually consisted of the route the patrol was going to run, a time check to make sure everyone's watches were on the same exact time, pertinent information about threats, and how the patrol was to handle an ambush or an attack. Sherman listened for the time check and usually what radio frequency he was to transmit off of, but the rest of the stuff seemed to be information for people other than himself. The brief took about thirty minutes, and Sherman always thought it could go quicker; no one wanted to be standing out here with all of this gear on, sweating their asses off and listening to all of this stuff. *Let's just get going,* he thought to himself. The Marines started to mount the vehicles, and he was directed to a vehicle Bean was standing in the back of. It was a vehicle that had four seats and then a flat area in the back, almost like a four-seat pickup truck with a bed. Bean was standing in the bed of the vehicle manning a mounted M249 squad automatic weapon. There were senior Marines buzzing around the convoy asking last-minute questions.

"Tank, what's your blood type?"

"A positive," he replied.

"Jones, are you a right-handed or left-handed shooter?" Left-handed, Jones replied. "Well then you need to be on the other side of the vehicle."

Last-minute adjustments were made, and the patrol started to slowly move forward. At this point Sherman had been on probably fifty patrols, and they seemed to go out like clockwork, every hour on the hour like a bus schedule. They drove through the streets, poverty around every turn, and when the vehicles slowed down kids would swarm the vehicles. "American, give me food, give me water," the children would beg, their hands laid over the other as if they were at church prepared to receive communion. Many Marines would save the candy or treats they received from their MREs, or bring an extra apple or orange from the chow tent on patrol to give to the kids. Water bottles were handed out, and some Marines would give the kids full MREs, knowing they were only issued three a day.

The streets seemed to always be lined with people, a very eclectic bunch. Some would be wearing old sports teams shirts, or shirts with brand names like Nike or Adidas. Others would wear a suit jacket over a t-shirt matched with a pair of shorts. Many of the people carried weapons. Sherman was now seeing larger caliber weapons than he did before. He was especially on edge when he saw people carrying AK-47 assault rifles. He assumed those were the same people that were probably shooting at them on night patrols.

There was no rhyme or reason to some of the ensembles that were seen during a patrol. Mostly that was because these people weren't using these clothes as a fashion statement. Rather, they were wearing them for their original intention, to cover their bodies, and it did not matter if they matched or what the writing may have been on the clothing. Many people wore the traditional African clothes, men in long flowing skirt-like garments and women wrapped in brightly colored garb with matching headscarves piled high on their heads. It was entertaining to see what was around the next bend and witness all of the interesting things taking place in the crowd, but it was mentally exhausting trying to take in all of these details and process them into possible threats. It seemed as if things were always on fire, piles of trash cooking over open fires and just random fires burning. The air smelled rank and musty. It smelled of rotting meat and smoke, dirty clothes, and body odor. The details were hard enough to process without the many distractions, but adding in the wafts of smoke that was driven through or patrolled through with the changes of smells and thickness of smoke made the processing much harder.

Sherman's responsibility was to call into the base regarding any out-of-the-ordinary issues or pass information back to the base from any other vehicles in the patrol. He would send a situation report or a radio check every fifteen minutes to let the base know if they were running behind in the patrol, or if they were still on track to return to the camp as expected. Sherman sat in the front passenger side of the vehicle, the radio at his feet, the coiled radio cable running up between his legs and clipped to the outside of his flak jacket for easy access. His weapon rested on the door, sticking out of the open window facing the people on the lined streets as the patrol went by. As the vehicles slowed down again, Sherman noticed that among the people lined on the streets was a man who stood on the backside of a tree, slightly hidden from view of the convoy. As the convoy moved, so did the man, edging further behind the tree to escape detection. He was wearing a red and black jacket, one that almost looked like something a lumberjack would wear, and the front pockets were weighted down with heavy contents.

The people lining the street often tried to find small pockets of shade to stand or sit under. Every inch of shade was usually taken up by someone, but with this man it was different. This man stayed on the sunny side of the tree, directly in the sunlight, which blared down on him as the convoy slowly passed. Sherman continued to take note of the people on the side of the road, but he kept coming back to this one—this one continued not to make sense. He was now directly next to the man behind the tree. As the vehicle started to pass, Sherman could see he had a rifle. The man looked directly at Sherman as though he was waiting for the perfect moment, and then their eyes locked and stayed locked. Time slowed almost to a standstill, and Sherman felt the impending doom unfold as though he was causing it to happen. The man never broke eye contact with Sherman, and as he started to raise his weapon, he seemed to start firing before the weapon was fully raised.

Sherman watched as if he was a spectator. The sound of the gunfire instantly dulled his hearing, and he could only hear muffled sounds and ringing, lots of ringing. The side of the vehicle jumped and crashed with every AK-47 round that impacted it. Sherman tried to scream, or did scream, or was screaming—he wasn't sure if he was screaming or what he was screaming, but could feel the tearing of the back of his throat as if he was screaming at the top of his lungs. He was locked in and focused on the man. Sherman swung his weapon around towards the side of the vehicle to aim in on the attacker, but his weapon crashed into the door frame before he could point it at the man. Sherman was a right-handed shooter and he was unable to get the weapon in his shoulder and still reach the angle toward the man at the same time. The Somali man continued to fire. This time he was just a few feet away from the vehicle, and he didn't let up on the trigger.

The crowd was running in different directions and gunfire now seemed to be coming from every direction. It seemed as if every Marine on the convoy was now shooting. Sherman had to get out of the vehicle. He bumped the door open with his shoulder and jumped out., He was close enough to the man to grab him now; they were just a few week away from each other. As Sherman put a foot on the ground, the radio handset still connected to his flak jacket and the radio on the floor of the vehicle, the radio jumped and pulled tight on his flak jacket, causing him to be jerked back towards the vehicle. He landed on his butt.

Sherman aimed his weapon towards the man while still on the ground. He saw the man's knee through his sights as he pulled the trigger and fired on the man, then his waist as he continued to fire, his stomach, his chest. Still firing, Sherman continued to raise his weapon as he aimed at the man's face. The Somali man was looking directly at him, just as he was a few minutes ago while leaning against the tree. Sherman pulled the trigger for the final time and the man instantly no longer looked like a man. The body crumbled to the floor in a pile.

Sherman unhooked the radio handset from his flak jacket. "Guardian, Guardian, this is Tarawa mobile, we have been ambushed," he barked into the handset, unable to tell if anyone was able to hear him over the background sound of gunfire and yelling. His ears were still ringing, and there was a heaviness in his head that made it difficult to know if they could hear him. He thought he was screaming, but was unsure. He turned to evaluate the situation and saw two of the front vehicles in a heated gun fight. Dropping the handset, he started to make his way up the vehicle convoy when he was stopped by a Sergeant and told, "Get the fuck back to your vehicle, they are fine up there, we are getting the fuck out of here." Sherman turned and ran back to the vehicle, and as he reached for the door handle he saw the side of the vehicle riddled with bullets. He thought to himself, *Luckily no one was sitting behind me.*

That's when he noticed Bean, kicking and writhing in the back of the vehicle. He was moving like he was screaming, but Sherman couldn't hear him. Sherman could feel his face start to get warm and the blood rush from his head. He jumped into the back of the vehicle. Bean was covered with blood and laying in a pool of blood that was running down the back of the truck and off of the tailgate. Sherman didn't know where to start; the vehicle started moving, and the blood seemed to be coming from everywhere, but he noticed a lot coming from Bean's chest. Sherman took his hand and placed it on the wound; his hand seemed to sink into his chest, as if his fist was being inserted into a huge hole. Sherman felt the urge to vomit, but couldn't.

The vehicle's speed quickened and they were both being covered with the dirt and dust from the high rate of speed traveling on a dirt road. Sherman, with his fist still in Bean's chest, laid himself on Bean's body, attempting to cover the wounds and keep them from being covered in dirt and dust. With Sherman's chest on Beans chest, his head next to his head, he could feel him crying, feel him sobbing, but could not hear him. Time seemed to slow down; it was as if nothing was going on outside of that vehicle, and he and Bean were the only people in the universe. He could feel the pressure of Bean's body against his hand as it pressed against and into his wound, he could feel the rush of fluids pass through and around his hand, his heart beating on his hand as if it was a bass drum. The soundless screaming continued; he could tell Bean was screaming by the rush of air that passed onto Sherman's face and skin. The vibrations of the soundless screams were as intense as the sounds of gunfire around him. Things were bad, very bad.

With the stickiness of the blood, the warmth of both of their tears as they ran down their faces and met where their heads touched, he didn't know who was holding who harder; both grasped each other hard enough that they would later leave bruises where the fingers gripped each other's skin. Sherman laid like that until he felt someone forcefully pulled him off of Bean. He wasn't sure who it was or if it was still a threat, it all was happening so fast. They were back at the base and unloading Bean from the vehicle. Sherman laid in the back of the truck, laying in Bean's blood, people standing above him and screaming at him, "Are you hit, are you hurt?" He could read the guy's lips and could tell he was trying to find out if he was hurt, but he wasn't concerned about himself. *Get away from me, go help Bean,* he thought.

He actually might have screamed it. He actually wasn't sure if he was hit; he didn't feel any pain, and he hoped he wasn't shot, but he actually didn't care. He felt the emotions overtake his whole body as he laid there in the back of the vehicle, covered in blood, staring up at the blue sky and crying, the cumulus clouds shifting and changing shape as he felt the breeze on his face and the sun's warmth on his skin. He could feel the tears run down the side of his face, hot and stinging, as if his emotions were supposed to be painful. These emotions didn't come from a physical pain or an emotional pain, but an internal and eternal pain. This wasn't regular crying; this was something different. This was a kind of crying that would forever change Sherman, and he knew it.

Chapter 4

As a young Marine, Sherman deployed to many places throughout the world. The years of being in the Corps started to stack up. 3 years turned into 10 years which quickly became 20 years. He truly enjoyed being in the Marine Corps, and didn't understand why some people would prefer to only do four years and then go back home. Sherman took advantage of all the training the Marines offered and he became very good at much of it. He was a natural at shooting a weapon and took a special liking to hand-to-hand combat. He must have trained thousands of hours in hand-to-hand combat throughout the years.

There was a shift in Sherman as the training became more advanced, and with it came a higher degree of equipment and leadership. The shift was one of self-importance and an understanding about his place in the world, and these grew in importance the more levels of training he went through and the more types of training he did. Patrolling, survival and evasion schools, Spie rigging. Sherman volunteered for everything. Any opportunity that came up to train, Sherman wanted to do it. He was very proficient in his craft and felt that knowledge was power. The more he knew about explosives, tracking people, guerrilla warfare, and the psychology of war, the more he felt he could be placed in any situation and not only survive, but strive. He was a difference maker.

The war seemed to come out of nowhere. After the towers fell in New York, everyone knew something was going to happen, but Iraq wasn't the first place any of the Marines thought about. Sherman certainly didn't think of it. After deploying to Somalia and Eritrea throughout his career, he knew he was capable of whatever the heat and desert had to throw at him. He was ready. Sherman was no longer a young Marine. He wasn't old, but he was older and wiser. He was a leader, and people treated him as one. As someone that makes the rules and decides the outcomes. The strength in his words and actions had weight.

Sherman spent many hours in the desert on security patrols, leading military vehicles from Baghdad International Airport to the outlying military bases. Many of these vehicles had resupplies of ammunition or food. Some were filled with mail. On almost every convoy Sherman found himself in either a firefight, or had insurgents take pot shots at the convoy from a far-off distance. Much too far for Sherman or the other Marines to return fire and still have an accurate ability to hit their targets. So, they would just have to watch the insurgents shoot at them, take cover, make sure no one got injured, and keep the convoy moving. It was a very frustrating time for Sherman.

Sherman spent two years in Iraq. During his second tour he participated in Operation Phantom Fury, where he led his Marines to assist taking the city of Fallujah back from insurgents. The battle was long, hard, and bloody, and Sherman lost a lot of friends and Marines during that battle. The days and nights were long and hot. There were times when the missions were almost unbearable. To help himself mentally get through the trying times, Sherman continued to tell himself, *That which does not kill you only makes you stronger.* He was led to all of these places in his life for a reason. He was meant to protect those who could not protect themselves. He was here to rid the world of bad people, and God put him in all of these scenarios to build him into who he wanted him to be, and to complete the missions that he wanted him to achieve. War was tough, but Sherman was tougher. Or so he would like to think. Millions of dollars were spent making Sherman into the Marine he was, and it all paid off during his combat tours and tours in other hostile areas of the world.

The years of being a Marine were weighing on Sherman and his time to step aside and let the younger Marines take over was upon him. Sherman had mixed feelings about it. He was highly trained, and loved the grind and misery of the training and putting what he'd trained for into practical application on the battlefield, but the excitement of new challenges was almost more than he could bear. He loved the Marine Corps and everything that he'd gained from it, but the pending retirement made him feel like he was taking on a whole new challenge in his life.

Sherman was nonetheless highly motivated to take on this next chapter of his life with as much drive and determination as the last 21 years of the Marine Corps. He was drawn to the thought of not having to be always spot on, overly disciplined, almost like having the ability to make mistakes without dire consequences. The belief that he could be a little more laid back, a little more civilian-like. The thought made him almost giddy. He knew that with his abilities and credentials, he would be able to run circles around any and all coworkers he may have on the civilian side of life, and that challenge motivated him greatly. The thought of retirement came almost with a sense of relief, like someone had released a pressure valve and all the pent-up hostility was being released, like the pressurized air being released from an air compressor. The more pressurized air that was being released as the days went on, the more excited and motivated he became. It was almost too much to control, too much to bear. The future was going to be incredible and he could not wait to get there. No more guns, no more mistakes that could cause someone to die, no more bad. Only good.

As it turned out, civilian life wasn't what Sherman thought it would be. It wasn't long after retiring that the "good life" of being a civilian started to weigh on him, and Sherman quickly realized that he wasn't a civilian and probably never would be. He was and always would be a Marine. He realized that life would never be the same. He was unable to cope with the feeling of being a nobody, slogging through the days without any feeling of accomplishment or purpose. *There has to be more,* he thought, *there has to be a purpose, there has to be a sign or a path that needs to be followed. Is this really it, is this life, is this what he is meant to be? Protecting those who cannot protect themselves is the only way I will ever be able to function in the world and still feel like a productive member of society.*

Sherman snapped out of his daydream. He and the other managers sat in the break room in between training sessions, the greasy pizza ordered by the company sitting on the table, oil soaking into the cardboard that contained it. His fellow managers were each their own level of sickly, obese, and unmotivated. As usual, the conversation turned to the normal bitching and complaining that he had become accustomed to hearing while working there for the last few years. Everybody's failures were someone else's fault, no accountability for one's own actions. "As soon as I find another job, I am going to quit this shithole and tell the boss to stick this job up his ass," one coworker said, as another chimed in, "Yeah, I have a second interview with another company later this month, and if all turns out I will be making more money, working less hours, and will not have to put up with this shit any longer." Sherman just smiled, because he has heard this same spiel for months from the same people. It was at a point now that it was almost comical.

"So, when are you leaving?" a coworker asked Sherman as their attention turned to him. He was always the odd man out; he didn't take lunch breaks with the other guys because they always went to fast food restaurants, and he was meticulous about his body and the types of foods he ate. He didn't enjoy eating fast food, and didn't drink alcohol or even soda. Everyone was always amazed that a retired Marine would have accepted a job like this. "Me, leaving? I don't know." The only reason he accepted this position at this company was because he doubted himself and his ability to be successful on the civilian side of life. He knew that after 21 years, Marines listened to him because they had to. He could punish them in ways that were less than desirable, and that kept everyone in line. But that wasn't the case on the civilian side of things. On this side of things, he would have to prove his leadership ability by earning the trust of his employees and proving them that he could lead. That didn't take long; he was an outstanding leader both in the Corps and as a civilian. He garnered many medals in the Corps and many awards and accolades as a civilian leader.

"We didn't think you would have been around as long as you have."

"Me neither. I'm not sure if this is the place for me, I'm just trying to find my niche out here in the civilian world," Sherman replied.

"What are you good at?" his coworker asked.

"Good at? Locating, closing with, and destroying the enemy," he stated with a slight smile.

"Well, I'm not sure if there are too many of those opportunities out here for that," another fellow employee mused from across the break room.

"Yeah I know, tell me about it . . . I wish I could go back to killing people for a living, I was so good at it," he said as the room broke into laughter. The boss popped his head in the doorway of the break room. "Lunch is over everyone, back to the training room . . ."

Sherman contemplated the question his coworker had asked about what Sherman was good at in life. He was pretty much good at everything, but he was only highly trained and great at one thing. That one thing was killing people. He spent the afternoon daydreaming about it. He couldn't shake the thought. On the ride home from work, he thought to himself, although it was said mostly in jest, *In reality, is the possibility there? If I could be a great leader in the military and on the civilian side of life, why can't I be a great protector on both sides? I have all the attributes, I was pretty good at it in the military, why let all of the training go to waste?*

He had always heard the discussions about making yourself marketable when leaving the military. He was a communicator, so he had some basic skills in the field, but he was by no means an expert. He had a solid foundation in leadership and could be a valuable asset to most businesses or corporations, but that wasn't his main skill. Marines are highly trained to ensure they can complete one basic task, which is to kill the enemy with efficiency and accuracy. Marines have many jobs in the Corps. There are mechanics, administrative clerks, communicators, artillerymen, infantrymen, and many other job titles. But the one thing the Marine Corps preached since the first day is that every Marine is a rifleman. It does not matter what your job field was; you must be able to shoot a rifle, perform hand-to-hand combat, know and understand different weapons systems, plan and utilize tactics and military schemes, and of course, be able to destroy the enemy by all means necessary. So why not market that skill? There had to be a place that he could put that skill to work—maybe become a cop, or a government contractor?

The possibilities were there, but Sherman would probably run into the same issue he was meeting now. How many cops or government contractors truly put these skills to use on a daily basis? Not many, he would presume. Why spent 90% of his time with the political correctness and menial parts of those jobs when he could put 100% into protecting those who couldn't protect themselves? He loved that phrase, he loved that job description, and he loved the possibilities. With every ride along at work, every meeting, every situation that was life shattering and of the utmost importance, he felt like he was wasting away. He felt like his razor-sharp edge was dulling. He knew it was only a matter of time before his edge would be gone. If he was going to make this happen, it had to be now.

Make a decision. What is it going to be? Yes or no? His inner voice demanded an answer.

What am I talking about? Sherman asked himself. *Am I truly considering killing people? Does this really make any sense?*

Of course it does, is this natural selection? He argued with the voice in his head that was trying to make sense of all of this. *Maybe it is God's way of telling me this needs to be done.*

As the days passed, he had trouble sleeping. He would wake up in the middle of the night with ideas and ways to make this work, places he could hide after the deeds had been done, different scenarios that would ensure he wasn't caught. The plans seem to be falling into place. He was unable to shake the feeling that this was a sign, that this was somehow what he was meant to do, and the urges just continued to get stronger. *Okay, I will give it one week,* he thought to himself. *If I receive a real sign, something a little more concrete, one way or the other, I will take it as my cue to proceed or change my plans.*

Two days passed, and Sherman received no sign, no symbol or overwhelming shift to tell him one way or the other if this was a good plan or not. Three days passed, then four, and five. He still had trouble sleeping, and it seemed like all signs were pointing towards carrying this out. His dreams were getting crisper with greater detail and ways his plan could be achieved without getting caught. He dreamt of the perfect extermination; he referred to it as an "extermination" rather than committing a crime because that is how it was portrayed to him in his dreams. He didn't like to think of it as a crime, because he truly did not see it that way. He was doing something that rightfully needed to be done, but with the political correctness and the softer side of the world these days, bad people slipped through the cracks, and it was his responsibility to catch them as they fell through. Or at least, that is what he was starting to believe.

On the sixth day, he sat at his computer looking at the normal websites he frequented, the sports websites, celebrity gossip, and national news sites. While on one of the celebrity news websites, an ad on the side of the screen caught his eye, sandwiched in between the advertisements reading, "Lose weight with the newest weight loss pill just recently approved by the FDA!" and "Build muscle without working out!" This also looked like an advertisement, but maybe it was less of an advertisement and more of an informative site, with the glaring headline, "Are there sex offenders living in your neighborhood?" along with a picture of a blurred-out adult male's face and a small map with flashing red dots on it. The headline was bright and yellow, flashing like a Las Vegas Casino street light trying to tempt you to enter their establishment.

For such a horrible product, the marketing of the advertisement was almost celebratory. *What type of article or advertisement is this?* Sherman thought. He was hesitant to click on it because he didn't want the pedophile search to be on his computer, but could not resist finding out the answer to the question. Could there really be pedophiles or sex offenders living in his area? Would that even be allowed? Don't they ship those types of people off somewhere? They aren't allowed to just blend back into the normal population, are they?

He clicked on the advertisement and a website popped up for him to input his information. Street name, town, zip code, state, and for some reason country, as if the prior information wasn't enough for the site to have a basic idea of what country that address was in. He put in the address in of a local Chinese restaurant, as he once again didn't want his information being logged on this website.

Sherman was stunned when the results were returned. The site showed a map of his neighborhood, and he noticed the local elementary school, the main crossroads, but what caught him off guard were all the red dots on the map. They were everywhere. It looked as if the map was suffering from a bad case of the measles or chickenpox. Each red dot represented an address, a name, and an offense. He clicked on a random red dot on the outskirts of town to find that this individual was a twenty-year-old male that was arrested for statutory rape against a seventeen-year-old female. The details of the arrest weren't listed, but the fact that he would now have to register as a sex offender for the rest of his life was listed along with the last time he registered. *Does he deserve to die?* Sherman wondered. *Is this the one? Could this be a case where a father called the cops on his daughter's boyfriend, or something? There is probably more to this story than what is listed.* It didn't say "rape", it was listed as "statutory rape".

Not sure of what consisted of the statutory part, Sherman clicked on another red dot. This one was a little bit further from the center of town, a forty-eight-year-old male convicted twice of lewd acts with a minor. Just the word "lewd" by itself made Sherman's stomach turn. This was a two-time offender, thus he obviously didn't learn from the first time. He wondered if this guy was still doing this type of stuff but wasn't getting caught. He continued searching through the red dots. A man getting caught for flashing in the park, a female teacher fondling a male student, a father molesting his stepchild, and the list of disgusting individuals went on and on. He spent hours on this site, reading every disgusting detail he could, all the while thinking, *How are these people not being beat up every day? How are they hiding in plain sight? How is this fair to their victims that have to live every day knowing that this person took from them and are able to walk the streets like nothing happened?*

The nights became more and more sleepless, and Sherman knew what he had to do, but was still unsure as to how to do it. The killing part would be easy. The details of getting away with it would be greatly more difficult. Everywhere he went, the anger of the word *lewd* would follow him. Lewd? Against a child? A defenseless child. His stomach churned; he could not and would not let this one word escape his mind. This had to be the sign, this has to be God's way of letting him know that this was okay. This is what he was destined to do. After all, today was the seventh day. He said he would give it one week and wait for a sign, and this was day seven.

There seemed to be more signs pointing towards going through with this then there were signs saying that he shouldn't. There was still a part of Sherman that thought this was wrong, wrong enough to not want to go to jail, but at the same time the urge was so strong that he knew there was a balance that had to be achieved. *Do your due diligence, research, and plan, and if it all makes sense, maybe the punishment would be worth the crime.* Would he be willing to spend the rest of his life in jail? *Yes,* he thought, *to free the mind of a child and let them feel like they can live the rest of their life without worrying that the monster they have nightmares about still exists, yes, a million times.* It would be worth it even just for one child. So then let it be done. His mind was made up. The research must begin.

Chapter 5

Sherman knew that from this point forward, everything that he did or didn't do could be traced back to him if he were to get caught. He had to be very careful about what actions he took from here on out, and how he could best keep them from being traced back to him. He couldn't just go around shooting people, could he? No, he couldn't, it had to be better planned than that. It had to be quiet, just like in the Corps. The closer you can get, and the quieter it can be, the better.

This person doesn't know who I am or what my intentions are, so I could technically get close to him without him even knowing, Sherman thought. He returned to the website to get all the information he could. Name, address, offense, every last detail he thought he may need. This would be the last time he would visit this website, as to not trigger a pattern on his computer. He wrote all the information down on a small napkin and placed it into the front pocket of his jeans. Knowing he might have to look inconspicuous, he decided to change into jogging clothes so it wouldn't be odd for someone to see him running. He transferred the napkin into a small zippered pocket on the inside of the waistband of his jogging shorts, designed for maybe a key or an identification card. He decided that, instead of taking his car and possibly being seen by someone that might write down his license plate number, he would travel by bus.

Sherman walked to the local bus stop and took a bus to the outskirts of town. Still dusk, he decided to scope out the house of the offender. As he approached the address, located on a long street lined with big shade trees and perfectly manicured front yards, it was a picture perfect suburb. One would never assume a sex offender lived on this block. The house was a two-story house with a two-car garage, a Buick in the driveway with a license plate frame that stated "I would rather be golfing" in words surrounding the plate. *Oh, you think you are a chameleon,* Sherman thought to himself, *blending into the crowd, being sneaky and assuming everyone is unaware of your deeds?*

There wasn't a great deal of information for Sherman to retrieve just by walking by the house. As he was passing by the house, a man walked out of it and headed towards the Buick. He was an unassuming man, about six feet tall; a little on the heavier side, but not fat, just a little out of shape but not thin. He wore Dockers and a three-button shirt with a logo on the upper left side, but he couldn't read the writing. Just as he walked past the house, the Buick left the driveway and drove up the street. *Should I be taking notes? Should I be writing the time down?* Sherman thought. *Should I be tracking every time he leaves his house and returns? Why didn't I bring my car?* He wondered. *I could have followed him. What a dumb plan, what am I going to do? Walk by his house every day and gather more information? This is stupid,* he thought. *Maybe I should just forget about the whole thing.*

His level of frustration peaked because he seemed to be letting the plan get away from him, he was losing control of the situation. He had to regroup, rethink his plan and solidify what his next steps were going to be. He was just going to leave and regroup. He decided to walk the five or so miles back to his house instead of taking the bus. The walk gave him plenty of time to rethink his plan. *Maybe I should just forget the whole thing,* Sherman thought. But then, the thoughts of the child popped into his head. Was she a little blond girl? A brunette? He wondered. Maybe she liked to sing, or dance, maybe she had a dog that she loved with all of her heart, and maybe she would never be able to trust a man again. *This motherfucker!* his inner voice screamed. The anger inside him kept building as the thoughts of the little girl swarmed his mind.

I have to do this, I have to plan this right, I have to stop being scared and protect this little girl, Sherman thought. He didn't know the girl, but every time he thought about this man, this vision of this girl came to mind. She was starting to take on a reality, she was starting to be someone he felt he knew and needed to protect. He didn't sleep much that night. This couldn't continue to drag on; he wouldn't be able to handle many more nights like this. He was so driven to get this done, it had to happen, and had to happen soon.

But what if he was forgiven? What if God forgave this man for his actions? What if the man had repented for his sins? *Repented? Who cares, the damage is done,* he argued with himself. But what if he is a changed man? How long ago did this even happen? He pulled out his napkin to check for a date the offense or offenses took place, but there was no date for the offenses. *So what?* he thought again, *maybe it happened two weeks ago,* he continued to argue.

Okay, I will track him again. If he has repented or gives me the impression he has repented, I will leave him alone; if not, I will continue, he agreed, as if having a conversation with someone else.

A week passed. Sherman had been studying the moon patterns to know when there would be the least amount of moonlight. Tonight was set to be the perfect night for stalking his prey. He tracked the moonlight, and tonight would be the only night of the month with no moon. It was the perfect setup to move around at night with little to no visible light that might allow him to be spotted by neighbors.

The plan was for him to go back to the house tonight, do a little snooping around and see if he could spot anything out of the ordinary. He would then take whatever information he could find and add that to the information he gathered the last time he went to the house. The final addition to the research would be to then follow the man in his car to have a better understanding of where he went during the day and see if he was living his life as a changed man, or someone who continued in his disgusting ways.

As night fell, Sherman decided he would once again walk the five miles instead of possibly being spotted on the bus, in case he was caught or in case people would be questioned. The walk wasn't a bad walk; the weather was nice and he didn't have many items to carry. He wore a backpack and dressed in jeans and a long-sleeved tee shirt. The backpack contained a handheld GPS device he received while in the military, which he brought along in case he got lost or had to run away for any reason. He also carried a small package of baby wipes in case he had to wipe his fingerprints off of something; a few snacks, because it may be a long night; and a couple of pairs of rubber surgical gloves, in case he needed to confiscate any items while there. He purposely did not carry any weapons, because this was just going to be an information gathering mission. His cover would be completely blown if he was caught carrying a weapon.

As he approached the neighborhood, the plan was to walk down the next block over so he could try and get a view of the back of the house. He had already scoped out the front of the house, so now the back was next. As he walked down the block behind the house, Sherman could see the peak of the house through the trees and knew he was just about behind the house. He couldn't get a good view, as the house behind it was in the way and there were trees separating the houses. For a second he thought of walking up the driveway of the house behind it and jumping over the fence, but was worried someone might see him.

As he decided what he should do, he noticed the house next door to this one had a "for sale" sign on the front lawn. He continued to walk past the house and to the next corner. He figured the plan now was to walk back to the house with the for sale sign, see if there was anyone living in the house, and if not, walk up the driveway into the backyard and then reevaluate the situation. As he walked up the driveway, he didn't see any lights on in the house and it seemed to have been empty for a while. He made his way into the backyard and ensured that he stayed within the shadows of the tall bushes that lined the area. He was able to make it to the corner of the property that shared the same corner as the house he wanted to stake out. There was a wooden fence on his side and a smaller chain link fence on the other property.

Sherman didn't want to make any noise, so he climbed the wooden fence very slowly, then jumped from the wooden fence over the chain link fence and into the yard while trying to keep the lowest silhouette as possible to not alert any of the neighbors. As he remained in the shadows of the yard, he could see the light from the house shining into areas of the backyard. He inched closer to the house once again not to alert anyone or anything; after all, he had no idea if there was a dog, an alarm, any light sensors in the yard that once tripped, would turn on a spotlight. He paused for a minute under a large bush in the yard next to a tin shed. His heart was racing and he couldn't catch his breath. *Calm down,* he thought to himself, *relax, you haven't done anything yet, just scope the place out and let's get the hell out of here.* After calming himself down, he agreed with himself, *let's get this done, and get out of here. Take some notes, and get going.*

He moved closer to the house to get the best vantage point he could. His heart racing, the anxiety of what he was doing started to sink in. He felt that rush of being on a patrol where he had no idea what could happen. It was the civilian equivalent of playing hide and go seek when the person who is "it" walks by the spot you're hiding in, and all you can do is hold your breath and hope they don't see you. Sherman had a clear vantage point to see through all of the windows in the back of the house; it looked like a kitchen window, a window for a dining room that led into a living room area, and a larger living room window. The glow of the television flickered and lit up the wall behind the couch, which faced the yard. The television must have been on the wall facing the couch, as he couldn't see the television; he was only able to see the reflection of the television lighting up the entire living room.

Inch closer, he thought. He did so as if he was a sniper trying to get the optimal position, slowly crawling on his belly, moving at the speed of a snail. Then he spotted movement in the far left window, the kitchen window. He could tell someone was moving, but could not see who it was. He froze; he lowered his face down onto the concrete of the back patio. As he waited to see if he was compromised, a part of him was afraid to lift his head from the concrete of the back patio in fear that there would be someone looking back at him. *This is insane,* he thought. Every time he doubted if he should continue, the image of the young child popped into his head. This time in a free flowing summer dress, her hair in ponytails as she skipped around with her friends clutching a Barbie doll, and then quickly the fear and anxiety dissipated.

He tracked the person from the kitchen through the dining room and then lost him at that point; his prey didn't seem to go as far as the living room or couch. He had to get a better vantage point, so he once again slowly crawled to his right so he could see the area between the dining room and living room windows. As he continued to move between huge ceramic planters and towards a big stainless steel barbecue, he was able to see that the man he saw walking down the driveway a few days before was sitting at what seemed to be a small desk-like area. He could see the glow of the laptop on his face as a small screen image reflected off his silver-rimmed glasses.

Now what? he thought. *Am I just going to sit here and watch him? What a stupid plan,* he said to himself. *No, it is not stupid, what is he looking at on the computer?* he argued with himself. A rush of anger raged through him. *Yeah, what if he is looking at child porn or something.* The overwhelming feeling of having to see that screen subdued his entire body. He needed to make his way around the house. Maybe the kitchen had another window he could look through, he couldn't tell from his vantage point. He was going to have to move back into the shadows, make his way around the glowing squares in the yard being portrayed by the light emanating from the house's rear windows, and make his way around the left side of the house.

It took him about thirty minutes to move about twenty feet, but he wanted to ensure he wasn't seen. He now stood next to a large air conditioning unit that maintained an incredibly loud humming sound. He was grateful for the air conditioner's sound because it seemed to have masked some of his movement toward this side of the house. He was able to stay out of the light of the window and see at an angle what was on the computer screen—which turned out to be nothing of any importance. He believed it was a news site; he couldn't see exactly which one, but it looked like there were some headline stories and what he believed to be maybe a political website. He settled in; this could be a little while.

An hour went by, then two, without a great deal of information being gathered. Sherman started to get tired and switched back to his spot in the back of the house next to the barbecue as he tracked the man through the house. The man switched spots from the kitchen, to the couch, to the computer on many occasions, and instead of following the man to every spot, Sherman often just waited for him to return. This time the man was at the computer, the man was there for a little while, and Sherman decided to move back from his spot next to the barbecue back to his spot outside the kitchen window. As he got there, he could not believe his eyes. This piece of shit was looking at children on his computer, half-dressed children in compromising positions. That was the evidence he was looking for, and the rage started to build. Sherman knew that this guy just sealed his own fate.

Sherman watched as the man sat in front of the computer and started to touch himself. He clicked through pictures, and the more graphic the picture, the more excited the man seemed to get. Sherman couldn't take it anymore; he had seen all he needed to see. He would leave here, go home, set a plan in motion, and then come back and kill this man. His mind was made up; there was no question that this man deserved to die and would not be allotted the opportunity to get caught a third time.

Sherman slowly left the loud hum of the air conditioner and made his way back to the back yard. He was so angry he could feel the heat in his head building, and his ears were burning. He couldn't think straight. *Get a gun,* he thought, *or maybe a knife. Lure him to a playground and then kill him.* His mind was awash with what was happening. With the details vague but as clear as they ever were, he started to put the plan in place.

Slowly dodging the light on the back patio, Sherman stepped onto the grass towards the corner of the yard, assuring he remained in the shadows. While he was slightly crouched but still somewhat standing, he heard from behind him a male voice say, "Hey, what are you doing?" and he turned to see the man standing there just a few feet away.

Caught off guard and unsure of what his next action should be, all Sherman could muster up was an unsure "What?" as a response.

"What the fuck are you doing?" the man responded as his voice rose and got more authoritative. The man started moving towards Sherman, and the distance between them was quickly getting shorter. Things went a little fuzzy at that point as the fight-or-flight mentality kicked in. The first thought he had *was attack, attack before you are attacked. Do not let up until you have destroyed the threat.* He pounced on the man with the speed and agility of a Marine on patrol being attacked by an insurgent.

The battle was fast-paced and heavy. Sherman lunged for the man's throat while sweeping his leg out from underneath him. The man quickly fell to his back as he was mounted by this younger, more agile opponent. Sherman choked the man with his hands as they both struggled to get the upper hand. The man swung wildly from his back, catching Sherman on the side of his head with solid blows. The blows hit him hard on the side of his head, and as they did, he saw flashes of light that made him question if he was losing consciousness. The fear of this man getting the upper hand started to set in; the man was still fighting hard, and didn't seem to be affected by being choked. *Isn't he supposed to lose consciousness by now? Why isn't this working?* he thought.

Sherman tightened his grip around the man's throat as he felt the bones in his fingers start to ache, the man's knees crashed and banged into Sherman's back with devastating force. The man started kicking his legs wildly, and Sherman heard the sound of metal clanging against the concrete of the patio. He looked down to see the man's unbuckled belt bouncing on the concrete. He removed one hand from the man's throat and grabbed a hold of the belt buckle, and with a few solid tugs, he felt the belt slip from the belt loops and become free. He quickly looped the belt around the man's neck and pulled at the belt as hard as he could.

The man still fought and struggled. Sherman rolled him over onto his stomach and mounted his back, wrapped each fist around an end of the belt, placed his knee in the center of the man's back, and leaned back and pulled with all of his might. He could feel the skin on his hands start to burn and slip under the intense pressure of the belt. He could sense the fight leaving the man's body; the less he struggled, the harder Sherman pulled, as he knew he was winning.

It seemed to take forever, but at last it was done—the man's body went limp. Sherman collapsed on the man's back and lay there momentarily as he caught his breath. The adulation of what he had done rushed over him. He could feel the free spirits of the little girls being released into the world, and he smiled so hard as he laid upon his victim that his cheeks started to hurt. Then, like a tidal wave of emotion, he thought, *fuck, I just killed a man and I am laying on him in his backyard.*

Now what? he questioned to his inner voice.

RUN, the voice cried out.

He stood, looked around, and for a minute started to head to the back fence. *Wait, calm down. Don't run, think, think this through. A burglary, make it look like someone broke in and killed him. Yeah,* he said to himself, *ransack the place and set it on fire. Yeah, set this mother fucker on fire. Burn it all down.*

What? his inner voice said. *Are you insane?* Then it dawned on him that yes, yes he was insane. Suicide, the guy killed himself—he couldn't live another moment knowing what he did, so he killed himself. With that, he went back to the man, struggled as he lifted him up in a fireman's carry type position over his shoulders, and carried him back into the house. *The bathroom,* he thought—*everyone kills themselves in the bathroom.* He put him down on the floor of the bathroom and figured he would put him in the tub and slit his wrists. *Wait, can't they tell if his wrists were cut after he died or before? I think they can,* his inner voice confirmed.

As he was searching around the bathroom for a believable suicide, he looked back at the man, the belt still wrapped around his neck, the postmortem bruising starting to form around the pressure of the belt staining his neck in purple, red, and blue hues. It dawned on him; he killed himself alright, but he did it by accident. He propped the man up against the wall under the towel holder and then returned to the living room, the computer monitor still displaying the half-dressed child. He went back onto the patio to where his backpack was tossed during the tussle and removed a pair of the rubber surgical gloves.

Putting on the gloves, Sherman returned to the computer. He removed the laptop from its docking station and brought it to the bathroom. There, he looped the ends of the belt over the towel rack and secured the belt to it using the belt holes. He lifted the man up just enough to where his weight was being supported by the towel rack. His body was still in a semi-seated position, his torso against the wall under the towel rack, his lower body just off the ground, enough to be hanging. He positioned the laptop on the toilet facing the man. He then shimmied the already unzipped and unbuttoned man's jeans down his legs until they were just below his knees. He did the same with the man's boxers and placed one of his hands in his lap.

Looks believable to me, he thought to himself. *What do they call that? Affixation? Or something like that*, he chuckled to himself. He doubled-checked the area to ensure there was no trace of him having been around. Sherman then made his way back through the house, and with an ear-to-ear smile, he slowly closed the sliding glass door behind him, retrieved his backpack, made his way through the grass while still in the shadows of the bushes, over the fences, down the driveway, and on his way home. He had almost a skip in his step as he smiled; he could not have felt better about what he had done.

Sherman reached into his front pocket and retrieved the napkin, opened it up, read its contents, ripped it into four pieces, and while he walked home, he ate the napkin pieces, as if with every bite that melted in his mouth and swallowed, he was erasing the existence of this predator. As he continued to walk home, the reality of what he had done started to sink in, and he started to second-guess his ability to get away with his crime. He started to get scared. *What if they find my DNA at the scene? What if they see blood where we tussled on the patio, was there blood? Am I bleeding?* All of these questions raced through his head. *I have to get out of here. I have to run, I have to hide.* Panic started to set in, and Sherman was not handling it well.

Chapter 6

Back at his apartment, Sherman knew they would be looking for the killer. Saying the word "killer" to himself made him physically sick; he didn't see himself that way, but he now had to face the harsh reality of his actions. He killed a civilian man, and now will be labeled a killer. He grabbed the essentials from the apartment and decided he was going to run. He could not stay here; it would only be a matter of time before the police came knocking on his door. He was sure that the police would find his DNA at the crime scene. He must have dropped beads of sweat somewhere in the house, or maybe they would find a shoe print. He racked his brain on other areas he might have screwed up, and could not remember if, when he was hiding behind the stainless steel barbecue, he actually touched the barbecue and left fingerprints. He replayed these moments over in his head all evening and into the next day. The more he thought of the intricate details, the more sure he was that the police were there right now and collecting his finger prints, DNA, and other information that would point directly to him. Unless he was just going to sit in his apartment and wait for a knock at the door, he was going to have to take action. He would run, run far, run long, run now. He locked up the apartment and made his way to the street with just his backpack filled with the bare minimum needed to get by, some clothes, some hygiene equipment, and a few other odds and ends.

His plan was to not have a plan, do things that could not be traced, or think things through as if he were a person investigating someone. He had options; many of his Marine buddies did their time and then moved back home. Many of them were from states far away from his own, and the Marine bond would be enough for him to give someone a call to see if he could crash for a few nights. Being a city kid, he should probably go somewhere down south, it might be less likely the police would come look for him there. They would assume that being from the city, he would stay in the city or go to another city where he was most comfortable. But he would stick out like a sore thumb; most small towns down south all know each other, and surely would recognize a stranger that just showed up. There were too many people who would be able to see him in a big city. Televisions are everywhere, and he would have to spend a good portion of time out in the open to survive.

The major cities would have to be out for now, maybe something a little in-between, not out in the sticks, not in a small town, but not in a big city. Seattle? Seattle, Washington was basically as far as he could get from where he was right now, but did he know anyone in Seattle? He racked his brain, trying to think of where Marines he had met through the years were from. *Not one damn Marine from Seattle*, he thought to himself. And then it hit him: Mikey. Mikey was from Oregon. He vaguely remembered a conversation about him being from Oregon City, Oregon. Tank had made great fun of Mikey for being from a city that was named after the state; *how original*, he thought. Only to be reminded by Mikey that Tank was from New York City, New York. They both got a pretty good laugh out of that. So, it was decided— Tank was going to make his way to Mikey in Oregon City, Oregon.

As he stood on the street, he contemplated the best way to make his way across the country. He wanted to find a way that would be the least trailed if he were to get identified from the crime scene. He couldn't just buy a plane ticket, because he would need to show identification; the same would be true if he bought a bus ticket or tried to get on a cruise ship. He wouldn't be able to just drive his car, because once again, if they identified him from the crime scene, they would be able to post what car he was driving and he would take the chance of someone seeing him as he crossed the country. He would also have to stop for gas, so he would wind up on a gas station camera or noticed by other patrons. There had to be a way to make this work; he had to think with a tactical mind state and think about what a person would have done before there was technology to trace back to a person.

The first settlers traveled by wagon; that obviously was not an option, but to break it down to the most basic modes of travel, he had to rule out everything. He couldn't walk, he couldn't bike, take a car, bus, plane or boat, he couldn't take a train, and he couldn't take a . . . Wait, a train. A train. Couldn't he take a train? Not like an Amtrak train, but a freight train. He used to see freight trains just outside the city limits that would carry new cars. He wasn't sure where they went, but knew that they were freight trains and were traveling west. He could get on a freight train and travel across the country on a freight train. Freight train riders didn't often get identified, did they? He couldn't remember ever hearing or seeing a story about a fugitive being found, identified, or caught by trying to hop a freight train. He was intrigued by the idea, but more intrigued about making it work and living the temporary life of a hobo.

The local freight trains around him went to Chicago, which would be far enough to get him out of the city and give him time to figure out his next move. When he arrived at the train yard, it seemed desolate. He was expecting to have to climb over fences, possibly run from dogs, and time a guard's patrol routine. None of that was necessary. He literally walked up to a train and saw a door he would be able to jump up into when the train was leaving. The train yard consisted of a large number of trains all lined up next to each other. Some faced one way, some faced the other, and it seemed as if there was no rhyme or reason as to how these trains were parked. It almost gave the impression that this was the final resting place for freight trains, but Tank noticed that some of them moved during the time he was there so it must have been an active train yard. He was unable to figure out a way to tell what trains were going where, as they didn't have signs on them and there wasn't a train station he could go into to look up train routes. He was just going to have to take a stab at it and guess.

As he walked around the train yard, he saw trains that carried livestock, pens for what he imagined would be cows, train cars that carried automobiles, stacked three high, probably headed to some far off dealership. There were train cars that had an open top that were piled with what looked like coal. There were also regular box cars and lumber cars. Sherman spent a great deal of time watching trains come and go, and they all had a common theme: as one freight train came into the yard, the train to the right of it would start up and make its journey out of the yard within a twenty-minute window. Sherman decided that he was going to take his chances with the regular box car. He scouted out the area earlier in the day and determined that many of the box cars were unsecured, and a few of them had the doors locked into the open position. Getting onto the train would not be a problem; the issues would come with conductors or train yard security. The train Sherman would take still had eight trains in front of it before it would depart the yard. It looked like it was going to be a long wait, as the trains arrived every twenty minutes to a half hour, and then the next train would leave between five and fifteen minutes after that. Figuring he was going to have to wait a few hours, Sherman retrieved one of the MREs (Meal Ready to Eat) he had thrown in his bag on the way out of his apartment and started to eat. As the time passed and the time for his departure came closer, he noticed that more people started to arrive around the outskirts of the train yard, people who looked to be homeless. He assumed they were probably thinking the same thing he was and would be jumping on one of the trains, if not the same train he was going to get on. It provided a good opportunity to maybe get some information. Sherman approached an older gentlemen that had a rundown look and a face that looked like it was made of leather. He wore dirty clothes, and talked through a lazy southern drawl. Sherman avoided the introductions and tried to stick with the matter at hand. "How's the weather? I mean, some weather we are having, huh?" Sherman wasn't sure why he thought that was a good approach to this man, but he couldn't think of anything better to say. What was he supposed to say, "Hey, would this train get me far away from here? I just killed someone and am in kind of a rush to get out of here"? The stranger was very nice and helpful, and he explained to Sherman that he was what is known as a snow bird—he stayed north during the summer months and migrated south for the winter. The train Sherman was looking to take was the same train the stranger was taking. He advised Sherman to wait until the watch guard checked the train, and then he should be clear to board. He stated that he knew a lot of the watchmen, and many of them just want to check the trains because it is their job. Once that was completed, they didn't care what happened after that, and there were many people who hopped the trains.

As the conversation continued, the stranger pointed over Sherman's shoulder, and as Sherman turned and looked, there was the watchman. He seemed to be giving a halfhearted attempt a checking locks, shining a flashlight at things, and occasionally bending down to possibly look under the train. Once he was out of sight, the two men gathered up their belongings and made their way to the train. Sherman assisted the stranger into the box car and the man in turn gave Sherman a hand and pulled him up into the car. The car was clean, a little dust and dirt from traveling with the doors open, but a typical run-of-the-mill freight train box car—nothing too fancy, this would do nicely. Sherman settled into the far corner of the boxcar and waited for the train to start moving.

Sherman assumed it would be a few hours to get out of New York and into Chicago, and then he would be able to figure things out. He watched out of the freight door as the dusk turned to night, and as the time ticked away he started to take inventory of what he had done. As the night got closer and the air darker, he was more alone with himself than he has been in a while. He started to replay the entire scenario that got him into this position in the first place. He pictured police officers swarming all over the dead man's house, the snapping of flashbulbs and the collection of tiny fibers and hairs being placed into plastic bags. The pictures in his mind were vivid and clear. He did not regret his actions, but he did regret the sloppy manner in which he performed the actions. Sherman must have dosed off while deep in thought, because he awoke to his body feeling sore from laying on the hard wooden floor of the box car. It was dark, there was no moonlight, and he could barely see his hand in front of his face. The rumble of the car against the tracks made it difficult for him to hear anything going on around him. He assumed he slept for a solid eight hours and continued to doze in and out of sleep. When he finally awoke to the sunlight shining on him through the boxcar door, it was hot—sticky hot. He was uncomfortable, and covered with a light coat of dust and dirt from the travels. The train was still moving, and Sherman could tell from the landscape that the city of New York was far behind. He now was traveling through long stretches of plains and rolling hills. He could tell he was alone in the boxcar, and his riding buddy was no longer riding with him. He was unsure if the train had stopped at some point or if he missed his stop. He was hesitant to turn on his cell phone because he knew that it would be able to be traced, so he was unsure of the time. He also was unsure of how long it would take to get where he was trying to go. *How long does it take to get from New York to Chicago?* he asked his inner voice. A conversation ensued with himself, reminding him of the old math questions he was given in elementary school: *If a train leaves New York headed to Chicago...* Chicago was only a few hours away from New York, he thought to himself, right? How long could it take? He continued the back and forth banter with himself. He could quickly turn on his phone, google the answer really quickly and then turn it off. He had a mental battle with that one, and he almost felt like he had to physically restrain himself from taking out his phone and doing that. What if he was way off course? *You are not off course*, he argued with himself. *It's like twelve hours away*, his inner voice convinced him. *Twelve hours? Not a chance*, he barked back at his inner voice. *Can you get halfway across the country in twelve hours?* At this point he was getting unsure of his plan. He was a little upset that he didn't plan this out better, or even ask the stranger how long the trip would take. He asked him about the weather, so that was good? What a dummy. The one important question to ask, and he completely neglected it.

He was starting to feel like he was born on this train and had been on this train forever. He had been on this car long enough to be hungry a half a dozen times. He started to use events like these to have a better understanding of how long he could have been on the train. He got on the train when it was becoming dusk, he slept through the night, he woke up to the sunlight, and had eaten once last night and twice today. The sun was high in the sky, so he assumed it had to be around midday. It was definitely longer than the twelve hours he originally calculated. Or at least the twelve hours that his inner voice calculated; Sherman still didn't believe it was an accurate time frame. He started to contemplate maybe jumping off the train at the next available opportunity; he assumed if he paid better attention, he might realize when the train came to a roadway crossing and slowed down. So far, the train had been traveling at a pretty good speed, and everything outside the door seemed to be the middle of nowhere. Even if he did jump off now, he would have to walk for what seemed like miles to get anywhere. He didn't have a great deal of food and had very little water. Jumping off the train at this point didn't seem to be a viable option, so he settled in and enjoyed the ride the best he could. After all, this may be the last time he ever got to feel this free. He scooted to the box car door and hung his legs outside of the train, looked at the sun bouncing off of the plains and distant pastures, and just tried to soak it all in. He laid his head back and let the rays of the sun soak into his closed eyelids, and for that second of his life, he was calm.

The view started to quickly change outside the boxcar door, so much so that Sherman felt the need to crouch down in the corner of the car in his attempt to be as well-hidden as possible. The landscape now was more of a bustling suburban town. The train slowed down a few times and Sherman remembered passing the train crossing barriers as the train horn blared and the ringing sounds of bells reminding drivers to stay clear of the tracks. The time was coming close to get off the train. He saw a few spots that would have been perfect to get off, but for one reason or another he didn't jump, still hoping for a better spot. The train came to a complete stop, and Sherman assumed this might be the final stop. It wasn't at a train yard, and it seemed to be no longer on the main train tracks but on an alternate track that ran alongside them. He assumed this was as good as a place as any to get off. He gathered up his stuff, strapped his pack to his back, and jumped off of the train.

He was in what seemed to be a small town. There were a few coffee shops, some gas stations, and a convenience store. The town wasn't over bustling with people, and he made his way to one of the coffee shops. He chose one that looked like a mom-and-pop place that had the least likely chance of being monitored by video cameras. He made his way into the coffee shop and was happy to see that they had a television tuned into the news. He might be able to see information of the events and progress of his crime. He ordered a small coffee and paid in cash. While he waited for his coffee, he used the men's room and saw in the mirror that he was looking dirty and a little rough from the travel. He looked unshaven and unkempt. He did his best to wash up in the sink and make himself as presentable as he could. He left the men's room and sat down within view of the television, but not so close so that someone would notice he was interested in the news. There was no mention of the crime, and he believed that was partially because there was local news being mixed with national news and he didn't believe his crime would make the headlines of either. Maybe if he went over to the convenience store he could get a few newspapers that might have more information. He finished his coffee and made his way a block or so to the convenience store. When he entered the convenience store, he noticed there was a large section of local Chicago papers as well as newspapers from many different areas—the Daily Mirror from London, the Chicago Tribune, New York Times, The Indiana Republic, and many others. He gathered up the New York Times, The New York Daily News, The New York Post, and to not make his selection too obvious, he also purchased the Daily Mirror and the National Enquirer.

He took his papers to the nearest park and sat on a park bench. He thumbed through the paper and attempted to make it look like he was a person that just happened to be sitting on a park bench and reading a newspaper, but in his mind he wanted to frantically get to the part of the paper that had local crimes. He checked the Times first; no mention of any murders or crimes. It was a Manhattan or city paper, so he didn't think there would be a great deal of information about the crime in that paper. He then checked the Post and the Daily News, and he was surprised to see the same thing—no mention at all of the crime. There were plenty of crimes being reported, some not far from where his was committed, and many of them were less newsworthy than his. Why was there no mention of it? Were they trying to keep it out of the media because they had leads they were still following? Was this their way of trying to lull the culprit into thinking no one was looking for them so they could surprise them when they return to their normal life? There had to be more to this than what he had been able to gather. Could they really not be looking for him? Could he have gotten away with the crime?

He sat on the bench for hours, thinking, contemplating, trying to figure out what law enforcement could be thinking and what their next moves may be. How could he get more information about this crime? There had to be an untraceable way to get more information. He had to find the way and truly know if they were looking for him. It seemed that no one noticed when a bad person was killed. Maybe there was an understanding with law enforcement that it was okay. Maybe they knew this guy's background and were glad that someone got rid of him. No mention in the papers, no mention on the news. That was strange, but a calming strange, a strange that seemed to lean towards no one caring, or that those that did care, didn't know. They would have to have bigger crimes to solve than what seemed like a child predator dying by his own asphyxiation. Maybe they weren't interested in solving the crime. Maybe they had closed the case before they opened it.

The night started to fall and the air grew colder. The original plan was to sleep on the park bench for the night and then get back on the train in the morning on the way to Mikey's place. But it was getting far too cold to sleep in the park, and although he could do it, he didn't see the need to. There had to be a place he could go that was relatively warm where he could spend the night. He thought about some of the places he saw when he first got off of the train—a few delis, convenience stores, a laundromat, some bars. He was sure he could probably go to the bar, act drunk, and find a way to spend the night in the back room or something, but chose the laundromat instead. He couldn't remember if it was a 24-hour laundromat, and figured if it wasn't he would then use the bar plan. As he walked back to the laundromat, the temperature was dropping and the wind seem to make the cold that much more unbearable. His ears were numb, and his nose was running; he really hoped this laundromat was 24 hours. He knew when he was walking to the park that he wasn't in a good part of town, but always knew from growing up in New York that if you minded your own business, no one really messed with you. This night would be different. He could see a group of people from about a block away that were in his path and all hanging out on the sidewalk and leaning on cars in the street. His initial reaction was to cross the street, but he felt that he was too close to do that now and it would show that he was scared or intimidated. He was not scared or intimidated, but didn't want to give that impression to bolster the people in his path. As he got closer, the late teenagers and early twenty-year-olds seemed to take notice that he was approaching. Sherman really believed he would be able to walk right by the group of people and continue on his way. The yelling and screaming didn't start until it was too late. They verbally pounced on him as if they were drill instructors, barking commands at him from every direction. There was a great deal of "What set you claiming?" questions and other inquiries into who Sherman was and why he was walking on their street. He assumed that if he just kept moving and they didn't physically touch him, he would be fine with a little yelling and screaming. They all wore black bandanas, some around their heads, others around their biceps, and one had an entire shirt made of what looked exactly like the bandana material the others were wearing. Sherman assumed by all of these observations that there was a pretty good likelihood that they were all gang members. One gang member stepped directly in Sherman's path and caused him to have to stop. A female stepped towards Sherman and one of the gang members grabbed her by her hair and slapped her "Where do you think you are going, hoe?" It seemed like that was the breaking point for the gang members. He instantly felt people's hands on him; they pushed him, pulled at his backpack, and he felt a hand or two try to reach into his pocket. He tried to walk around them, but they were relentless in their pursuit to harass and intimidate him. Sherman was extremely angry, but knew if he wasn't able to control himself and his emotions, it would only make things worse. He couldn't stop thinking about the girl who just got abused by one of the gang members. The more he thought about it the angrier he became. He attempted to walk around the guy standing in front of him and banged chest to chest with a guy standing next to him. That guy took it as a challenge.

"Oh, shit, you want to fight me, bitch?" The man raised his hands up and took on a fighting stance, one that seemed more theatrics rather than a productive stance to protect himself from impending blows. Sherman continued to move through the crowd and did so at a snail's pace. It seemed to be only inches at times, but so far there was a little pushing and shoving but no actual punching. As he continued to move, it seemed that the gang members started to lose interest. They started to thin out until there were just a few of them. One big one stopped Sherman and demanded that Sherman get on his knees. Sherman could see that if he could just get past this one last gang member, he would be home free. He attempted to side-step the man, but the man gained ground in front of him again. This time Sherman heard the distinct sound of a 9mm Beretta charging handle being pulled to the rear and released as a round was chambered. "Get on your fucking knees, bitch." Sherman could feel the thudding of the barrel on the side of his head, just above his ear. He immediately put his hands up "Ain't no one said put your fucking hands up, get on your goddamn knees." For a split second Sherman thought of fighting back, or maybe just running. Worst case scenario, he'd get shot. But for some reason, he slowly lowered himself down to his knees. His hands still up, he wanted to say so many things, but feared his strong New York accent would just incite them more. He kept his mouth shut. He quickly assessed the situation; they were on a relatively busy road, so the chances of them shooting him right here were probably slim. The man with the gun probably wanted to show off in front of his friends and do something to embarrass his prey. So why put Sherman on his knees? He started to get worried, and as he did, the man with the gun took the gun off of the side of his head and placed it in his mouth. He could feel the steel of the barrel banging up against the top and bottom of his teeth almost hard enough to chip a tooth. "Yeah, suck that gun you little bitch." The crowd around him laughed and barked out some more commands. "Piss on that bitch," one shouted from somewhere behind him. "He looks like he likes sucking dick, give him some dick to suck." Sherman realized this could potentially get a great deal worse. The man tilted the gun in Sherman's mouth, causing him to look up at the man. The man gyrated his hips as he moved the gun in and out of Sherman's mouth. As the man pulled the gun out of Sherman's mouth, Sherman seized this opportunity and grabbed the man's calf with his right hand, and with his left, grabbed the guy's crotch as hard as he could and quickly attempted to stand up. He then struck the man as hard as he could in the stomach to knock him off-balance. The man stumbled back, fell, and landed on his back. In what seemed to be all in one lightning-fast motion, Sherman pounced to his feet and ran as fast as he could over and past the guy. A few of the gang members gave a halfhearted chase, yelling some profanities and vowing to kill him when they caught him, but with the clothes they were wearing and their lack of cardio, Sherman knew he was no longer in danger of being chased down unless they jumped in a car, and that did not seem to be the case. He ran the rest of the way towards the laundromat. It was a cold night, and running helped warm him up, but he also wanted to ensure he put as much distance between him and the gang as he could.

As he approached the laundromat he noticed there was a great deal of activity around it. People seemed to be coming in and out, so he could tell from a distance that it was still open. He walked through the front door and the wave of warm air hit his face, the smell of cleanliness, and freshly dried clothes filled the air. There were a few people doing their laundry and others seem to be doing the same as he was, just trying to find a way to get out of the night's bitter cold. He picked up the remnants of a newspaper he saw on one of the tables and made his way to the back of the laundromat. As he read the paper, he made it a point every few minutes to get up, open a dryer, check to see if the clothes were dry, close the dryer and restart it to give the impression he was there to do laundry. He did this for about an hour before he realized that no one cared that he was there, and cared even less to see him continue the charade of pretending he had laundry in the dryer. There seemed to be a guy sitting towards the middle of the laundromat who had the same intentions as he did. He was a relatively young guy, and wasn't dressed overly nice but wasn't dressed like he was homeless. He had extremely baggy clothes on and wore what seemed to be brand-new sneakers. He didn't seem to be doing laundry, or at least Sherman didn't see him going through the motions of checking dryers or moving clothes from a washing machine. People continued to come in and out throughout the night. The traffic died down as the night got later; the clientele that was coming in later at night was a younger crowd who didn't seem to be coming in to do laundry. Many seemed to be coming in to get out of the cold, and as Sherman paid closer attention, he realized that most of them were coming in to see the guy in the baggy clothes. They would come in, hang out with him for a little while, and then leave. Sherman couldn't see exactly what was going on, as he was sitting on the opposite side of a bank of washing machines. He could see the patrons from about the waist up while they spoke to the man. Often the man would stand up when they addressed him and would sit back down after his guests left.

Sherman made his way around the bank of machines and walked down the aisle on the side of the baggy-clothed man. The man was sitting as Sherman walked down the twenty feet or so of aisle. As Sherman got about ten feet away from the man, he stood up. Sherman continued to walk by the man, but noticed he had tattoos covering a good portion of his neck and face. Sherman made eye contact with him and got the feeling that they both may have looked a little longer than they should have; it was almost like two dogs being walked on leashes that could only get so close to each other without actually being able to make contact. As he passed by the man, Sherman gave him a head nod and greeted him as most New Yorkers do. "Hey, how you doin'?" It came out more as a hello than it did the typical *how you doin'* that is often times mocked and mimicked by non-New Yorkers. The man responded with his own head nod but never answered the inquiry. Sherman continued his path and exited the laundromat. He stood in front in the cold for a few minutes and made a point to walk out of the man's line of sight so it could be assumed that Sherman went outside to possibly have a smoke break. He stood out front for about forty-five minutes as he watched endless amounts of people walk in and out of the laundromat. At this hour of the night, that had to be unusual behavior—none of these people had any clothes when they entered or when they left.

It was getting a little too cold to continue to stand outside, so he made his way back into the laundromat. He turned down the long aisle that ran in front of the baggy-clothed man, and as he did, he saw the man standing with his back to Sherman, a long brown bandana folded and hanging from the man's back pocket and almost reaching down to the back of his knee. Another man stood in front of him and was facing Sherman as he made his way down the aisle. The men were talking to each other, and as Sherman passed both men, it dawned on him: the baggy-clothed man must be selling drugs from the laundromat and using it as a place to stay warm while peddling his wares. Sherman passed the men and made his way back to the rear of the laundromat. He opened a dryer, checked the clothes, closed the dryer, did a half-hearted huff to give the impression that his clothes were taking far too long to dry, and went back to his seat and opened the paper.

The more patrons that came in to see the man in the baggy clothes, the more agitated Sherman became. For every older female, he thought that she was probably a mother or a wife. The younger girls were someone's daughter or sister. The men were the same; the older were probably fathers, the younger probably sons and brothers. Sherman figured that for every person that walked through the door to purchase drugs from the baggy-clothed man, there were probably three or four people affected by the fact that these people were doing drugs. The baggy-clothed man sat there in between sales without a care in the world while his customers had to live the life of a drug addict, affecting every aspect of their lives and the lives that were around them. The hate for this man was building within Sherman, and he at times would doze off, staring into space and thinking about grabbing this man and stuffing him into a washer or dryer, turning it on, and just leaving him in there until he drowned or burned to death.

Of course, those thoughts quickly passed as Sherman assumed there were cameras in the laundromat. Sherman just couldn't wrap his mind around the lack of caring that had to be obtained to sell people something that you knew was going to destroy every aspect of their lives and not feel somewhat responsible for that person's pending demise. The more Sherman thought about it, the angrier he became. The man in the baggy clothes was getting a big gold star next to his name in regard to becoming the next eradicated piece of garbage on Sherman's list. If Sherman was to take out the baggy-clothed man, he could positively have an effect on tens if not hundreds of people that this man sold drugs to. Would some of them buy drugs from somewhere else? Sure. Would some of them see his death as a sign that maybe they should change their ways and attempt to straighten out their lives? Hopefully. There was no true way to know for sure, but at least that was what Sherman was hoping for. How do you not trade one negative act towards a bad person for the possibility of a hundred positive acts towards assumed good people?

Tina was a girl Sherman saw come into the laundromat who spent some time with the guy in the baggy clothes. She stayed with him for a few hours throughout the night and gave the impression they may have been more than just friends. She was a pretty girl that didn't look like the rest of the clientele that came in and out of the laundromat. From what Sherman could tell, she was of Hispanic descent and was in phenomenally great shape. She was short, but had long dark hair that made her look shorter; she was a little unkempt, but more in a tomboyish way, rather than someone who didn't take care of themselves. Sherman spent the remainder of the night dozing in and out of sleep or hanging out in front of the laundromat for short periods of time. On one of his returns back into the laundromat, he could hear the man in the baggy clothes and Tina yelling at each other. There didn't seem to be any intelligent points being made in the conversation, just a great deal of yelling and screaming. The girl stormed out of the laundromat crying. Sherman continued to mind his business and took his seat again at the back of the Laundromat. He started to brainstorm the details on how he could possibly take out this drug dealer without anyone knowing; he could easily follow him out to the parking lot and strangle the man to death and leave his body in the parking lot. The local police would probably give him a medal for getting rid of this piece of garbage. As Sherman continued to daydream about the possibilities, he snapped out of his daydream and came back to reality. It wasn't too long after that the man in the baggy clothes decided to leave. There went his chance. He didn't want to follow him out of the laundromat—since it was only the two of them there, he thought it might look too obvious and cause trouble, leading to someone seeing an altercation, and that wouldn't be good for Sherman's current situation. He chalked it up as one that got away and nestled back into the chair to attempt to get a little more sleep.

Chapter 7

It was now morning, and Sherman knew he was going to have to start making his way to the train yard. The laundromat was connected on one side to a small restaurant and had an open parking lot on the other side. As Sherman departed the laundromat, he headed through the parking lot to go behind the restaurant and see if maybe he could scrounge some food from the restaurant dumpster. He had some money on him, but wanted to save as much as he could in case he needed it for an emergency, and eating a few things that might seem safe out of the dumpster did not seem to be a big deal to Sherman. As he turned the corner of the building, he saw Tina sitting on the ground with her back against the rear of the building. She didn't look the same as she did in the laundromat a few hours ago; instead, she seemed disheveled and dirty. At first Sherman walked by her, but then he decided to stop. "Are you okay?" he asked. She ignored him, or didn't hear him. She didn't motion towards him or give any sign of acknowledgment. "Excuse me," he said again, this time louder than the first. "Are you okay?" This time he crouched down in front of her. Up close, he could see that his original assessment of her in the laundromat was off; she had the remnants of a black eye that was now yellowed, her eye was slightly bloodshot, her clothes were dirtier than he originally thought, and she seemed out of it. She was wearing nice clothes and seemed to have a nice purse, and seemed out-of-place sitting in an alleyway behind a laundromat and a restaurant. Sherman tapped the lady's arm and asked again, "Hey, hey, you okay?" it was like she was snapped out of a trance, "What? What do you want? Leave me alone," she said as she pushed Sherman's hand away from her.

"I don't want anything, I just wanted to make sure you were okay, I thought you might be hurt or something."

"No, I am not hurt," she said through slurred words and in a trancelike state. Sherman introduced himself as Tank and took a seat next to her against the wall. "Why are you out here?" he asked.

"Because Ricky is a fucking asshole." Sherman assumed that Ricky was the man in the baggy clothes. It baffled Sherman that a woman who seemed to at one time have the ability to have any man she wanted somehow ended up with the man in the baggy clothes. It actually kind of angered Sherman; he had a bunch of sisters and had a soft spot for women being treated right in general. It bothered him that someone would mistreat women and then leave them on the street to fend for themselves. "Why do you put up with his shit?" he asked.

"Because I love him," she responded in the clearest sentence she had spoken since the conversation started. Sherman felt as if he was counseling this woman and trying to convince her to no longer settle or let this man treat her the way he had. Sherman was more concerned for this woman than she seemed to be for herself. The conversation went on for hours. They talked about their original paths in life, how she and Ricky were high school sweethearts, and where things all went wrong with the drugs and him beating her. She spoke of him beating her on a pretty regular basis, but spoke of it as if it was her doing, it was her fault, and how she "always pushed him too far or didn't know when to just walk away." Sherman felt like he was having a conversation with someone who was trying to convince him to see her angle and why was all right for Ricky to beat her. She did a lot of crying towards the end of the conversation, and Sherman believed she started seeing her own worth. "Just leave him," he said. "Do you have anywhere to go?"

"I could go back to my parents' house in California." Tina was a runaway. She had left her middle class home in California so she could live out her dream with Ricky as he took a job across the country. They started out living the American dream and wound up in the middle of a nightmare—or at least for Tina, that's how it turned out. "You are right," she said, "I should just go home." Sherman had some money. It wasn't a lot, but it might be enough to get her on a bus and get her home to her family, and there she might be able to start over. But she had to tell Ricky first; she couldn't just leave, he might chase after her and make matters worse. "You should tell Ricky it's over, and then we can get you in touch with your parents and on a bus. We can do that right now, we can have you on a bus by this time tomorrow." The more he spoke, the more the glimmer in her eye shined. He could tell she liked the idea but lacked the courage to see it through.

"Will you come with me?" she asked.

"To Cali?" he replied. "No, I can't go to Cali, but I can make sure you get on a bus and get back home where you belong."

"Will you come with me to tell Ricky it's over? I don't want him to try to convince me to stay or make me stay."

"That I can do. I will help you be strong and tell him you won't put up with the way he treats you and that you are leaving. You have to tell him you are leaving." This might be the opportunity that Sherman was looking for. She would lead him right to this piece of shit who deserved what was coming to him. This must be a sign; this morning it looked like this opportunity was lost, but God's plan had put Sherman right back on track again with ridding the world of horrible people. Sherman was excited, but didn't want to show it; he reiterated the terms of him going with her and continued to give it a somber spin, although inside, he couldn't be more excited. She agreed to his terms and they discussed where Ricky lived and how the best way to get there was going to be. Ricky only lived about a mile or so from the laundromat, and they decided it would be best if they just walked rather than taking a bus or taxi. As they walked, they talked about the future.

"You should call your parents and tell them you're okay and that you want to come home." Sherman figured that would be the motivation she may need to follow through with this plan; he figured if she already told her family she was coming home, she would have to see it through. "I promise I will call them as soon as we leave his house. I have to focus on doing this first. I haven't seen or talked to my parents in a few years, and they probably think I'm dead by now. I'm actually getting kind of excited to go home, it feels surreal, but it feels like it is the right thing to do. I'm glad I met you, Mr. Tank."

They practiced her speech as they got closer to the house, Sherman advised her to just keep it short and sweet, to not accuse him of anything and basically just tell him she was leaving. "Ricky, you have hurt me long enough, I always loved you, but you hurt me bad. I am not going to let you hurt me anymore, and I am leaving." Quick, simple, and to the point. After that, Sherman would be there to make sure that things didn't get too out of hand. He was anticipating a little bit of screaming and yelling, but figured in the end, Ricky might be fine with her leaving.

As they approached the house, it appeared run down and looked as if a slum lord ran the place. There was a strange looking car in the driveway that looked like a sedan or old mans car that had big shiny wheels on it. The wheels were much bigger than the wheels that were supposed to be on the car. Sherman thought they looked ridiculous. The house had a front porch that needed a lot of repairs, the house needed to be painted, and the landscape was overgrown. There hadn't been much attention given to this house in quite some time. As they walked up the front walkway and onto the rickety porch, Sherman could feel the anxiety in his chest start to grow. He felt like he had to jump up and down a little bit and shake the anxiety out; he felt a buzz running through his body. It wasn't fear, but could very easily be mistaken as such. The only light on the porch was the remainder of the sunlight that was shining through the trees, and dusk was setting in, the afternoon light was fading into evening. Tina knocked on the door, which seemed like an odd thing to do because she has been with this guy from high school. Why would she knock on the door of the place she was living? For a split second, Sherman contemplated that he may be getting set up; was she sent to go and find an unsuspecting victim, cry, have the victim then convince her to tell her boyfriend that she was going to leave, go back to their house, have a secret knock on the door and then rob the victim? It was all happening so fast; should he just turn around and leave, or was his mind just making this up?

His mind was not making this up. The door flew open, and there stood Ricky with a Bersa .380 pistol in his hand "What the fuck you want?" The pistol was at his side, but the question was directed at Tina. "Ricky, you have always hurt me, I . . ." Ricky raised the gun and pointed it at Sherman. "This a cop? You here to arrest me?" Sherman's hands went up. "Um, no, I am not cop, and I am not here to arrest you." His response sounded practiced and a little too calm; it was almost like he was responded to a Jeopardy question. "Alex, what is 'no, I am not a cop and I am not here to arrest you'?" "I will take insane gun-wielding drug dealers for 200, Alex."

Ricky looked past both of them to see if there was anyone watching this unfold. "Get in the fucking house," he demanded, motioning and waving the gun toward the inside of the house. *Do not go inside that house,* Sherman's inner voice calmly but sternly told him. *I agree, that would not be good*, he silently responded to himself as he felt his legs moving him as he walked into the house. *What the hell are you doing? I said DON'T go into the house*, his inner voice now screamed. *I HAVE NO IDEA WHAT THE FUCK I AM DOING*, he shouted back at himself. He yelled it so loud that he questioned for a second if he said it out loud.

He now stood in the living room of the house; it was dimly lit and smelled of mold and old food. The house was dirty, but not as dirty as he would have expected from the occupants.

"Tina, why the fuck is there a cop standing in my house?, Why Tina? Fucking answer me, Tina!" Ricky didn't leave much room in between the accusations and questions for Tina to respond. She kept attempting to stick to her script, and Sherman heard her reciting bits and pieces it. "I am not going to let me hurt you, I mean you hurt me, Ricky . . ."

"Hurt you, bitch? Leave me?"

"Ricky, I am leaving 'cause you hurt me."

"Oh, I will fucking hurt you. Leave me? Yeah, right." The arguing seemed to get louder and with no direction, and panic started to set in for Sherman. Sherman, with his hands still in the air, started having a conversation with his inner voice. *Look around and find your exits, stay calm, think this through, and get out.* He noticed he wasn't far from one of the windows; he could get a running start and toss himself out of the window, and chances were the man in the baggy clothes would be too concerned with what was going on with Tina and not even give chase. The gunshot caught him completely off guard. He wasn't expecting it, but was looking right at it when it happened. He was in a daze and not mentally in the room while discussing his options with himself. The room slowed down, and he saw what happened in super slow motion before the sound and reactions caught up. The small puff of smoke as the bullet left the barrel. He thought the time between the bullet leaving the barrel and actually striking Tina in the head just above her right eye could have been a full minute; she was turning to look at Sherman as if to wonder why he wasn't taking any action. The sound quickly caught up, and Sherman was surprised that he didn't even flinch when it hit. His ears rang and his awareness of the situation heightened, and his body moved almost before he could realize what he was doing. He stepped into Ricky's inner step with his left leg, wrapped his arm up and over the arm Ricky was using to hold the pistol. He had him in a standing arm bar and shook his arm with great force, He could feel the pressure against Ricky's elbow, which was on the verge of snapping. He continued the upward pressure until he could feel the weapon shake loose, fall out of Ricky's hand, and make a solid *thud* on the ground. He let Ricky go, pushed him to the floor, and turned towards where he heard the sound of the weapon hitting the floor, picked up the weapon, and turned back towards Ricky.

They were only a few feet away from each other. Ricky was now sitting on the floor and attempting to get back to his feet; the pace was fast, and Sherman quickly tried to close the distance between him and Ricky to keep Ricky on the floor. Ricky got to his feet as Sherman reached him, and Ricky was in the middle of throwing a punch at him. Ricky was shouting something, but Sherman could not hear him; his ears were still ringing, and his inner voice was giving a play by play of what he should do next. *Sherman, step into him, wrap the arm, grab, twist, pull, grab, get the gun, duck, look out here he comes . . .* He could hear the barking directions of his drill instructors during hand-to-hand combat, the Sergeants before patrols on how to apprehend an enemy combatant, the reminder in many voices that "It is him or you, only one of you will have the luxury of going home, who wants it more?" Sherman wasn't concerned for the punch that was being thrown; he knew he was out of the range of getting hit by it. Ricky had his left shoulder forward as he missed the punch, and Sherman was basically standing on his left side now that he was able to avoid the punch. He raised the pistol and shot Ricky at close range, right above his left temple. His body instantly went limp and crumbled to the floor.

FUCK, RUN! Burn the house down; get an axe, chop up the bodies, his inner voice screamed. *Calm down, think, slow down, breathe Sherman. Sherman, you're not breathing,* He responded to himself. Sherman attempted to control his breathing. His ears were still ringing, but there was an inner peace that he felt. He was standing in a room with two dead bodies, but still felt at peace—he enjoyed the quiet. His ears were warm and his body felt heavy; it was a relaxed heavy, it was a just-after-a-long-massage heavy. The kind of heavy that makes you want to lay down and take a nap. But he knew there was work to be done, that the work was just getting started.

His plan was to drag the bodies into the tub in the bathroom and cut the bodies into pieces. Then dispose of the pieces somewhere and then get on the train towards Oregon. *Okay,* he thought, *I could use the sheet off of the bed, the shower curtain, I can check to see if there is a tablecloth in the kitchen.* He made his way into the bedroom to get the sheets. It was a modest room that didn't have too many bells and whistles. The sliding doors on the closet were open, and Sherman could see the kind of clothes Ricky enjoyed wearing. That might help Sherman out later on; he could use these clothes when discarding the bodies, and in case anyone saw him, they may think it was one of the local gang members. Curiously, he walked over to the closet to check the sizes on some of the clothes just to see if it was a viable option. They all seemed like they would be a decent fit, all would be baggy, and he figured that would be the point. It would break up his body type and make him less recognizable.

As he was looking through the closet, he saw the hand grip of what looked like a rifle or a shotgun leaning against the back wall of the closet. Sherman squatted down to get a better look at the weapon. He was amazed to see an AK-47 assault rifle staring back at him. It was the old wooden butt stock and handle kind. It had a banana clip in the magazine weld and a string of ammunition hung around the upper barrel area. Sherman had no business touching this weapon, but his curiosity and intrigue got the better of him. He reached for the weapon and pulled it out of the closet, ensuring not to disrupt anything else if he could help it. It seemed to be a well-kept weapon, oiled in all of the right places and no buildup of carbon. Maybe if Ricky took care of his women the way he takes care of his assault rifles, he wouldn't be lying dead on the living room floor. Sherman kept discussing with his inner voice the damage that could be done with this weapon, and whether there was a possibility to take it with him. He knew it wasn't, but he reveled at the thought of it. Nightfall was coming, and whatever plan he was going to put in place, he was going to have to do it now. He carefully took clothes out of the closet and started dressing himself up to look like a member of the local gang. He even had the brown bandana hanging out of his back pocket. He thought to himself, *How could anyone dress like this?* He could barely move, and felt very restricted in these clothes. It was as though he had potato sacks hanging off of his body.

He returned to the bodies and stood over them as he thought about his next steps. *Maybe I should cover myself in trash bags before cutting up the bodies*, he thought to himself. *Cutting up bodies?* his inner voice responded. *Do you hear what you are saying?* it continued. *You are talking about cutting peoples' bodies into pieces, we can't do that, can we? I don't know, I guess we could, if not, then what are we supposed to do? Just walk out the front door and have another horribly planned out murder on our hands? Hell, make that a double murder. We can't just walk away, that is out of the question.* He questioned his inner voice, but then put his foot down on not walking away. "Asphyxiation?" he chuckled to himself. "Wait, yeah, asphyxiation," he responded as if the solution to his problem now became very clear. He stood over the bodies to gain a better understanding as to how he wanted to position them. Looking down at Tina it saddened him to realize what a horrible tragedy it was for such a young life to be wasted. Although It made him sad, he didn't have time to be sad right now, he had to stay focused and figure this out. He knew that anything he did was going to be analyzed by law enforcement when they arrived. Maybe he didn't want to move them at all. As of right now, the scene looked completely untouched by him. He didn't step in any of the blood, and as he thought back to when he entered the house, his hands were up and he didn't touch anything. He returned to the bedroom and searched for something to write on; he found the pen first, and then a pack of

115

notebook paper that was opened on the floor near the closet. He slid one piece of paper out and stood next to the clothes dresser. He wrote:

Tina,

I can't believe you did me like this. I always loved you and you hurt me bad. For you to be unfaithful against me with someone from the black rag gang hurts me real deep. I cannot live like this any longer. I cannot have you live like this if I am gone. I wish it didn't have to end this way. I love you.

After writing the note, Sherman read it back and thought to himself, *What are the chances that this guy was educated enough to write this letter and not butcher it up with grammar and typographical errors?* Then he questioned, *why would he write her a letter if he planned on killing her?* He took the piece of paper and stuffed it into his pocket. He got another piece of paper:

Girl you did me wrong. I can't live knowing you did me like this. This is what you want. Be with the black gang if you want. I always loved you. I want you to hurt with this as much as you hurt me with what you did.

Sherman wrote the letter with his left hand, as if that would throw the whole investigation into a tailspin. He didn't want the letter to be too long and overanalytical, but still wanted to give the impression that he was going to kill himself over his girlfriend's infidelity with a member of the rival gang. He left the letter right on the dresser and made his way back to the bodies. He was going over all the details in his head; he could walk away now, and the investigators would at least have to think that the possibility was there that he might have decided to kill himself and she came home, an argument ensued, and things escalated into a murder-suicide. Was he missing any details? He racked his brain, trying to run the scenario through his head over and over to decide if there was anything he was missing. He continued to stand over the bodies and saw a keychain hanging from Ricky's belt loop. It was a regular clip-on keychain that had a few keys on it, and as Sherman bent down to get a closer look, it looked like a house key or two and a couple of car keys. He went into the kitchen, pulled a paper towel from the roll, and returned to the body. With the paper towel covering his hand from touching the key ring clip, he removed the keys and held them in his hand on top of the paper towel. *Maybe I can drive the rest of the way to Oregon?*

Hell no, they will be looking for the car if it was missing from the house, dumbass, his inner voice responded. He returned to the kitchen and pulled a few more paper towels from the roll. He returned to the living room, picked up the AK-47, and made his way to the front door. The nightfall made the front of the house very dark, and Sherman had to wait a minute or so on the front porch while his eyes adjusted to the darkness. He walked to the driveway side of the porch and looked up the driveway; there was an older model car in the driveway with huge, shiny chrome wheels. The car looked ridiculous, Sherman thought it looked like it had wagon wheels on it or something. He made his way off the porch and up the driveway, making sure that he took notice of exactly where the car was sitting. The car was backed into the driveway, and the front tires were in line with a basement window that was next to the driveway. He got into the car, laid the rifle on the passenger seat, and placed his paper towel-covered hands on the steering wheel. He started up the vehicle and slowly started to roll out of the driveway.

He rolled down the final turn towards his destination; he was driving for about three minutes and once again his heart was pounding. He stopped the car in the middle of the street and jumped out. With the element of surprise, he ran to the sidewalk and made his way down the sidewalk, about two houses away from where the gang members stood. They didn't see him or notice him until it was almost too late. He tried to focus in to where the girl was so he could have her leave with him but she was no longer there. He raised the weapon and placed his finger on the trigger, pulling the trigger as fast as his finger would allow, as the muzzle lit up with the flashes of fire shooting out of the barrel. The flashes temporarily blinded him, but he knew his aim was on target as he could hear the screams and bodies fall to the floor. He mostly shot the weapon from the hip, but at times saw a moving target and took aim with the weapon in his shoulder. There seemed to be half-hearted attempts to return fire at him, but they were off their mark and were impacting against trees, ricocheting off of the sidewalk, and whizzing by high over his head. He remembered thinking it would take a great deal of luck for one of these bullets to hit him because they were all over the place and there didn't seem to be any well-aimed shots. His adrenaline was high, but his actions were calm. He controlled his breathing, took well-aimed shots, and made sure no one had the opportunity to run. He was in his element; the controlled chaos was invigorating, the smell of the gun fire, the flashes of the muzzles, the sounds of battle, his heart racing at breakneck speed. He was ridding the world of more evil-doers, those who prey on the weak, break the laws, beat women, and harass innocent people. Tonight they would not get away with it—tonight they would pay for their actions. Some attempted to run, but Sherman quickly closed the distance between him and the runners and mowed them down. He moved closer to his victims as he stepped around bodies. Some laid limp and others writhed in pain, as they must have only received wounding injuries. When he made his way from one end of the sidewalk, through the victims to the other, he turned around and returned to those that were wounded. Placing the gun to their heads, he ensured no one would live when he was done.

He came to an injured gang member and rolled him over. It was the one that put the gun in Sherman's mouth. Sherman leaned over the man and whispered in his ear, "Open your fucking mouth," just as the man had Sherman put the barrel of the rifle in his mouth. "Open your fucking eyes," he demanded, and the man obliged. "I want you to see my face, look at me." With the barrel still in the man's mouth, Sherman gyrated his hips a little bit, blew a kiss at the man, and pulled the trigger. The night was now silent.

Sherman tucked his head down and made his way back to the vehicle. He could see house lights in the area start to go on, and knew people were starting to take notice of what just happened. He jumped in the car and made sure he spun the wheels, making a loud screeching sound as he sped away. He slowed to a normal driving speed as he turned the first corner, then returned to the house and backed the car into the driveway. He had to get out a few times to check and make sure that he had parked it exactly where it was. He grabbed the rifle and keys with his hands still covered in the paper towels. He entered the house with his newly acquired house keys and closed the door quietly behind him. As he returned to the bodies of Ricky and Tina, strangely he was a little surprised that everything was exactly the way he left it. Not that he was really expecting anything to change, but it was the first thing that he noticed. He returned to the bedroom, wiped down the rifle, and returned it to the back of the closet. He returned to Ricky's body and slowly clipped the keys to his belt, ensuring not to disturb any of the crime scenes. He stood over the body and said out loud, "Okay, Ricky is about to kill himself and writes the note . . . No, Ricky finds out about his girlfriend cheating on him and then takes revenge on the rival gang, then comes home to kill himself, writes his girlfriend a note, she unexpectedly comes home, they argue, and he turns it into a murder-suicide." *Sounds good to me*, he thought. Sherman stripped out of the gang member's clothes that he was wearing over his own, stuffed them into his backpack, and made his way to the front door. He used his paper towels to ensure he didn't leave any trace evidence as he opened and closed the door behind him. He made his way to the sidewalk and started walking back towards the laundromat. The weather was cold, and he wanted to walk with his head down and hands in his pockets, but feared that he would look like a "suspicious character" if someone saw him from afar. He walked with his head held high and his arms lightly swinging at his side as if he was going for a leisurely stroll in the park. He didn't want to overdo it, but thought he was putting on quite a convincing show. His inner voice was not amused and continued to remind him in different ways how he could correct his acting.

121

As he walked into the laundromat, the warmth hit his face and it was welcoming. Sherman took the clothes out of his backpack and threw them into a washing machine. There were a few bottles of detergent lined up on the machine next to his, as if the person using the machine had it there while they were doing their laundry. There was a bottle of detergent, a bottle of bleach, and a bottle of fabric softener. Sherman grabbed the bleach, poured about three cups of the bleach into his washing machine, and started the machine. He went to the back and plopped down in his seat.

It was late, and he was tired. He feared the police would come in and haul him off, but also knew it might be a while before they would be able to hash everything out. Every so often he would hear what he thought was a siren in the distance, but they seemed to be getting further away rather than getting closer. The traffic in the laundromat was just as it was before; the same type of clientele would walk into the place, look around, see that the man in the baggy clothes wasn't there, and then make their way out of the laundromat. Some left right away, others stood inside and waited, hoping that he would show up. *What a surprise that would be if he showed up,* Sherman thought.

Others walked around the place, left, and then waited outside as if to hope he might at least drive by. *Nope, he ain't doing that either,* Sherman thought as they waited outside. He spent the night dozing off and abruptly waking up at times when people walked in. He slept on and off throughout the night, and now that morning had arrived, he decided it was time to go back to the train station and continue his journey. It was a little later in the morning than he planned to leave, but he didn't really have a timeline or schedule that he had to stick to. He left the laundromat and started walking up the road. He thought about returning to the convenience store to buy another newspaper, but thought that might be a little suspicious. Instead he walked a little ways and got a paper from a machine outside of a gas station. He tucked the paper under his arm and continued on his way to the train station.

Chapter 8

As Sherman arrived at the station, he was still unsure as to where he was going. Did he still want to make the trek all the way across the country? He didn't see any reason to still do that. He was on the run for his original crime, and there was no mention of anyone looking for him. His inner voice told him to go back—Go back to New York, lay low for a little while, and get a feel for who, if anyone, was looking for him. He was under the assumption that at this point, if there was any information or he was a wanted man, the papers would have said something or the news would have mentioned him. There was no mention at all in any form of media, so he assumed he was safe to return. If anything was to turn out from the events of the last few nights, he would be a safe enough distance away that it would not be assumed that he left New York, traveled to a small town outside of Chicago, participated in a gang massacre, and then casually traveled back to New York as if nothing happened. He returned to the same track he got off of and went to the opposite side of the track. He sat a little distance away from the tracks and down the steep hill that the tracks sit on, leaning against a tree to await the arrival of the slow passing train. He consumed some of the snacks he had in his pack and opened up the paper he purchased at the gas station.

The story about the gang was all over the newspapers. Sherman wondered how they could get so much information about the situation, then get it printed and distributed in a paper form to so many outlets when the events only took place a handful of hours ago. He assumed that with the internet and greater technological advances, if the newspapers were going to survive, they better be quicker and more relevant and not just report news that is older than people would want to read. The headline read, *Gang Violence Massacre* and showed a picture of police cars parked in the street out in front of the house where all of the gang members were hanging out. There was a small picture transposed in the bottom corner of the larger picture and it was a picture of the outside of Ricky's house. Sherman turned to the article and started to read. The article started with, *James "Ricky" Ricardo was the main suspect in a gang-related mass murder and murder-suicide. Motives and details are still being obtained as law enforcement services continue to process both crime scenes.* There was mention of both gangs, how Ricky fit into one gang as opposed to the other, why the two gang sanctions were rivals, what might have triggered the massacre, and then the choice of weapon and a halfhearted attempt by the author as to why gun laws need to be more strict and assault rifles needed to be banned.

It wasn't a very well-written article, but it provided many details on what the law enforcement was thinking. Sherman didn't read anything that would suggest that law enforcement was thinking of any other motives or participants in the murders other than those that were already discussed in the article. Sherman thought there was no way that traveling through states and killing people could be this easy. There had to be more to it than this; how did all of these killers get caught when he had butchered a ton of people, and no one had any idea as to how it happened? All his exterminations to this point had started and ended almost accidentally, and it seemed that he had gotten away with all of them at this point. He imagined how much easier this could be if he actually sat down and planned every detail out. He could do this forever and never get caught; he could do this and continue to protect those who could not protect themselves. He was starting to like the new life he was leading; he was beginning to feel important again, and finally starting to feel like he was a valuable member of society.

Could it really be this easy? Could there be more people like him out there who had the same desire and passion to rid the world of horrible human beings? He was intrigued by the possibility, but also, his outlook on criminal investigations was forever changed. Maybe every article he had read about murders and suicides weren't what they truly were, and there were outside participants that staged the scenes to give the impression of how they wanted the media to report the crimes and who they were going to hold accountable in the eyes of the media, the public, and eventually the court system. Sherman's mind was running wild, and with every thought of the possibilities, the more excited he became. He saw the world in a different light, and he saw the need for his services greater than he ever had before. He once saw what he was doing as a positive action through negative means, but he now was losing sight of any negative aspects of his actions and only saw the positives of what he was doing.

His mind raced with the possibilities. He could really turn this into something. He had found something outside of the military that he was just as good at and where he was needed by the same people he was protecting while serving in the military. Instead of fighting overseas against an enemy that may or may not truly be understood by the American people, he was able to fight and protect them in his own country, closer to the people that needed him to protect them. He was honored to be able to do this at home, in his own country, on his own soil, and for the people he so deeply loved. The American people.

He hopped on the slow-moving train as if he was an expert and had been doing this his whole life. It was a great deal easier getting on the train this time than the first time. He made his way to the corner of the dark train car and plopped down, almost out of exhaustion. He'd spent many times physically, mentally, and emotionally exhausted throughout his time as a Marine and his body had become accustomed to dealing with exhaustion. He had a few hours to kill, so he decided to take another long needed nap in hopes that he could wake up refreshed and clear-headed enough to rethink his strategy and decide on the best new course of action.

Sherman slept hard and soundly, and he dreamt about the consequences of his actions. He truly didn't believe what he was doing was wrong; well, he knew the physical act of killing someone was wrong, but he believed there were right reasons to do wrong things. His dream had members of his family, friends, old school teachers, and random strangers questioning his actions and calling him names like *murderer, serial killer, sick,* or *insane.* He unsuccessfully tried to explain why it was okay, why God would approve, why someone truly had to do it, and how the world would benefit when it was done. It made great sense to rid the world of the bad people at all cost necessary. At one point in the dream, he found himself in a court of law explaining his case to a judge that wholeheartedly agreed with his actions and commended him for his bravery. He did question his sanity in some of the points made, but many of the points were from people who were never asked to constantly train for years to perfect the ability to take a life to defend the constitution of the United States against all enemies foreign and domestic. Didn't anyone who was asked to sacrifice themselves and their safety have to be a little bit insane? Didn't firemen have to be a little bit nuts to run into a burning building? But they willingly did it to save lives, even at the cost of their own. Cops had to run into harm's way with bank robberies in progress or a burglary in progress to protect innocent people; didn't they have to be a little bit out of their minds to be willing to do that? These were domestic enemies he was killing, so why didn't they understand or praise his noble actions, why weren't they glad someone was performing the actions they wouldn't be able to bring themselves to do?

Sherman woke abruptly to the train wheels screeching and the car vibrating violently. He braced himself as he got to his feet and saw that he was traveling next to a large river. The train was coming to a halt to allow cars to cross the tracks and travel over a large bridge that took them to the other side of the river. It was a large bridge in comparison to others Sherman had seen, but it wasn't like a huge Golden Gate Bridge. In terms of bridges, this was probably one of the smaller ones leading into the city. He assumed the bridge was one heading into Brooklyn or Manhattan. Sherman grew up in Queens, and didn't spend much time in the city; he knew landmarks, but wasn't an expert on directions or which bridge led to what boroughs, or even how to get around the city very well. As the train stopped, he jumped off onto the gravel and started making his way down the side of the train tracks. As he approached the bridge and made his way onto the walking path crossing the bridge, he realized that this bridge didn't lead into the city, but to the outskirts of the city. He wasn't able to even see the city from this side of the bridge, and would have a better view as he got further across the bridge and to a higher vantage point.

The bridge was busy with traffic and the water below was rushing at great speeds. He took a minute to marvel at the crossing of the paths of all of these humans as they drove over such a powerful force of nature without giving it a second thought. He stood at the midway point of the bridge, watching the water run by, and thought about the power of the water. It looked calm and refreshing, but he knew it could be powerful, dangerous, and unrelenting if it needed to be. He shared a moment of respect with the river, marveled at the comparison he just drew between the river and himself, and continued over the bridge. He crested the bridge and could see that the city was further off in the distance than he'd thought. He had a few highways to pass over or under and then some industrial-looking areas, and he would be back in the city.

But something didn't look right. He wasn't sure what side of the city he was on, but the skyline looked different. He usually couldn't pick out many of the buildings of the skyline and often only recognized the Statue of Liberty, depending on what side of the city he was looking from. But here, he didn't recognize any part of the skyline, and one of the buildings appeared to have florescent lights tracing around the entire top of it or something. He assumed he must have been coming from the north of the city, maybe from near the Bronx; he didn't spend much time in the Bronx, so that would explain why he was unfamiliar with this view or angle of the skyline.

He was continuing on his journey when he heard a very distinct sound coming from behind him. It was the quick siren blast of a police car, really short, and really loud, almost as if it was making the sound for him to move out of the way. He was on the end part of the bridge's walking path and not in the way, so that couldn't have been what the police officer wanted him to do. The car was slowly moving behind him, and as he stopped and turned around, the police car came to a halt on the side of the road. The driver's door opened as a police officer exited the car and motioned for him to come over to the front of the car, which he did.

"Did you just come off of that freight train?" the officer asked.

"No Officer, I was walking on the tracks and crossed the tracks as the train passed." Standing on the passenger side of the car with his hands on the hood of the car, the police officer stood next to him and continued to fire off questions. He took the backpack off of his back and placed it on the hood of the vehicle. Sherman looked back in the direction from where he came. He saw the bridge and the tracks, and he thought for a second that he might be able to outrun the cop long enough to get on a passing train, but what if he got caught? They would know something was up for sure then. He glanced at the side of the car as he looked back towards the police officer, and saw it had a badgelike emblem with big bold letters declaring, *Philadelphia Police.*

Well, that explains why I didn't recognize the skyline, he thought. "Where are you coming from?" the police officer asked.

"New York." As soon as the words left his mouth he cringed, but what else could he have said? He couldn't have said Chicago. A vagrant who just got off of a freight train coming from Chicago would seem way too suspicious.

"What brings you to Philadelphia?"

"I am looking for work, I figured this is a good a place as any."

The police officer was now standing behind him and half-heartedly patting him down. "Got any weapons? Anything in your pockets that will stick me or hurt me?"

The police officer was pulling his pockets inside out and placing the contents on the hood of the vehicle. "No, sir, no weapons or anything in my pockets you should be concerned with."

"Got I.D.?"

His heart sank. He didn't feel like he was keeping up with the conversation quick enough and that he was taking too much time answering questions. He was very nervous, but knew if this police officer stopped him for a reason, he would have already been put in handcuffs. He wasn't in handcuffs, so he assumed the police officer was just making a routine stop on a person he thought hopped a freight train. The police officer started going through his backpack. Sherman tried to think hard about anything that might be in there that would get him in trouble, but nothing came to mind. The contents looked like the belongings of someone who was traveling or being a survivalist or something like that, nothing out of the ordinary. The police officer removed a bunch of plastic cards being held together by a rubber band. He held it up in Sherman's direction "One of these your I.D.?" and before he could answer, the police officer was thumbing through the cards. He retrieved Sherman's retired military I.D. "Marine, huh? Well, thank you for your service." Sherman got a kick out of this comment, because this police officer had no idea the service he was actually providing and how it was truly helping the police officer out.

The police officer was making his way to the driver's side of the vehicle, still holding Sherman's identification in his hand, waving it towards Sherman's direction. "If everything checks out and you don't have any warrants, you will be free to go." With that, he got into the driver's side of the vehicle. Sherman started to sweat, and his level of nervousness had to be visible to the cop. Sherman started to think about all the times he had been pulled over for speeding, or when he was a teenager and got a ticket for drinking in the park, jumped a turnstile. He just knew something was going to pop up, and once they got him to the police station, they would somehow know of his actions. It seemed as if the police officer was in the car forever. How long could it possibly take for them to decide if he had a warrant? He half-expected for the police officer to come bounding out of the car, gun drawn and barking commands for Sherman to get on the ground. What if he did? Sherman thought maybe then he would run. He couldn't just give himself up; he would have to make some attempt at getting away, wouldn't he? Yeah, he would.

He started to look around and make an escape plan. He would first run back the same way he came. The cop wouldn't be able to bring his car against traffic over the bridge, so Sherman would have to outrun the police officer. The police officer was a little overweight and had a belt with all sorts of stuff hanging from it—his gun, pepper spray, a taser, and probably a half-dozen other things Sherman wanted no part of. Maybe running wouldn't be such a good idea.

"Looks like you're clean," the officer said as he made his way around the car. "If you're looking for work, ever consider becoming a cop? We're always looking for veterans to join the force, and they will take some of your military time towards your retirement on the force. Plus, they waive the age limit for retired service members." Sherman barely heard any of what he was saying, more concerned with gathering up his stuff on the hood of the car. "I will look into that," he responded, not exactly sure what was being asked of him. He quickly grabbed all of his stuff, but didn't want it to look obvious that he was trying to be quick and not too suspicious. He swung his pack onto his back and turned to walk away when the officer spoke again.

"Hey man, thanks again for your service, it really is appreciated. My Dad was a Marine. I was going to join the Corps, but the Navy got me first, then the police department came calling." The cop was standing at the front of the car with his hand outstretched in Sherman's direction. Sherman grabbed the man's hand in a firm handshake; the two men locked eyes, and for a split second Sherman thought that this wouldn't be the last time these two would see each other. Although he hoped differently.

Sherman made his way down the road, the police cruiser getting smaller and smaller behind him. He saw the police officer sit in the driver's seat, but that he still had the door open. *He must be doing paperwork or something,* Sherman thought. He didn't want to look back too many times as he thought it would look too suspicious.

The city was dirty. Trash blew through the streets, and there seemed to be a great deal of misplaced people throughout. Some seemed homeless, while others seemed to be just choosing to live on the streets. There were many panhandlers and young adults and teenagers; all were dirty and seemed to relish this lifestyle. Sherman felt he would fit right in.

He came to a park that was nestled right in the middle of some skyscraper buildings. The park was shadowed by the buildings, and he wondered how these trees ever got any sun. The park was old but well-kept; it had a swing set, merry-go-round, and a seesaw that looked to have been originally built in the 50s. The green paint on the playground equipment was thick. It looked as though the city maintained the equipment as well as the landscaping. Sherman sat on one of the benches and contemplated his next move. He was here in a city that he didn't plan on staying in, he had nowhere to go, nothing to do, and didn't have an overabundance of money. He might as well get back to doing what he was good at. He was sure there was someone within the city that would fit his requirements. Maybe he should get back online and look for another pedophile on the website he got the first one off of. The mistake he made with his first victim was that he left too much up to chance and didn't control the variables of the situation. He believed it was just a matter of time before they found his DNA, fingerprint, or something he had left behind.

Deep into thought, Sherman barely noticed the small group of dogs sniffing around the park. At first Sherman was greatly intimidated by these dogs, as he knew from past experiences that you could never be too sure as to what one loose dog might do, and here there were four loose dogs. He made sure he didn't do anything stupid, like try to get up and run or to show too much fear. He once heard that dogs could smell fear. He never understood how that changed a situation—does a dog smell fear and feel like they now have the upper hand and feel the need to be violent? Or is it just something people should be aware of, but doesn't change the situation?

The dogs continued to sniff throughout the park and were getting closer to him. One of the dogs that looked like a complete mutt came and sniffed his shoes. The dog hung around for a few seconds before something one of the other dogs was doing caught its attention and it ran off with the others. Sherman breathed a sigh of relief that the situation had turned out the way it did and these dogs didn't smell his fear and decide to all attack him. Sometimes Sherman let his fears overcome the reality of a situation. When it came to uncontrollable variables, it made him feel uncomfortable. Not knowing what a pack of stray dogs would do, was one of those situations.

He returned to his thoughts. Sherman knew if he researched another pedophile and went to their house, he would be at risk of leaving some sort of evidence. He had to come up with a better plan, one that would be less likely to get him caught. He had more important things to think about right now, like where he was going to sleep for the night and where he was going to get food.

Sherman searched around the buildings in the area and found many of them had basements. One in particular had a long entrance way that went down a steep ramp and led to a heavy metal door. The door opened to a brick wall, and the hallway ran left and right from the entrance. Sherman poked his head in and looked down both directions of the hallway. The hallway was very long and very dark. He had to let his eyes adjust to the darkness. There were rooms that were brightly lit far down the hallway on either side.

He entered the basement and made his way towards the first lit room. The room had a steady hum and racket of working machines, and there were about twenty washing machines and dryers. There was a long counter for folding clothes, a deep sink in the corner of the room that had a mop bucket in front of it, and a mop in the deep sink. There was a small bathroom off the corner of the laundry room with only a toilet and a pedestal sink. It was dirty and unmaintained; the type of bathroom a man would have no problem using, but that a woman would have refused. All the machines were quarter-operated machines and there was a coin operated detergent vending machine on the wall. It looked as though this was the community laundromat for the building residents.

He left the room and continued down the long hallway. The basement smelled of mold and dust, sitting water and rust. As he got further away from the light from the laundry room door, the hallway got darker and darker. He walked for a couple of hundred feet and found himself almost in complete darkness. He worried if there were other people in this hallway; if there were, he couldn't see them. They could be standing within inches of him and he probably still couldn't see them, it was that dark. He slowly took his backpack off his back and opened it up, rifling around for the book of matches he had in one of the side pockets. He removed a match, struck it, and the room lit up. He was no longer in a hallway; it seemed to have opened up to his left into a big room or open area. There was no door leading into this area, it just opened up from the hallway. The walls were covered with graffiti and there seemed to be broken wood or old broken furniture throughout the room and back wall. The light from the match wasn't enough to see to the far back wall, so Sherman blew out the match and walked to the area the light last lit up. He struck another match to see that the room went back a great deal further than he thought. He could now see the back wall and the windows at the top of the walls that led to the outside of the building.

He walked to one of the windows and stared out of it. The window was about eight feet high, just below where the ceiling met the wall. He could see that the window from the outside was under the ground level, but within a small half-circle area that led to ground level. The window was too small to crawl through, or at least he thought it was. It was one of those windows that were about a foot or so across and maybe eight inches from top to bottom. It was a rectangular window. Sherman guessed that in an emergency he might be able to get through, but seriously doubted it. He turned back towards the room and figured he would spend the night here. It was a warm spot, with not a lot of people coming through, and dark enough to scare away anyone with any kind of fear of the unknown. He just hoped that he wasn't the only homeless person who had this spot in mind and hoped to not run across them in the middle of the night.

Chapter 9

Sherman slept well, waking up refreshed and ready to take on the world. Other than a few late-night laundry dwellers and a few nighttime noises like car alarms going off on the street and the occasional arguing from passersby, he didn't run into anyone and no one came down into the room he was in. He looked for a good place in one of the corners of the basement where he could stash his backpack. He would be less conspicuous and would blend better walking the streets if he wasn't carrying it. There was a far corner in one of the rooms further down another hallway that had a bunch of old trash and pallets stacked up. They had about an inch of dust and settled dirt on them, so he knew this was not a frequented part of the underbelly of the building. He was extremely hungry, and took to the streets to see if he could find a dumpster or trash can to get some wastefully discarded half eaten food. He was surprised to see how much food gets thrown away that was perfectly fine. He found a hot dog in a garbage can that looked like only one small bite had been taken out of it, as if a mother and child got hot dogs and the kid didn't like theirs after taking one bite, so the mother took it and threw it away at the next garbage can. Sherman didn't mind; it seemed fine for him to eat, and it kept him from having to spend any of his own money.

He continued to try and think like a man on the run, trying not to be in the areas where there were cameras, trying to stay away from making too many transactions with people that might recognize him if he was on some sort of wanted list back in New York that he didn't know about or maybe some national database. For all he knew he could be all over the internet and a great deal of people may be able to recognize his face. He wasn't sure but wanted to err on the side of caution just in case. He also didn't want to do anything stupid that would get him stopped by another cop. The game plan was to go to an internet café, the library, or anywhere he could find that had the internet and get back on the site he used to find the first pedophile. Sherman knew he was taking a great risk of leaving a trail, because wherever he was going to use the internet, chances are they had cameras, and they could probably trace what websites he was on. He was concerned, but not overly concerned. If he played his cards right like the first one, did his research, and was smart about the way he conducted himself, he might be able to pull it off and not make the mistakes he made that time. He needed to ensure he was going to stay disciplined and do his homework the right way with this one. He would need to research, conduct surveillance, determine if they had been rehabilitated, and if they hadn't, then take action. He would use the same game plan as the first one, hopefully with better results that could not be traced back to him.

He walked down the street eating his hot dog and wondering, as he passed hundreds if not thousands of people on the streets of Philadelphia, how many of them had secrets, how many of them had these skeletons in their closets, and how many of them could make his list for actions in their lives. The image of the computer screen with all the red dots flashed back into his mind, and the possibilities of these people all walking the streets made him sick. He walked past businessmen in suits and city workers, men and women, young and old. He assumed many were good people without twisted and sick secrets, but he wasn't overly convinced. He would have never believed the red dots were out there until he saw them with his own eyes on the computer screen.

Sherman continued to walk and wondered if the sick feeling he was having in his stomach was from the possibility of these people or from the hot dog he ate out of the garbage. At this point, it could have been either. About a half a block up, he could see a sign hanging over the sidewalk that said *The Joe and Net.* It had a picture of a cup of coffee trapped in a fisherman's net, and under the picture it said *Internet Café.* Sherman thought the name was pretty lame and didn't quite understand it until he saw the storefront. He looked in through the large windows in the front of the store, and saw that there were computers lining the walls of the store on high counters. The place was packed, and people were drinking coffee and had plates with pastries and snacks they enjoyed while surfing the internet. It definitely wasn't the place Sherman thought that he should use to do his research, as there were too many people and too much interaction without enough privacy.

He continued to walk down the street, passing more business people on the way to work. The traffic was congested, everyone was in a rush, and no one seemed to pay any attention to what was going on around them, just the way he liked it. The more he blended in, the better. He came to a corner where there was an older lady sitting against the wall with a dog. She was holding a sign that was asking for money for some reason or other. Without ever coming to a full stop, he turned in her direction while still walking and asked, "Is there a library around here?"

"Yeah, Sixth and Arch," she responded.

Sherman pointed down the street he was already traveling. "Down here?"

"Yeah, three blocks and then up one." She pointed to the left when mentioning the "up one" part of the directions. The library was right where the directions suggested. Sherman walked three blocks and went up one block, and there it was—a tremendous old brick building. Sherman walked through the huge doors. The doors felt like they were twenty feet high, and were heavy, but glided open like they were on ice, smooth and effortless. The quality of the doors and workmanship of the building was impressive. Sherman walked through the door and was instantly blown away. The doors closed behind him, and he could feel the seal of the air when they did. The room was mostly made of wood and the smell of paper filled the air. Not the cheap paper smell of newspaper, cardboard, or printer paper, but the rich deep smell of novels, knowledge, information, and authenticity.

Sherman quickly scanned the place and instantly felt almost guilty or a little disgusted in himself that he had come to such a beautiful place to gain access to the internet instead of coming to submerse himself in the history or the reading of a good novel. It made him feel a little cheap or gave him the feeling of cheating. He saw a sign pointing towards the back of the library that read *Internet Access.* He followed the sign, and as he walked by the thousands of books, he felt as though they were shaking their heads in shame as he passed them up to make his way to the computers.

The computers did not match the place. He was expecting new, high-speed computers with clean-cut lines and high-resolution screens. What he found were old bulky monitors and tower computers that were once white and had now yellowed from the sun through the windows. They weren't very appealing, nor were they very impressive to look at. Sherman got the feeling that the library wanted the focus to remain on the books and not on the computer technology. So they provided the internet service but were not going to go above and beyond that. They would continue to put the bulk of their resources and continue to remain focused on the books. Sherman liked this, and mentally felt a tip of his cap was in order.

Sherman did all he could to not look too conspicuous. He didn't want to look up to the ceilings for cameras, but didn't want to just sit at any computer and then look, see a camera pointing right at him, and then have to get up and move to another computer. He also didn't want to stand in the room without taking a seat at a computer, or look as though he was looking for something. He didn't want to make it look as if he was looking at books while he was trying to find cameras, because he believed it would be odd if he was looking for a book, randomly decided he was going to use the computer, and then never got a book. He walked into the room, sat at the first computer that he saw, and immediately thought, *I did that entirely too quick. I wonder if it looked like I ran in here and sat down as fast as I could, as though the music stopped during a final round of musical chairs.* Now he felt suspicious, and he was already in the chair and facing the computer, so there wasn't much he could do about it now.

He turned the computer on and was prompted to agree to some terms about computer use and monitoring of the computers by the library. He almost got up and left, but didn't have a better plan as to how he could get the information. He agreed to the terms and was welcomed by the computer's desktop screen. He clicked on the internet connection and then stopped, drawing a blank as to where he saw the site originally. He couldn't just type in "Pedophile site," as that would raise a red flag immediately. He racked his brain, trying to remember where he saw the site; he vaguely remembered that it might have been a side advertisement on his email, but wasn't sure. He surely wasn't about to pull up his email on this computer and then enter a pedophile site. How would he get to a pedophile site? he wondered. How do pedophiles get on those sites without getting caught? He figured he had to think like a pedophile to catch a pedophile. What was he missing? How could he make this work? Maybe he needed to take a different approach. Maybe instead of him hunting the pedophiles, he could have the pedophiles hunt him.

Okay, if I hunt down a pedophile and kill him in his house, I have a ton of details I have to overcome to make it the perfect crime. What if I had the pedophiles come to me and killed them in the perfect spot? Then I could control the details and outcomes. He remembered watching a show a few years ago where the producers would have a person go online and pretend to be a young boy or a young girl and strike up a conversation on a chat line with a pedophile. They would then have the pedophile come to their house for a prearranged agreement for sex, and then when the pedophile would show up, the host of the show would pop out from behind the scenes and question the pedophile as to why he was there. They would have printed-out transcripts of the online chat about sexual questions and intentions and would really let the pedophile self-incriminate themselves before they left the house and were arrested by the police who were waiting outside for the pedophile. The forty, fifty, or sixty-year-old pedophiles always swore they were only there to play video games or talk to the young kids, but never ever had any intentions of doing anything sexually. Often the police would later check the pedophiles' cars and find a bag of sexual toys, condoms, candy, and alcohol in the trunks in preparation for their time with these children. Sometimes these animals would have the audacity to bring these items into the house with them as they introduced themselves to the bait child the producers had answer the door. The bait child was always an of-age police officer that looked really young, or who could pass as a teenager from a distance, and they would dress them up to fit the part. It worked rather well, and they arrested many predators due to this show.

So that's what he would do; he would go online and meet a pedophile, lure them to a park or dark alley, and kill them. That of course was just a generalization of his idea; he had to think out other details. He now had somewhat of a plan, he just had to finalize it and narrow down the finer details to increase his chances of getting away with it. If he did it in a park, it would have to be late at night and needed to look like a random act. A dark alley could be a little trickier, unless of course he made it look like a random meeting of someone who walked down the wrong alley at the wrong time. Either way, he believed he could make this work.

Back at the library, Sherman sat in front of the computer screen, his reflection staring him in the face as he tried to figure out how he was going to find the perfect target. He knew he first had to find an internet place to meet his victim. He assumed that the meeting would most likely take place in a chat site. Finding a chat site without using a search engine turned out to be a great deal more difficult than he would have thought. He ruled out using Google, Bing, or a Yahoo search engine and settled on going to the AOL home site. Under the "lifestyles" tab on the top of the home page were opportunities to enter chatrooms. He clicked on the link and was directed to a page with many chatroom options. The list of rooms seemed to go on for hundreds of pages: "Over Thirty", "Dog Lovers", "Sports Junkie", and "Friend

Search" were just a few that stood out. There were chatrooms for every category imaginable. Many had somewhat vague titles, but one could easily assume they were for other products or services. Sherman was pretty certain that he wasn't going to stumble across any chatrooms labeled "Pedophiles", so he was going to have to find a way to get creative and think like a young boy or girl to attract someone preying on young boys or girls.

He decided he was going to pose as a young girl, as he thought he would be better able to attract scum quicker. Now the problem was trying to figure out where he as a young girl could go to attract predators. He figured it would have to be in a young girl chatroom; maybe one that had to do with makeup, boys, or actors? His thought process was somewhat limited, because he didn't have any insight as to what these young girls would be thinking about and what chatrooms they might frequent. He scrolled through a few pages and found a common theme with boy band type-chatrooms dedicated to the love of individual singers in these bands or the bands in total. He clicked on the "CCA Nation" chatroom. CCA was a national boy band who's full name was "Caution, Cuidado, Attention", but were known more commonly as CCA. Many of the posts were in regard to trivia information, band dates, or concert experiences. Many of the posters posted information they believed was exclusively known to them. A poster that went by the name

"Mrs. Alonso", a spin off of one of the band members last name to give the impression she was his wife, or hoped to one day be. She posted that the favorite food of one of the band members, Deacon, was pizza. She posted this information as if she had an inside track into the eating habits of the band members. Others argued her knowledge of the band and offered greater truths regarding how they personally knew that Deacon's favorite food was indeed hamburgers, or pasta, fish and chips, or his mom's meatloaf. It seemed for as many posters were in this forum, there were just as many theories and different types of favorite food, all of them seeming to have rock-solid proof as to why they knew what his favorite foods were.

Sherman attempted to add his two cents, but was quickly prompted to sign up with a username to be able to post information on the site. He wanted to make a username that was descriptive and luring at the same time, something that was cute, but not too sexual for a young girl. He decided that he was going to be a thirteen-year-old girl, and he created the username "PrettyinPink13." Now that the name was created, it was time to set the bait. He entered the forum and typed, "I agree with Mrs. Alonso, I know his favorite food is pizza because he mentions it in a bunch of interviews." It didn't take long before Sherman found himself in the middle of what seemed to be a feeding frenzy about the band and all aspects of their eating habits. Within the mixture of rebuttals and insults came a few requests to "Private Chat." He assumed that this was other posters requesting to have a private conversation away from the group. Sherman spent some time entertaining private chats, and found that most of them were young boys who wanted to get to know Prettyinpink13. After a few questions and responses, it usually was quickly realized that an online friendship was not going to work and the requesting posters would move on.

A few of them either didn't take the hint, or seemed to be a little more intelligent in asking their questions, giving Sherman the idea that these posters may be older. Three in particular caught his attention; the main one in the group was "DeliveryBoy2013." Sherman chatted with this one for a little while, and didn't seem to be too far out of line until the very end of the conversation. Sherman could feel that the question string of "What is your favorite food?" "Where do you live?" and "Favorite band?" questions seemed normal. But the subtle "Do you like older boys?" "Do you have a boyfriend?" and "We should meet up" seemed a little fast-paced and out of line for normal teenage chatter.

Sherman looked down on the monitor and saw that he had been speaking with this poster for about forty-five minutes, and knew he was pushing his luck with the amount of time he was spending on the computer. He knew he had to somehow sink the hook in a very subtle way without scaring the delivery boy away. "I do like older boys, but how much older?" he typed. The response was going to be very telling as to the intent of the delivery boy. The anticipation Sherman felt while his fingers hovered over the keyboard was almost unbearable; with this response, he could have his next target, another making the list. His heart was pounding and he noticed he was holding his breath with anticipation.

"A lot could be learned from older boys. We could teach each other some fun stuff." Sherman's anticipation almost made him jump out of his chair and fist pump the air like he was Tiger Woods sinking a thirty-foot putt at Augusta National. He knew that he had just found his next victim and he couldn't be happier. "I like learning new stuff, and age is just a number. There is nothing wrong with having fun, I like fun," he typed back. Sherman could anticipate the responses on the other end of the chat, and he knew that the delivery boy was going to have to seal the deal and possibly ask some questions that were going to ensure Pretty in pink wasn't a police officer or someone who was setting him up to get in trouble. Sherman was prepared for anything this person could ask, but also had to ensure he really wasn't talking to some seventeen-year-old kid that was assuming he was talking to a thirteen-year-old girl. The relationship would have to be built, and maybe a little bit of trust would have to be created. Sherman knew this wasn't going to happen in one chat session.

"I have to get off the computer, my mom just got home. Will you be back on tomorrow? About the same time?" He asked.

"Yeah, sure, same time tomorrow," the delivery boy responded, and with that Sherman logged off and made his way out of the library and back to the basement. He had a little bit of a hop in his step; he was enjoying the thought of getting rid of another one. The planning phase was one of the most intriguing parts of the chase. The fear of doing it wrong and getting caught against planning it right and it running smooth was one of the greatest challenges he had been faced with since retiring from the military. His mind was racing with details, ideas, and escape routes. The ball was in motion. If he was who Sherman thought he was, the "delivery boy" would die, and he had no idea that his fate had already been decided.

Sherman returned to the library at the same time the next day. Sherman sat in the same seat, logged on the same way, made some small talk with who he thought were the regulars in this chatroom, and just waited for the "delivery boy" to show back up. It didn't take long before he received a message.

"Hey, it's you again. I was hoping you would be online. What's happening?"

They made some small talk, but Sherman was in no mood to spend a great deal of time with this guy getting to know each other. He had to ensure he was who he thought he was, sink the hook, set the meeting place, and then dispose of this menace to society. Sherman stomached the small talk for as long as he could but very quickly got more and more disgusted with the whole premise of what this predator was trying to do. Sherman cut right to the chase. "So, do you want to meet up?" He sat in anticipation to the response. Was this guy just out to have internet fun with young kids, or was he really who Sherman assumed he was and willing to take it further? To a physical level?

"Sure, that sounds fun but being a little older than you, I don't want you to be worried or concerned about the age difference. I believe that although I may seem older, I have always felt younger than I actually am. I really like many of the same things you like and since chatting with you I feel like we have a really cool bond."

Sherman wanted to smash the computer monitor. The anger in him was growing by the keystroke.

"Where do you want to meet?" flashed across the screen. Sherman looked at it as if he had hit the lottery. He thought for sure that he was going to have to find a way to Jedi mind-trick this guy into agreeing to meet him at a place of his choosing.

"There are a lot of fun places around here where we can go. I know a really cool park we can hang out at." Knowing that this guy was not about to agree to meeting in a park, Sherman just waited for his response to see if he had a better idea, as he was sure he did. "A park sounds fine, but I was hoping the first time we meet could be somewhere a little quieter where we could get to know each other. Me being older and all, I don't want anyone to get the wrong idea, I really like you, and think that we should get to know each other first together before hanging out in public. Would you want to come to my place?"

Well, that was a shock. *Come to his place?* Sherman wasn't expecting that. Was Sherman being set up? Why would this guy offer for an underage kid to come to his house? If he acted inappropriately, she would know where he lived. Unless he had no intention of letting her ever leave his house. This thing had just taken a weird turn, and Sherman no longer looked at it as just ridding the world of a pedophile, but also saw this guy as a possible worthy opponent. Maybe that wasn't the right wording, but he now saw this guy as maybe someone who would give him a run for his money. If this guy had the ability to kill, maybe he might be a little bit harder to kill than Sherman anticipated.

Sherman knew he didn't want to agree to go to this guy's house, that was for sure. He wanted him in the basement. He wanted him on his turf, in a familiar spot to him. "Oh, okay, he wrote back. "There is a place me and all my friends hang out when we just want to chill and not be bothered. It is over near the laundry room of the Manor apartments, they have a basement laundromat. Do you know where that is?"

Delivery boy responded, "I don't know off the top of my head where it is, but I know the area, I am sure I can GPS it. I can catch a train to the area and then walk the rest. I believe that isn't far from the station. What time do you want to meet?"

Sherman wasn't sure what would be a good time. What time would be the least busy with people? *When do most people do laundry?* he asked himself. "Some time during the day, I guess?" Sherman sent this assuming that most people did their laundry after they got off of work, so later in the day, or at night might be busier. He was trying to think of all angles and anything that would trip him up. So far, so good.

"During the day would work for me, how does tomorrow sound?" the delivery boy responded.

"Tomorrow is okay with me too, how about at like 3?" Sherman typed.

"Sounds like a plan, tomorrow at 3 at the Manor apartments laundry room."

And with that, the date was almost set. "Well, not AT the laundry room but right near it. Once you go down the ramp of the basement towards the laundry room you will come to a wall that you can only go left or right, the laundry room will be down the hallway to the left, where we hang out is down the hallway to the right. You continue down the hallway through a little bit of a dark area, and then it opens up to a room with light. No one ever goes down there and bothers us because I don't think they like walking past the dark part of the hallway. We can hang out down there for a little while before my mom comes home."

"Okay, sounds good to me. I look forward to hanging out and getting to know you, I am all excited now."

Sherman's skin crawled with that last sentence from the delivery boy, but he knew there were still a few more details that he would need before he was sure this would actually happen. "How will I know it is you?" he asked.

"That is a great question. I wouldn't want you to just assume it is someone else. How about I wear something that makes it really obvious that it is me? I have a Mickey Mouse t-shirt I could wear. That and a pair of blue jeans. And I can also wear a hat so there is no mistaking me. I have a really cool light blue trucker's hat that I can also wear. I am super pumped up to see you tomorrow, I can't wait. See you soon."

Yes you will, yes you will see me soon, and if all goes well, I will be the last person you see. Once again, there was a great deal of work to do, and Sherman felt that overwhelming sense of purpose that he hadn't felt in many years. The mission was put in place, the details needed to be hashed out, and then the mission needed to be completed.

The delivery boy was excited and pumped up for this meeting, but nowhere near as excited and pumped up as Sherman was. Sherman was almost jumping out of his skin with the thought of it. At the same time, he had a great deal of nervousness and anxiety about ensuring that all of this would go off without any issues, and that he would be able to figure out how not to get caught. The cat-and-mouse game of it all was just as exciting as completing the mission.

The preparation was going to be difficult, but the more work that needed to be done, the more Sherman reveled in it. Nothing easy is worth doing. Many thoughts kept crossing his mind. Should he use a knife? A brick, a meat grinder, a gun? How was he going to craft the perfect murder, and how was he planning to dispose of the remains once it was completed? He searched through the basement for the perfect spot, the perfect timing, the perfect scenario. The more he thought about it, the more details arose that he thought he was overlooking. His heart raced as he ran through them in his mind while his inner voice loved all the details and the planning. But his true self wasn't sure how he felt.

Actually, Sherman wasn't sure which was his true self anymore. Was it the bloodthirsty animal that he had become, the person who thrived on the destruction of others, or was it the kind-hearted person that many would describe him as? At this point he really didn't care. He knew what he was doing was beneficial to those who couldn't do it for themselves, so he was happy being whichever he needed to be. In the basement, in the room down the right hall, through the dark hallway, in the corner he sat, thinking about many scenarios and many details. A knife would be bloody. A gun would be loud and messy. Maybe a rope? Strangling someone might be loud and could have a struggle Sherman might not be physically prepared to overcome. After all, he had no idea what this guy looked like, how big he was, how strong he was, or if he had the intention of killing Prettyinpink13. So many things to think about, so many issues. He couldn't go to a store and buy materials, because that was how people got caught. They would be on the security camera buying ropes, tape, knives, and tarps. It was clear as day from an outside perspective what they were attempting to do and why they purchased all of those materials.

Maybe he could kill him, cut him up in the deep sink, put his body parts through a meat grinder, and then feed the chopped-up meat to that pack of stray dogs he ran into the other day? *They would never find the body,* His inner voice chimed in. *Well, unless they collected a bunch of dog poop.* But that could be way too messy, and there was so much that could go wrong with that plan. What if the dogs didn't like the taste of the delivery boy? Sherman would be stuck with a couple hundred pounds of chopped meat. His inner voice quickly shot down that idea.

He walked down to the laundry room to check out the place and make sure there weren't any cameras. There wasn't anyone in the laundry room when Sherman walked in, and he immediately thought, *Maybe I should have scoped out the place to see what hours were most busy and then waited a few days before making the meeting day and time.* But he hadn't, so here he was, rushing through the details to find the perfect way to make this all happen. No cameras in the laundry room, no cameras in the basement, no cameras on the building outside. That was one detail he wouldn't have to be nervous about. As he made his way down the ramp, Sherman grabbed the brick that was propping the outside metal door open. The door slammed behind him, and he returned to the dark part of the basement and tried to get some rest. He had a big day ahead of him tomorrow, and wanted to make sure he was going to show up to battle as the best version of himself he could. Well-rested and overly prepared to be successful.

The next day, Sherman paced with anticipation. The day was here, and he was as motivated and prepared as he could be. "Giddy" wouldn't be the right description, but it was close. Since he found out that there was a possibility this person could possibly be coming to do him harm, it made him feel like he was actually more preparing for battle and less like he was getting rid of a weak person who preyed on young children. The possibility that this person could maybe fight back or make Sherman work harder for the prize excited him and made him anticipate the encounter on an entirely different level. As the time ticked on, the adrenaline grew. He woke up before dawn as he always did. He was well-rested and had slept soundly. He anticipated restless sleeping and that he'd wake up tired and groggy, but for some reason, even on a concrete floor in a cold, damp basement, he slept soundly and woke up well-rested. Maybe it was because his body knew what was coming and how he was going to need to respond to the day's events.

With each hour that passed, the excitement, adrenaline, anxiety, worry, and fear grew. The area that Sherman slept was in the dark hallway area in between the laundry room and the lit room near the end of the long hallway that would be the meeting place. It looked like a long, dark hallway, but if you were to shine a light in that area, it was an actual cutout from the hallway that went back about twenty feet into the darkness. Sherman felt relatively safe sleeping there, because even if someone decided to walk down the hallway through the darkness towards the lit room, they wouldn't assume that there was a cutout of the hallway and would just keep walking though the darkness. The only people who would come into the area would be people who knew it was there and who wanted to be in the darkness, like maintenance workers or homeless people. So far, Sherman hadn't run into anyone else in the darkness. But the area was so large and so dark, there could be people in there with him that he may not even know were in there. Once again, so far so good.

Time was ticking by; twelve o'clock, one o'clock, two o'clock. The time was here. Sherman had his brick, he had his ambush spot, and he was as ready as he could be. He was going to be in the lit room, behind the open door, when the delivery boy entered. He was going to close the door behind him and then bludgeon him to death with the brick. He was then going to drag the body into the darkness, wait until nightfall, and decide on his next course of action once his adrenaline calmed down. He sat in the darkness and waited. And waited. And waited. It seemed like forever. There were moments that he second guessed what he was about to do. There were moments that he questioned his sanity. He questioned his mental health. There were moments that he was disgusted at what he had become. Then his inner voice would remind him that people like him were a necessity in this world. And although he may not understand it right now, it was for the greater good. It might be mentally painful for him right now, but in the darkness was where people like him shone the brightest. And although he agreed with his inner voice, he also questioned how all of this was the right path for him.

At 2:50 p.m., he came out of the darkened area to watch out of a small window in the hallway that had a clear view of the sidewalk leading to the basement. There were many people that walked by. Sherman at first thought it could be any one of these people who were going to meet any manner of other people to do dastardly deeds towards kids, or the elderly, or selling drugs to the weak. His mind was racing with how shitty his opinion of society now was. 3:00, still no Mickey shirt. 3:10, 3:15, 3:20. While watching hundreds of people walk by, he started to think that maybe he'd changed his mind. Maybe the delivery boy decided against meeting him. Maybe he scoped out the place and saw him earlier in the day, maybe the day before, or maybe he was preying on someone else right now and decided not to show up at all.

Off in the distance and down the road, Sherman spotted a light blue hat bobbing in the crowd. He wasn't sure if it was a man or a woman wearing it, but he could feel his breath start to quicken. He could feel the blood start to pulse and throb in his temples; his cheeks started to get hot with every step the blue hat took towards him. As the hat got closer, Sherman could tell that it belonged to a man. He wasn't a big man, about 5' 9" tall. He had a wide build, but didn't look overweight. He seemed to have a belly but he wasn't obese. The man's shirt started coming into sight. He was wearing a Micky Mouse shirt and a pair of denim shorts, white calf-high socks, and sneakers. He looked like he could be in his fifties, but a young fifty. He didn't look like he was in shape, but looked like he once had been, and Sherman wouldn't be surprised if he was extremely strong.

As the man continued toward him and made his way down the street, Sherman rethought his plan: *get behind the door, brick, body, darkness.* Check, check, check. The man stopped in front of the building and looked up at the apartments. He looked as if he was assessing the situation. He stood there for a few minutes and then started to make his way down the ramp towards the heavy metal door of the basement. Sherman quickly ran down the hallway, through the darkness, into the lit room and behind the door. He looked down to pick up the brick, but it wasn't there. *Oh shit, I left it in the darkness. FUUUCCKKKK.*

Sherman looked down the hallway; no delivery boy yet. He ran down the hallway and into the darkness. He could hear the heavy door open, and the man cast a shadow down the hall as the metal door slammed behind him. Sherman didn't want to let the man leave his sight, but as he felt around in the darkness with his foot for the brick, he couldn't feel it. He knew it was there, but didn't want to go further into the darkness and lose sight of the delivery boy. He worried that he might pass him, or he might see him. As the delivery boy started walking down the hallway, Sherman could sense his hesitation in each step. It was like he knew what he was doing was wrong, but the reward was too great to not continue even though he was scared. Step by step, Sherman could feel the calmness wash over him. He could feel time slow down, could feel his senses heighten. He could hear his inner voice say over the thumping of his heart, over the dry swallows of his throat, *This is what we train for.*

The man entered the darkness, and at one point he was within inches of Sherman. He could smell his cologne and the rankness of his breath. No brick, no gun, no knife. It was game time. This animalistic rage came over Sherman as he reached out for the man, he was a taller man and out-weighed Sherman so he knew whatever decision he was going to make, it was going to have to be quick. He lunged at the man from the side, came up onto his tippy-toes, and wrapped his arm around the delivery boy's neck. Sherman positioned his other arm on the opposite side of the delivery boy's head and latched his hand onto his own bicep, then squeezed with all his might. The man's arms came up in a defensive mode and tried to pull on Sherman's arm around his neck. Sherman could feel the man gasping for air, and every time the man breathed out in effort to get more air, Sherman squeezed harder, and harder, and harder. The delivery boy tried to bounce Sherman off the wall of the hallway but the delivery boys backpack softened the blow. Time after time, the delivery boy used all of his fading strength to slam Sherman against the wall, only to be cushioned by the backpack between their bodies. The delivery boy went from one wall and then turned his back towards the other wall in the darkness, pushing to try to get Sherman off of his neck, and at this point, off of his back. The delivery boy ran backwards to slam Sherman against the wall again, but there was no wall on this side, just an open, empty dark space. They both came crashing to the ground.

Sherman locked his legs around the man's waist and continued to squeeze harder and harder. Sherman at one point became lightheaded from the sheer force he was trying to use on this man. He could feel him start to go limp. Sherman could hear the metal door open and then slam shut. Was he only pretending to be limp? Should he take the chance? Should he wait? Sherman continued to squeeze and decided he wasn't going to let go until he was no longer able to hold on. He started to count. He remembered from his training that if a person was choked for long enough without oxygen it would kill them, but he couldn't remember if it was a minute, three minutes, or eight minutes. The door opened and the metal door slammed shut again. So he decided to just continue to squeeze, and hopefully he could hold on for eight minutes to ensure the job was done. He continued to count, 135, 256, 330, and somewhere in the middle he mentally ventured off to try and figure out how long eight minutes of seconds were, and thought that he probably should have counted to sixty eight times. At 400 he knew he had to be close, and decided to count to 500 and then reassess the situation. Once he got to 500, he slowly started to let up on the choke hold. He didn't realize at the time, but his arms were pretty numb and he could feel the blood rushing back into his arms. His arms tingled as if they were asleep. He was more concerned about how he felt at the moment than he was about the man in his grasp. He laid there on his side, his legs still wrapped around the delivery boy's waist and locked together in front of him. He held him in a hug to see if he could feel him breathing, or detect a pulse. His adrenaline was so high and his own senses were so out of whack that he couldn't tell if what he felt was real, or if he was imagining it.

The metal door opened up again and slammed shut. Sherman hoped that it was just people coming to do their laundry or picking it up. He didn't know if he had the strength to kill another person if they came down here making trouble or wanting to know what he was up to. He was pretty sure at this point that the man was dead. He'd laid with him wrapped up for quite a while and the man didn't seem to move, breathe, or have a pulse. Sherman unwrapped his legs from around the man and pushed the man off of him and onto the floor. He felt the vibration of the floor when the back of the man's head hit the floor.

Sherman's inner voice said, *Damn, that must have hurt,* and that made Sherman chuckle.

He did a quick mental check to ensure he wasn't hurt. He sat there in the dark and took inventory of his body. His legs worked and his arms were okay, no head injuries. Everything seemed okay, but he did notice that he was sticky. He was sure it was blood, but wasn't sure if it was his own blood or the delivery boy's blood. His shirt was wet; he assumed again that it was probably a mix of blood and sweat, and he wouldn't be able to tell for sure until he was able to see in the light.

He got up off of the floor, looked down the hallway, made sure the coast was clear, and made his way to the lit room. His shirt was covered with blood, as was his pants. He had a good amount of blood on his hands, arms, and his face. Now the clean-up would begin, but not until nightfall. He went back into the darkness and laid next to the body, half-leaning on it and half-sitting next to it. He did this as if he was concerned that if he wasn't right on top of the body, it might somehow escape.

The hours ticked by as Sherman sat and listened to the hum of the machines and the opening and slamming of the metal door. The frequency of the door opening became less and less, and he eventually heard the locking of the metal door. He waited another hour or so and started to make his way down the hallway to the laundry room. There were a few machines that still had laundry in them, and Sherman thought to himself, *someone isn't going to be happy that their stuff is still down here. I guess they will have to wait until tomorrow to get it.* It was interesting that even in the position he was in, he was concerned about how others would feel about their current misfortune. He went over to the deep sink and started to wash the blood off of himself. He took off his shirt and his pants and tried to wash them in the deep sink. The blood was coming out, but he needed to wash them. He looked around the laundry room. There were a few empty bottles of detergent in the trash that he took out and turned upside down in hopes to gets some out of the bottles. There was a shopping cart in the corner of the room that had some empty laundry bags in it that probably belonged to the people that still had laundry in the machines. He took his clothes and threw them in the washing machine. He noticed that his underwear had some blood on the waistband, and took those off also. There he stood, naked, with only his socks on. He poured the remainder of the detergent from the empty bottles he found and then decided to wash his socks also. He peeled them off, tossed them in the machine, closed it, and then read the directions so he could decide which cycle would best remove blood from clothes. *Is it permanent press? Or delicate? Maybe just normal would work best,* his inner voice contemplated. Normal was the longest cycle, so that is the one he chose. 42 minutes flashed on the display.

Sherman at first leaned against the machine and waited. Naked. He then decided it would be best to do whatever he was going to do with the body now, while he was naked, rather than wait until he was clothed again. He grabbed the shopping cart and made his way back into the darkness. He scooped up the man under the arms as if he was trying to bring a drunk buddy home to his wife after a rough night of drinking. He dumped his upper torso into the shopping cart and then lifted his legs to dump them into the cart also, but every time he went to lift the legs, the cart's wheels would roll and he would wind up chasing the motion of the cart while holding his legs. The bare legs in shorts against his skin felt weird to him, but not weird that it was a dead body's bare legs; it was holding another man's bare legs while he was naked that made him feel uncomfortable.

After he chased the cart around in a small circle, the cart finally stopped and he was able to get the rest of the body in the cart. Sherman attempted to move the cart down the hall and into the lit room, but it wouldn't move. Every time he attempted to push the cart forward it wouldn't move. Was the body too heavy? Did a wheel break? He reached down to make sure the wheels weren't broken and he found the problem. There was a brick blocking the front wheel. *There you are,* speaking to the brick as if it was a lost pet.

171

He picked up the brick, and with a chuckle, threw it in the cart with the body. He wheeled the cart into the light and saw that the man was clearly dead. He had blood coming out of his nose and mouth, but didn't seem to have any other injuries. The amount of blood was a little strange, and it almost seemed like maybe this guy died of something else in the process. Why would he bleed this much from being choked? Maybe he had an aneurysm or something? That made Sherman feel better, as if he wasn't responsible for his death completely; it was like he started it and something else finished it. He was okay with that. But at the same time, he was okay with the fact the guy was dead.

Sherman took one of the laundry bags, wiped the blood off of the guy's face and body the best he could, and stuffed the bag down the front of the guy's shirt. He took the backpack off the guy's back and opened it up. What he found made him feel a great deal better. There was a bottle of vodka, furry pink handcuffs, a bandana, bungee cords, some kind of powder in a medicine bottle, and a knife. Sherman's first thought was to spit on the guy, but he didn't want to leave any DNA on him, so he just looked at him with disgust and said out loud, "You fucking piece of shit. You got what you deserved, and I am glad I was the one able to give it to you." He emptied the rest of the man's pockets and was surprised he didn't find a phone. He found $42 in bills, some change, and that was it. No wallet, no identification, no credit cards, nothing. And that made Sherman nervous. He couldn't figure out why that was. So he just sat there on his shoes, butt naked next to the shopping cart with the dead body in it waiting for his clothes to get finished being washed, contemplating his next move.

His inner voice chimed in, *okay, you sick fuck, what are we going to do with you now?* Sherman had some ideas, but wanted to wait until his adrenaline calmed down a bit before making any rash decisions. But everything ran through his mind; *get a hacksaw and cut him up? Too messy. Meat grinder and grind him up and feed him to those neighborhood dogs you ran into? Once again, probably too loud and too messy. Just dump him somewhere? No ID, no wallet, nothing? Maybe. Keep thinking. Where do bad guys dump bodies? Shallow graves in the woods? Throw him on the train tracks? Sure, why not throw him on the train tracks?* His inner voice jumped in, speaking in a tone that made Sherman sound like an idiot. *Why? Because it would show drag marks getting him there. Then they would be able to tell he was already dead beforehand, and that would just raise more red flags. I like the 'dump him somewhere' idea. Let's do that.*

Sherman sat and amused himself about how useful laundromats had been for him in the last few weeks. He came up with nicknames for himself like "The laundromat murderer", "The Maytag Murderer", "The fluff and fold

Killer", and the "Soak and Spin Psycho." He didn't so much like that last one, but he couldn't come up with too many others that made sense.

After switching his laundry from the washer to the dryer, and then completing that cycle, Sherman got dressed and was actually surprised at how much blood had come out of his clothes. You couldn't even tell there was any blood on them at all, and definitely couldn't tell that a few short hours ago he was covered in blood from killing someone. He gathered up his stuff, put his new belongings in his backpack, and pulled a laundry bag over the top of the torso. Sherman stuffed the Delivery Boy's legs into another laundry bag, pulled the laundry bag up to the man's waist, and pulled the drawstring tight. Sherman then retrieved the clothes from the dryer, filled up the other two bags with laundry, threw them on top of the body, and made his way to the loud metal door. Slowly, he unlocked it from the inside, pushed the cart out of the door, and was mindful to make sure the door didn't squeak or slam when closing it. Sherman wouldn't have been surprised if someone told him he took a solid five minutes to shut that door. He wheeled his new trophy up the ramp, onto the sidewalk, and into the crisp night air, looking for the perfect place to leave the delivery boy.

These wheels are really great, Sherman thought to himself. Often shopping carts had one wobbly wheel, or wouldn't be smooth when rolling. This cart was grade A. No wonder someone stole it. It glided around like it was on glass, and it really made Sherman's task much easier. His mind was no longer racing, and he was at ease with what he had done. He was still in the moment, still vigilantly focused, as the mission hadn't been completed yet—he was still pushing around two hundred pounds of waste he needed to dispose of. He wasn't overly concerned as he had a relatively good idea of how he was going to dispose of this one.

Sherman was getting more brazen with these tasks as he started to realize maybe not as many people missed these types of people as he first thought. This one was going to be a homeless guy. But he had to make it believable, so now he had to find a place where bums hang out without there being any bums there to decide what he was going to do. That would make things more difficult, as many of the homeless would probably have bedded down for the night in all of the perfect homeless spots that would make being unseen more difficult. He continued to push the shopping cart for what he figured was probably a half a mile. Off in the distance, he could hear the sounds of cars driving at a high rate of speed, so he assumed not too much further there would be a highway or an expressway that might help him in his endeavor. The streets were dead, and Sherman hadn't yet seen a person. No drunks making their way home after a late night at the bar, no late-night dog walkers, no one. Sherman wasn't sure if he was just getting lucky, or if it was somehow divine intervention just proving a little bit more that maybe he had truly found his calling.

As he approached the expressway, he quickly realized he was in "dead bum drop-off" heaven. There were a bunch of areas that had walking paths that went under the expressway, walking paths that went next to the expressway, and walking paths that went over the expressway. Sherman pushed the cart to the side of a walkway and went to recon the area to see what area would be best. He didn't have to go far to realize that there were a few bums on the walkway that went over the expressway. He quickly realized that this was probably due to there being no chance of rain tonight, so the bums chose to sleep under the stars; if there was a chance of rain, they would probably sleep under the expressway on the other walkway. The delivery boy was going to sleep under the expressway tonight.

Sherman went back and retrieved the shopping cart and pushed it towards the underpass. He couldn't believe how smooth this cart was; it was really distracting to what he was trying to do. He was more focused on it than his surroundings, and at times worried it might cause him to be caught or seen if he let his guard down. *Focus, dumb dumb,* his inner voice said. *We can discuss the cart later.* He found what he thought was the perfect spot. It was in the underpass, but away from the overhead lights. He dumped the cart over and the delivery boy spilled out onto the floor.

He made sure to not leave too many clues that he was here. He lifted each extremity up individually and placed it where he wanted it to avoid drag marks. He leaned the body on the wall as if it was sitting straight up, and then let it naturally fall to the floor on its side as if it naturally happened. He retrieved the bottle of vodka from his backpack, put it to the delivery boy's lips, and poured a little into his mouth. He then wiped the bottle clean with his t-shirt, making sure there weren't any fingerprints left on it, and placed it in the man's hand.

It took a little doing trying to pry his fingers open, as he assumed rigor mortis was starting to set in. Once he got the bottle to stay, Sherman gathered up the laundry bags, threw them in the shopping cart, and made his way back the same way he came. He looked back at the end of the underpass and thought to himself, *That looks pretty natural, a dead bum under a bridge. Let's see how that plays out in the morning paper.* He rolled the cart back to the basement, left the clean laundry bags in the cart, and cleaned up the area to make it look like he was never there, ensuring the clothes he'd removed from the washer and dryer were back where they belonged. He washed the brick in the deep sink and returned it to near where he found it next to the outside door, and then made his way into the dark hallway. He couldn't tell in the darkness if there was blood on the floor or any other of the delivery boy's possessions. It still bothered him that the delivery boy didn't have a wallet or any identification, and he wondered if it might have fallen out of his pocket during the scuffle. He searched as best he could, but didn't see anything.

Sherman went further into the darkness, leaned up against the wall, and fell asleep. He woke a few times throughout the night, questioning his decision and actions, and the more time that went by, the more freaked out, worried, and nervous he got. His mind was playing tricks on him, and he wasn't handling it well. *Am I losing my mind? Or is this my new reality?* he wondered.

Chapter 10

Sherman sat at the bar, still slightly in shock from what just happened the day before, but surprisingly less in shock than he thought he should have been. He had gotten accustomed to how his body and mind reacted after he completed these deeds. He was hungry, and he figured while he was here he might as well order something local. He'd heard all the hype about them, but never had one, so why not order a Philly cheesesteak? Lunch was on the delivery boy.

Sherman didn't drink much, or often, so being in a bar had its own level of suspicion. Who goes to a bar to just order food? He felt like maybe he should order a beer and then not drink it to make it look less obvious. "What can I get you, friend?" the bartender asked over the louder-than-usual music as he laid a napkin down in front of Sherman on the bar.

"How are your cheesesteaks?" Sherman asked.

"One of the best in the city," the bartender replied.

"Let me get one of those and an Arnold Palmer, more iced tea than lemonade, like a 75-25 split. I'm still nursing a hangover from last night." *What a genius order*, Sherman thought. Maybe that would make it less obvious as to why he wasn't drinking as he sat alone in a bar.

* * *

The Police Chief sat at his desk. He was thinking about the many crimes throughout the city that had taken place in the days before. He knew many of the criminals in the city, and knew most of their reasoning and ways of committing crimes. The Italians did things one way, as did the Asian mafia, the stick-up kids, the junkies, and the wannabees. But today he was stuck on a crime that didn't match the gang murders, or the random snatch-and-grab accidental murders. This didn't even match any of the numerous robbery murders that happened quite a bit around the city. He was going to have to hit the streets hard and talk to some of his informants to see what they knew, and if anyone might have seen anything.

"Grab your stuff, let's go up the block and grab a beer," the Police Chief said as he walked up to the Sergeant's desk. He tossed him his keys. "You're driving."

The drive was short, and they made small chit-chat on the way, a little about sports, a little about the murder details, a little brainstorming. They parked the car and made their way into the bar. "It's kind of loud in here today, don't you think?"

"You know what I think? I think you're getting old, Chief."

They found a table and sat down. "I'll go get us some drinks," the younger officer said, then went to the bar and ordered a round of beers for himself and his boss. He looked down the bar as he waited for his beers and saw the guy he'd stopped a few days before, the one who hopped off the freight train. *A vagrant?* he thought. He began to ponder the thought in regard to the murder case file on his desk.

The beers arrived, and he made his way back to the table. "Hey Chief, there was this guy I could have sworn I saw jumping off a freight train just outside of town the other day. I stopped him and got some info from him, and he came up clean, but there's just something about him I can't seem to shake. Maybe I should bring him in to ask him a few questions."

"About what?" the Chief asked.

"The murder," the Officer replied.

"Do you have probable cause as to why you would want to bring in this homeless guy over any other homeless guy throughout the entire city?" the Chief asked the younger officer. "Well, no. Good point." He paused. "Well, he was a Marine though, isn't that reason enough?" he said jokingly to the Chief.

"Well, if he was a Marine, you know he's a good guy. Us Marines are all good guys. Let's go talk to him," the Chief said. Technically they weren't going to question the guy about anything, just get a feel for him. They were both off-duty, out of uniform, and wearing civilian attire. They grabbed their beers and made their way to the bar.

* * *

Sherman sat at the bar. His cheesesteak was pretty good, it came with a side of French fries and coleslaw. He never understood why sandwiches came with coleslaw; he always thought there were so many other sides that could better go with a sandwich and French fries. He never ate the coleslaw and wondered how many people who got this added to their order actually did. It could only be about 10%, as it was an acquired taste and he assumed that most people just didn't like it. It seemed like a waste of money for the restaurant to include it with every sandwich and French fries that was ordered.

Suddenly, Sherman felt a hand on his shoulder. As he turned, he noticed the police officer that stopped him on the bridge the other day. He reintroduced himself and another guy that was with him. The other guy made Sherman slightly nervous; he stood looking at him a little as if he knew what he had done. He was originally going to give a fake name, but thought that maybe the police officer might have remembered his name and only asked as an icebreaker. That would give them reason to be suspicious if he had given them a fake name, knowing they knew what his real name was.

Why would they come up to me? Sherman thought. He wondered if they may know what he had done. He started to feel unsettled and panicked. The room started to get a little smaller, the air a little heavier, the crowd was greater, and he felt like he needed to get out of this place and fast. As he stood up, the older guy put his hand on Sherman's shoulder and motioned to the bartender. "Ryan, let me get a beer for my friend, my Marine friend."

Sherman's heart was racing, and he knew he had to do something—he just wasn't sure what he needed to do. He felt as though he was on the verge of a nervous breakdown. The young officer gave Sherman a head nod. "Hey, it's you again! We really have to stop meeting like this." The officer reached out his hand in an offer at a handshake. "Hey Chief, I want you to meet . . . what was your name again?" he asked as he leaned towards Sherman, raising his voice to ensure he heard him over the music.

"Sherman, my name is Sherman."

The Chief reached out his hand and firmly shook Sherman's hand. "Semper Fi. I hear you are a Marine."

"Yeah, a long time ago, but I guess you know what they say—once a Marine, always a Marine."

"Ain't that the truth, I still miss those days. Not the Vietnam part, but the rest, and all of the Marines, I miss the comradery a lot. I was lucky to find the next best thing in the police department, so it worked out in the long run. Let me buy you a beer."

As the Police Chief raised his arm to get the attention of the bartender, Sherman replied "No, that's okay, I don't drink, and I have a hangover. So I'm nursing that." Sherman was sure that response would work just as well on him as it did on the bartender. But the Chief replied, "Oh, really? You don't drink and you have a hangover, nice try."

The bartender made his way over. "Hey Chief, how's it going?"

"Things are great Ryan, Let me get a beer for my friend here. My Marine friend." He placed his hand on Sherman's shoulder and gave it a light tap and a firm grasp. Sherman didn't want to drink, but figured why not? Maybe it would take the edge off and make him relax a little. He'd never liked the taste of beer, and this beer was no exception. He wasn't sure if it was a regular beer or one of those micro-brew beers that were made with all of the weird ingredients like ginger and cumin. He knew from the first sip he didn't like it, but continued to drink it not to be rude.

Sherman couldn't believe he was sitting here with two cops after the night he had. He felt like maybe they knew. *Nah, there's no way they know. They don't have beers with suspects*, his inner voice teased. *If they knew, they would have dragged you out of here in handcuffs twenty minutes ago.* The evening continued with discussions of military service duty stations, campaigns overseas, and the normal complaints about the misery of being in the military. Especially the Marines. The younger police officer had been in the Navy, so there was a great deal of making fun of him in regard to Marines versus Sailors.

"Hey Sherman, if the Marines are so great, why are they not their own branch instead of being a department of the Navy?' the younger officer teased. Without missing a beat, Sherman responded with, "Yeah, we are a department of the Navy, the men's department." The two Marines laughed and gave each other some chummy physical responses, a high five, a light push, as they threw their heads back in laughter. The night dragged on, as did the beer drinking and military gamesmanship.

"Ryan, a round of shots for the boys," the Police Chief shouted to the bartender.

"Oh, no, I don't do shots." Sherman protested. After all, he'd finished his beer and had another, and this one came with a slice of orange on the glass, which was strange to Sherman. He also had a super dark beer that tasted like it was burnt, and at this point he was feeling a little tipsy and knew he should soon call it a night. "No shot for me," he proclaimed.

"Nice try, Marine. I haven't had a night out like this in a long time. You aren't going to ruin the fun so you can go to sleep. The night is still young." One shot, two shot, three shots. Was it an hour later or three hours later? Sherman had no idea, and reality was starting to slip from his grasp.

"I'm going to the bathroom," Sherman screamed over the music. He hopped off of the bar stool and it all hit him like a brick. The room was moving; not spinning, but moving. Every time he tried to focus on one thing, it would get blurry, focused, blurry again, and then spin. He found that closing one eye helped, but not much. He stumbled his way to the bathroom.

As he was pissing, Sherman leaned his arm against the wall and his head against his arm. *What have I done? I'm too drunk. You can't go around killing people and get this drunk.*

What? his inner voice said.

I kill people, Sherman screamed.

Who kills people? his inner voice said. *What are you talking about?*

Sherman picked his head up off of his arm. His vision was blurry and the room was spinning. He wasn't in the bathroom. He was at the bar; he'd had his head down at the bar. He focused his eyes on the Police Chief sitting next to him. Sherman could barely hold his head up.

"We all have, war is not pretty," the Chief said as he patted Sherman on the back. "War is not pretty, my friend." Sherman couldn't keep his head up anymore and placed it back on his arm on the bar. That is when he realized that he'd pissed his pants. His pants were soaking wet, and there was a small puddle under his feet on the floor. He could feel himself talking, but wasn't sure what he was mumbling, or to whom he was mumbling. "Now or then?" the Chief asked him. Sherman couldn't seem to let it go. He was going on and on about the evils of the world. Half was mumbled gibberish while the other half was spoken, as if he was giving a speech before congress.

"Where do we go? US. WHERE DO WE GO? You spend millions on us. You train us, and train us, and train us. For what? To go back home and sit on the couch? I KILL PEOPLE. I kill bad people. You have a badge. You have a gun. People come to you for help. But who helps you when your hands are tied? Who fights for you? Who fights for them? Who protects them when the demons come at night? I am the demon fighter. I kill the bad guys."

"Okay Sherman, maybe you had too much to drink. Let's get you home."

"I kill pedophiles, drug dealers, predators, I kill them all. One evil at a time. My training demands it of me. Of you. It demands it of us." He spoke the words into the crook of his arm on the bar, never lifting his head.

"Hey everyone, look at big bad Sherman, the killer, Sherman the killer," the Chief yelled, loud enough for people to see he was talking, but not loud enough to hear what he was saying.

"I prey on the predators. I hunt them, I draw them in, I stalk them and rid the world of them. Don't believe me?

Check the bridge. He preyed on young girls. I did that, I saved them, I was trained to handle these situations, and I did." Sherman never lifted his head from his arm on the bar. He was making his argument through his arm, almost shouting it at the floor. The Chief, who had heard everything he had to say, nudged the younger police officer and said, "You believe this guy? Some storyteller, huh?"

The younger police officer leaned in, equally as intoxicated as the others in his group. "Huh? What did he say?" the officer asked.

"Nothing, he is just talking a bunch of nonsense. I will be right back, I am going to take a piss," the Chief said as he walked away from the bar. Sherman popped up from the bar, stood up, steadied himself, jammed his hands into the front pockets of his jeans that were soaking wet from him urinating on himself, and started making his way to the door through blurry eyes and a spinning room. He made it to the front door and used his shoulder to open it. It was a beautiful night, but Sherman would not realize it in the state he was in. He walked at times with one eye open, both eyes open, and sometimes with both eyes closed in hopes that it would stop the world from spinning as fast and as hard as it was spinning. He laid down on his side, made himself as comfortable as he could, and tried to get some sleep. The spinning was worse as he laid there, and when he opened his eyes to make it stop, it was even worse than when he had his eyes closed. He was sure he was going to throw up, and started discussing with himself the possibility of just getting up and doing it before it came, or making himself throw up just to get the alcohol out of his system. As he argued and contemplated, Sherman fell asleep under the stars on a beautiful night on the streets of Philadelphia.

* * *

It wasn't unusual for police officers to come into the Police Chief's office and brief him on bodies that were found throughout the city. He didn't get reports on natural deaths or deaths that happened out of his jurisdiction. Mostly homicides, deaths of the homeless, and suicides. This morning was like all the rest. Almost every day, an officer would walk in and say, "Hey Chief, they found another body." But this time, one stood out to him.

"Hey Chief, we found another body. Across town, under the bridge, a homeless guy." The hair on the back of the Police Chief's neck stood on end.

"Homicide? What was the weapon used?"

"No weapon, looks like a natural cause of death. He was bleeding out of his nose and mouth, but so far, no reason to assume anything other than a natural death. Want me to have them run an autopsy report?" the officer asked.

"Not unless there is reason to, any background? Any information on him?" the Chief responded.

"Not yet, no ID, no belongings, other than a bottle of booze. We are running some prints. I will let you know what comes up when I get the results."

The Chief sat in his office alone, thinking about all that Sherman said. *Could it be true? Could this guy be wandering the city killing people?* He tried to remember all the things that Sherman had told him that night. He was pretty intoxicated also, so he was having a hard time remembering it all. *He mentioned bad people, he mentioned the guy under the bridge, he mentioned his training. Did he say the guy under the bridge was a bad guy? A drug dealer? Pedophile?* He couldn't remember, and now wished he would have paid better attention to what Sherman was saying. A retired Marine ridding the city of bad people? He had heard of worse things happening. *Like a vigilante, but not really. Don't vigilantes have a grudge to settle or something?* He asked himself. *Maybe he does. Maybe one of these people did him wrong?* He needed to find Sherman and make some sense of all of this.

"Hey Chief, the report is back. Turns out the guy has a background. He wasn't homeless. He lived in a motel across town. Not much in his room, just a few belongings, and he was renting the place weekly. Turns out this guy was a real sicko. Has a bunch of arrests for actions against children. Child endangerment, sexual assault of a minor, sodomy of a minor, and a rape charge from about fifteen years ago. A real piece of trash. Probably better he's dead. Want me to run an autopsy report?" he asked the Chief.

"No need. Natural causes. Send him to the morgue and let them process him." The Chief sat back and thought to himself, *You son of a bitch, you're really doing it. You are really continuing your oath of enlistment.* He was intrigued by the premise, but also realized that he was a law enforcement officer and it was his responsibility to arrest people when they did these things. *How many times have we arrested these guys, brought them to court, they let them go, and we arrest them again? It's like a revolving door. Maybe the door stops with Sherman. That's not so bad, is it? Hell, if that's the case, I got a few guys he could help me out with,* he thought to himself as he patted a stack of files on his desk. His heart quickened and his pulse raced a little bit. *This can't happen. Or can it?* He started playing out the scenarios in his head. *I mean, we are Marines, right? We were born again through the right of passage and forged by fire.* The thought of it made him see things in a little bit of a different light. *I'm not doing anything illegal if I just turn a blind eye, right? Maybe if I just don't look so hard in his direction, maybe?* He grabbed the stack of files on his desk, put them on his lap, leaned back in his chair, and threw his legs up onto his desk. He crossed his ankles and looked down on the stack of files. "Maybe, just maybe."

Chapter 11

Sherman woke up freezing. He was laying in mulch underneath a tree in the city park. He sat up and leaned against the tree. He was surprised that no one had woken him up or bothered him. He checked his pockets to make sure he still had his belongings. His head was pounding and he felt nauseous. It was still early. The sun was up, but not by much. It still hadn't made it up over the buildings, so it was cold and there was dew all over the grass. And Sherman—his pants were soaking wet, and he quickly realized that it wasn't from the dew. It seemed as if he'd peed on himself while he was sleeping. He was more drunk last night then he had been in many years, and he wondered what happened and how he got to the park. He remembered having a few beers with the police officers, but not much after that. The entire night was a blur. And most of it was just a complete blackout.

Sherman still felt pretty confident that all was fine, because if it wasn't, he wouldn't have woken up under a tree in the park. He would have woken up in a jail cell. And since he hadn't, everything must be fine. Sherman just rationalized to himself that he had a few beers, got a little drunk, and decided to sleep here instead of the basement.

Or maybe they were following him last night and he didn't want to go to the basement and show them where he lived, so he stayed in the park instead? Either way, he felt relatively confident that everything was okay. He got himself up and dusted off as much of the mulch on his clothes as he could, especially the wet part of his pants that now seemed to be stained red from the mulch. He still felt terrible, and on his way back to the basement he stopped to throw up twice. It was going to be a long, miserable day.

Sherman made it back to the comfort and sanctity of the basement. He stripped off his pants as if he was standing in his own laundry room in his house, threw them in the washer, went to the trash can for a few almost-empty bottles of detergent, mixed them together, and started the machine. He walked back into the darkness and sat on the floor. He still felt terrible, so he leaned back against the wall and immediately fell back asleep.

* * *

The night was chilly, but not unbearable. The Chief had his hood pulled up over his head and there was a slight cold mist falling from the sky. His hands were jammed in his coat pockets, and he looked like any other person on the streets at this late hour, or early morning hour, trying to keep from freezing to death. He was looking for one of his moles, his street people. He needed information, and knew just the person to find to get it. There was an underground process that was used by law enforcement towards the lower-level criminals in the city. The cops would let the low-level criminals continue to do their low-level crimes as long as when the cops needed some information, they would be willing to give up what information they had.

The Chief had been working these streets for many years and knew a great deal of the criminals of the city. He had quite an understanding with many of the homeless. He had seen many of them grow up on the streets. He wanted to find "Sherman", if that was his real name. He wanted to find him without anyone knowing he was looking for him, and to do this, he knew he had to dip into his bag of tricks and work the streets for information. The man who had all of the answers he was looking for was Cappy. Cappy was a homeless man who looked far older than his age would suggest, was missing the majority of his teeth, and came across as a very nonthreatening character. The community loved Cappy and almost treated him like the neighborhood mascot. People would often bring him food or clothes in the winter, but often avoided giving him money knowing it would go right to alcohol. The community wanted to take care of Cappy and make sure he was okay, while at the same time not contributing to his bad habits. Cappy was a very interesting fellow. He had great stories that spoke of Naval ships and wartime heroics, bodybuilding championships, law enforcement awards and recognition, as well as being a pilot for a commercial airlines, and at times a surgeon. Cappy spoke in codes, and there was no way of ever truly being able to tell what was fact and what was fiction. Cappy wasn't his real name; he had been given the name by some of his homeless buddies because he was at one time or another in his life a captain of everything, or at least that is how his stories went. An airline captain, boat captain, police captain, a military captain, and at times, Captain Kangaroo, Captain Caveman, and Captain Crunch. Cappy had a very well-versed understanding of the streets. He somehow knew everything that was going on, but could never explain how he knew so much. The irony of Cappy was that he spoke in codes, rhymes, and gibberish. But if you could decipher what he was saying, often the information would be spot on. The problem was figuring out how to decipher the information. If the Chief was going to find Sherman, Cappy was going to be the man to point him in the right direction.

Cappy was sitting in the city park on a small concrete wall. The rain didn't seem to bother him as he sat drinking his beer and nervously inventorying the contents of his shopping cart. The Chief sat next to him and said, "Hey Cap, how goes the night?"

"The night? The night goes as the day of yester, and yore, with the downward velocity of oxygenated hydronospheres, brother." Cappy never looked up from his cart, frantically rummaging as if the cart contained an inventory of precious stones and metals.

"Cap, I am looking for a new guy, someone who just came into town off of the freights." The Chief described Sherman. Cappy spoke as if he knew the man, but wasn't sure of his location. "He's a mole man, a gunslinger, a fast walker, the dog walker, sky walker, no talker, he was and will be the government. Watch him, the war machine, baby . . ."

"So you know him?" the Chief asked.

"Know him, Gnome. He is my brother, I gnome him, in the mountains, the Rockies. He's on the spin cycle, he is here, he is there, he is everywhere, catch him and he'll book. Book him, Donatello." The Chief attempted to write down any information that Cappy was giving him, but the way and speed in which Cappy spoke made it difficult. One bit of information caught the Chief's attention. Cappy mentioned booking him, or books, or something like that. There was a large group of homeless people that lived next to and underneath the steps of the Philadelphia Museum of Arts. Many people believed the building was a library. That is where the Rocky statue was located. *Didn't Cappy mention something about Rocky, or the Rockies? I think that is what he meant. Is that where I will find Sherman?* The Chief knew that there were good times and bad times to catch Cappy. Often, if you caught him within an hour or two of waking up, the information he provided was a great deal clearer. Once you missed that window, it was often a slurred mess of gibberish. The Chief figured he would call it a night and try again tomorrow. He didn't want to comb the streets asking too many people, because he didn't want the word to get out that he was looking for Sherman.

He hoped to get to the library steps early enough to catch all the residents living there before they started making their rounds for the day. The morning was brisk, but not as bad as it was the night before. Many people didn't know that the library steps, although very large and concrete, were also hollow. If a person was to go around the back side of the museum steps, they would find a small, hollowed-out area that gave access to go behind and underneath the steps. It was one of those hidden places in the city that many people didn't know about, but the cops knew about it and somewhat allowed the city's homeless to sleep under the stairs. It was a quasi-agreement so that the homeless weren't sleeping all over the city and making the city look bad or harassing tourists. It was an agreement that seems to work for both sides.

The Chief walked into the vast concrete area and took a minute for his eyes to adjust to the darkness. Most of the homeless in the city knew who he was and what he looked like, so he wasn't surprising anyone or able to be discreet when he entered the area. It could safely be assumed that they knew he was looking for someone; otherwise, someone of his stature would have sent some of his officers to check the area. The Chief wasn't sure exactly how he was going to tackle asking around for Sherman without it getting back to Sherman or without chasing Sherman away. That was his biggest fear—that Sherman would hop on a freight train the same way he got here. The Chief slowly walked around the homeless encampments. Cardboard walls were set up, along with some small tents, and electric lines ran connecting small, dim light bulbs hanging from the top of some of the tents. The Chief wanted to first just see if Sherman was here. He took about ten minutes walking throughout the area. Many of the homeless knew the Chief and saw him in a good and caring light. Some walked up to him and asked him how he was doing, who he was looking for, and how they could help. Some lightly confronted him about the city not doing enough for the homeless in the area, but most were cordial and nonthreatening.

The Chief said to one of the elders of the community, "Any Marines down here?" the Chief thought that might be a way to flush Sherman out without the Chief having to come out and specifically ask for him by name.

"Yeah, a couple," the old man replied.

"Any Iraq Marines?" he asked more specifically.

"Well that narrows it down, he is down on the end, on the left."

Wow, that was easy, the Chief thought to himself. He wholeheartedly expected to walk down to the end of the area and run right into Sherman. He made his way to the end of the long line of encampments and came to the end. There was a small green government tent with a pair of well-worn desert-colored boots with the very distinguishable Marine Corps emblem on the side of them. "Knock knock, Devil Dog," the Chief said as he faintly knocked on the side of the tent's slick material. No answer. "Hello, anyone home?" This time the Chief went down on one knee and started to unzip the side of the tent. He zipped it down about halfway and looked in on the body that was laying on its side facing away from the Chief. "Ding-dong. Wakey wakey."

The man in the tent rolled over and looked at the Chief. "What do you want?"

"I am looking for a Marine," the Chief said.

"Well, I am a Marine, what do you want?"

"Not any Marine, a specific Marine." The man sat up, realized who he was talking to, looked both ways out of the tent and said, "Meet me up near the statue. I don't want any of the guys seeing me talking to you. We can discuss it up there."

The Chief agreed and started making his way back down the line of encampments. "You guys stay safe down here, and if there is anything I can do, you know I am always on your side." He shook a few hands, talked with a few more people, and made his way out from under the steps. He walked around the steps and started to walk up them. The sun was up, but it was a cool morning. There were tourists already starting to race up the steps and jump up and down at the top of them like Rocky Balboa did in the Rocky movies. The statue was up at the top of the couple of hundred steps that it took to get to the top.

The Chief walked halfway up the steps, stopped, looked behind him at the city, and took a break. He wasn't out of breath, but he could feel his thighs and calves start to burn a little bit and realized he wasn't in quite the shape he thought he was in or that he once was in. He turned again and continued to climb up the steps, although slightly slower than he'd attacked the first set of steps. He made it to the top and walked around to the back of the statue. Now he was a little bit out of breath. As he rounded the back of the statue, he saw the Iraq Marine sitting on a small wall outlying the building. He walked over to him and said, "You got up here quick. I didn't even see you pass by me."

"I didn't, there is an elevator back here. I have been here for a few minutes watching you struggle to get up the steps."

The Chief smiled and shook his head. "An elevator? When did they put an elevator back here?"

"I don't know. Maybe 1885 when they built the building."

"They didn't have elevators in . . . never mind. Listen. I am looking for a Marine. He isn't in trouble, but I figured the best way to find one is to ask one. As you already know, I am also a Marine, and I know you are a Marine, and I am discreetly looking for a Marine."

"The new guy? I know who you're talking about. What's in it for me?"

"I don't know, what do you want?"

"A hundred bucks," the Iraq Marine responded.

"Make it fifty and you got a deal. But it be better be good information," the Chief said.

"Only the best info for you, Chief." And with that the Chief pulled out his wallet and handed the man a $50 bill.

"Oh wow, you got it like that Chief? You got anything smaller? I would hate to get robbed or not be allowed to cash it because someone would think it was fake from a homeless guy." The Chief understood his issue and took back the bill and gave him two twenties and a ten. "He stays down in the basement of The Manor Apartments. At least that's where he used to stay. I am not sure what his name is but I know he is a Marine. A pretty well-decorated one at that. We spent some time comparing notes. Turns out he was a few places I was and we both fought in Fallujah, just in different units. Nice guy. Hope he isn't in any trouble."

"No, he isn't in any trouble. He was stopped by one of my officers and he left behind a backpack I wanted to get back to him, that's all."

"Really Chief? Don't forget I am a Marine also, and we don't lie to each other if we don't need to. If you didn't want to tell me, I respect that more than a lie. The man left a bag so the Chief of Police is beating the streets looking for him? That doesn't make any sense. Don't forget where you came from. We don't lie to each other."

"You're right, I apologize. To keep from lying to you, and also to not give away too much information, I will tell you this: He is not in any kind of trouble, and I just want to talk to him. Everything I just told you is 100% the truth. From one Marine to another. You have my word." The two men shook hands, exchanged pleasantries, and the Chief made his way back down the steps again. Now he knew where Sherman was. The only question was, should he rush right over there and take the chance of him not being there, or should he wait until it was dark to have a better chance or running into him? He decided to wait until it was dark. There would be a much better chance of him being there. He actually hoped it would be raining. That would raise the percentage of him being there. *The homeless tend to go to their shelters when it rains. Well, actually everyone seems to do that when it rains, not just the homeless*, he thought to himself. He now just had to wait until tonight.

* * *

The Police Chief must have checked thousands of square feet of concrete basements throughout the Manor Apartments. There were only a few left, and it was getting later than he anticipated to be wandering around dark basements. He started to make his way down the long ramp leading to the metal door at the end. He opened the door; it was a loud, squeaky door, so he knew his element of surprise was gone. If Sherman was in here, he knew someone was coming in. He attempted to let the door close as quietly as he could behind him. As soon as the door completely closed, he was in almost complete darkness. He felt the nearby wall to see if there was a light switch, but there wasn't. He could see a lit room at the end of the hall and started to make his way to it.

* * *

Sherman laid in the dark, half asleep, half awake, but always on alert. The sound of the metal door opening and closing was a background noise that Sherman had become accustomed to. But he also knew the times during which the door was used more often than others. At times during a nice day, the door would be propped open by Sherman's freshly washed brick, and people would come and go without Sherman being able to notice. Other times, when the door was closed and it was busy laundry hours, the door seemed to constantly squeak open and slam shut over and over again. As the laundry hours slowed down, so did the squeaking and slamming of the door. When he heard the door squeak open this late at night, he assumed it was the maintenance guy who would come in, check the laundry room, and lock up for the night. It was a little early for lockup, but only about thirty minutes earlier than usual. Although, Sherman did find it unusual that the door squeaked open, but didn't slam shut. As if someone came in and held the door from slamming behind them. The maintenance guy didn't do that, and wouldn't have done that. Maybe someone was coming in to start a load of laundry? *If that's the case, they might as well kiss their laundry goodbye until tomorrow morning, because the maintenance guy will lock it up without any regard for your stuff,* his inner voice joked to him.

About ten minutes passed as Sherman anticipated the sound of the door opening and slamming shut, and then the sound of the keys locking the door for the evening, but instead, Sherman saw a flood of light shine down the hallway towards him. On the floor, on the walls, across the ceiling. The light was heading towards his dark hallway, slowly, unsure, but definitely heading his way. He stood up, slightly panicked, and headed further into the dark and behind a concrete pillar that would completely hide him from the light. He stood there and waited, attempting to anticipate why someone was down here, what they wanted, and what he needed to do to get them to leave. His pulse sped up, his blood started to pound, and he was getting himself prepared for whatever was about to happen.

* * *

The Chief walked into the lit room to see that it was a laundry room, just like many of the others in the area. Every basement didn't have a laundry room; only about every fourth building had one, and the other buildings were just expected to share it. If you lived in this building, it was very convenient. If you live in one of the far away buildings, it was a hassle to lug all of your laundry all the way over to this basement to wash your clothes. The Chief meticulously walked the perimeter of the room, checking to see if there were any hidden areas, any places for someone to camp out. Maybe a doorway behind the machines that could make for a good spot for someone to sleep in a warm area unbothered. Seeing that the laundry room was empty, the Chief walked back out into the dark hallway and looked down the hallway both ways. Both were dark. He closed his eyes and tried to listen, to see if maybe he could hear someone moving, or music playing, maybe a television. It wasn't unusual for the homeless population to steal electricity from somewhere and cut into it to run radios, small televisions, or lights. But he didn't hear anything.

He reached for a small flashlight that he kept in a small pouch on his belt. He turned on the flashlight and it flooded the area with light. He always thought that these basements look scarier at night, and now he thought they looked even creepier under the light of a flashlight. He inspected the area with his light. One direction down the hallway seemed to go on for a good distance. The other way, there was a doorway about twenty feet away with a combination lock hinged onto a hasp locking the door. He walked over to the door and gave the lock a little tug. It was locked. And from the outside, so there was a good chance there wasn't anyone on the other side of that door.

He turned and started making his way down the other way of the hallway. He shined the light on the floor to see if there was anything that was going to trip him up. As he made his way down the hallway, passing the door he originally entered from, the floor became a great deal dustier and dirtier. He could see that there were footprints and tire marks that looked like maybe someone had rolled a bicycle or cart or something down this way, but the foot traffic was much less than the area people used when walking to and from the laundry room. He checked the ceiling to ensure nothing was going to fall on him as he made his way down the hall. It was packed with pipes and electrical lines running down the hallway, with big metal brackets holding up all of the pipes and utility apparatus. The walls were concrete and looked like they were painted once every hundred years, but painted in a way that whomever painted them just put the paint right over whatever was already on the walls without properly preparing them first. They painted over cobwebs, dirt, holes, and anything else that protruded from the walls. The walls had graffiti written in marker, and in some areas, spray paint. "KAV WAS HERE" was sloppily written on the uneven and pocked wall. There were a few areas where people had carved their names into the concrete of the wall. H.K.L. was written and scratched out and replaced with the word YUCK. The Chief stopped to read a few other artistic expressions to see if maybe something would give a clue or help him in his endeavor. Nothing jumped out at him, so he continued down the hallway.

He could tell as he made his way down the hallway that it opened up into a larger area. If he didn't have a flashlight, he would have continued right through the dark hallway and into the room at the end without ever knowing that the opening was there. He slowed as he came to the opening and shined his light into the dark abyss. He didn't see or hear anyone, but was still hesitant to let his guard down. He shined the light throughout the room and saw an area where it looked like someone had been sleeping on the floor, or maybe a bunch of people. The thick layer of dirt on the concrete floor had been disturbed, and it looked like the dirt was clumped around a wet substance. Or it looked like it was wet at one time. He continued over the area and noticed that it could possibly be blood. It wasn't a lot of blood, but it was more than just a few drops. It could be substantial to whoever was bleeding. As he stayed in a squatted position he said, "Hello." He said it almost in a whisper, but loud enough for anyone in the immediate area of the room to hear.

* * *

Sherman watched from behind the pillar to see the flashlight shine throughout the area and then focus in on the floor where he and the delivery boy had scuffled. *Wasn't a scuffle, you killed him,* his inner voice reminded him. *Shut up, now is not the time,* he responded. It looked like whoever had the flashlight was inspecting the area and they had seen the blood. *Should have cleaned it up. Should have at least scooped up the part in the dirt. Very sloppy work. You know better than that,* his inner voice teased him again. *Please shut the hell up,* he responded in hopes that if he was nice and cordial, his inner voice would actually stop nagging him.

"Hello." Sherman heard it as if it was said an inch away from his ear. He froze, tried to control his breathing, and just stayed as still as he could. If this was a homeless person looking for a place to sleep, they would just find a spot, lay down, and go to sleep. They wouldn't want to disturb anyone else that was here in the dark, and wouldn't necessarily care if anyone else was here. It would probably be assumed that there was definitely someone else here sleeping in the dark and trying not to be bothered. So the fact that someone spoke in the dark told him it wasn't the run-of-the-mill homeless person. And then he heard it. Or he thought he heard it, but hoped he didn't hear what he thought he just heard.

"Sherman?"

* * *

He could sense that he wasn't alone. Still kneeling down next to the bloodied area, the Chief knew someone was in here with him. He could feel it. It was that sixth sense that he established and honed in the Corps to be in tuned and aware of his surroundings. He flashed the light around the area again. From corner to corner, along all of the walls, across the ceiling, and throughout the floor of the entire room. Someone was in here, but where? The room had concrete pillars evenly spaced throughout the room, and they were big. Really big. Big enough to hold up the entire weight of the building they were resting on. There could very easily be someone behind those pillars. And he knew there was. He just had to flush them out. *Let's just cut to the chase.* "Sherman?"

The silence was defining. "Sherman?" the Chief said again. Still nothing. The next plan was to clear the room. Walk to a corner, get your back to the wall and just go corner to corner with your back against the wall and the light shining into the middle of the room. If there was someone here, he was going to know it. "Sherman, if you are in here, say something now. It is the Police Chief and I am just here to talk to you. I promise you aren't in trouble, and I just want to discuss what happened at the bar the other night. Nothing more. You have my word. From one Marine to another, and we share that vow that we would not lie to each other."

* * *

Sherman stood behind the pillar. He almost breathed a sigh of relief hearing that it was the Chief. He was starting to let his mind get the best of him and was worried he might have to hurt someone else to keep them from hurting him. He stepped out from behind the pillar and into the light of the Chief's flashlight with his hands up. "Put your hands down, Sherman. I am not here as a police officer. I'm here as a Marine, and hopefully as a friend." Sherman put his hands down at his sides and said, "Why are you here if I'm not in trouble?"

"You said some stuff at the bar that I took as drunken bravado talk, but everything you said lines up. I know what you did, I know how you did it, and now I know where you did it." He motioned over to the clumped blood and scuffle marks on the floor. "I just want to know why you did it. I think I may know why you did it, because you spoke of it at the bar. But I was intoxicated and I want to make sure what you were saying is actually what I thought I was hearing. So this is your opportunity to tell me why. Man to man, Marine to Marine. One shot, so let's hear it."

Sherman sat quietly, thinking to himself, *If I tell him, he will arrest me. If I don't tell him, maybe he doesn't have enough to arrest me, but he probably wouldn't be down here if he didn't. Maybe I should find out what he knows first and go from there.* Sherman said to the Chief, "Tell me what you know and we can go from there."

"I don't know anything. Well, that isn't true, I know everything. I know that you said you kill people to protect other people. I know that you said when a fireman retires, they are still expected to run into fires and save people if they can because they were trained for that. When the police retire they still carry guns and are expected to help quell crime if they are put in a position to help. But when a Marine retires, where do they go? Do they just go home and sit on the couch and wither away and wait to die? After all the training they have, to be able to use that training to protect those who can't protect themselves . . .

"I know that you wondered where we go. Where we highly trained Marines go when we are no longer needed as Marines. I know what you said made sense. I know what you said gave me a sense of pride and a sense of understanding as to what you are trying to accomplish. I know that there is one less pedophile on the earth that no one is going to miss, and who no one will ask questions about. And I know that I need help.

"I know that there are more of them that slip through the cracks than get put in jail. I know that they make us look foolish in the revolving door of the justice system. I know that there is a stack of files on my desk that will get bigger. But mostly, I know that what you have done is a service. A service to those that need people like you. People like us. To continue that unwavering service to protect and shepherd the weak. I don't want to arrest you. I don't want to stop you. I want to help you."

Sherman stood there frozen, unsure if what he was hearing was what he was actually hearing or not. His inner voice was just as confused and in shock. *ARE YOU OUT OF YOUR FUCKING MIND?* because he knew that Sherman was contemplating the possibilities. "How do I know that you aren't setting me up or like, wearing a wire or something?" he asked.

"Sherman, why would I need to wear a wire? You told me you kill people. You told me you killed a bum that was a pedophile and that you dumped him under a bridge. I am sitting here in the exact spot that you killed him, right?" He stood there and motioned over to the blood again. Sherman slowly nodded his head. "Why would I need to wear a wire? I could have just stormed the basement with ten police officers and arrested you. I wouldn't have needed a wire, witnesses, or anything else. I am the Chief of Police, and I have all of the information I would need to put you away for a long time. Not to mention, I just asked you if this is the place that you killed him and you nodded your head. I wouldn't need any more evidence against you."

"I have to admit, I am a little apprehensive and somewhat scared of what you are telling me. Are you making me a proposition or something? I'm still kind of confused," Sherman responded. His voice a little bit lower and unsure of himself.

The Chief walked over to Sherman, and in a low drill instructor voice, said, "Sherman, there is no reason to be scared or apprehensive. We are Marines, and there is no greater bond. I give you my word. We work together or I haul you off to prison for the rest of your life. That should ease your mind on my motives."

Sherman was always afraid of the whisper. The whisper spoke louder than screams. But what did he have to lose? The gig was either over right here, or it would be over when the Chief decided it was over. He might as well roll with it and see if he could assist the Chief, get whatever he needed done, and then skip town.

"So let's start from the beginning so we can both be on the same sheet of music and we can build on our newfound relationship. Is this the first one? The only one? Or were there more?"

At first Sherman thought about telling him this was the first one, but he wasn't sure what he'd told him in the bar and didn't want to start off this whole thing with lies and distrust. So he decided to tell him everything. They sat in the basement the entire night, going over all the details of everything Sherman had done. Sherman felt a wave of relief come over him like he had been at a therapy session. The more he told about what he had done, the more the Chief seemed to be impressed and eager to work with Sherman. "Sherman. I have rapists, child molesters, robbers, domestic violence abusers. I have it all. We can just go right down the list and get rid of all of them."

"No, not all of them," Sherman retorted. "Just the worst ones. And we can't start at the top of the list, because that would look suspicious if the police department's top ten criminals just started dying off in order from number one to number ten. Choose a few, and let's brief each other on whatever files you have and then we can decide.

"I know one right off the top of my head. This is a guy that has been in and out of the system his whole life. His rap sheet is disgusting, and we haven't been able to make anything stick. This one is a no-brainer. I will get the file. We can figure out a ton of ways to make this one go down. But we will need some help. Do you have anyone in the city that you can trust?" the Chief asked. "I can't provide anyone. I don't have anyone that won't be traced back to me." the Chief continued.

"I might have someone. Rule number one—Only trust Marines. No one else. We have a common bond and one that cannot be broken. Only Marines that we can trust. What kind of crime is this guy most known for?" Sherman informed the Chief.

"Mostly crimes against women and children. He's a pimp across town. A real dirtbag, and rubs it in our faces every chance he gets. I have a personal hatred for this guy." Said the Chief.

"Okay, let me see if I can find someone to help that we can trust. I might have someone in mind." Sherman replied.

The Chief shook Sherman's hand and then pulled him in for a tight embrace. "I love everything about this," he said as he let Sherman out of the embrace. "Semper Fi, Marine," the Chief said as he turned and walked down the hallway. Sherman could hear the squeaky door open and slam shut. He sat against the pillar in disbelief. *This can't be real,* he thought to himself. *This is a set up.* He is going to jail for a long time. He was so torn on whether he should run. If he ran, he would for sure be chased. But if the Chief wanted him arrested, he would have already done it. He wouldn't have left the basement and given Sherman the chance to run.

Sherman's brain was going a mile a minute. He was scared. Really scared. And confused. He was for sure in trouble and needed help. Maybe he could kill two birds with one stone. Talk to the person he was thinking about on what his next steps should be, as well as maybe help him and the Chief with getting rid of this guy high on the Chief's list.

Chapter 12

The Sergeant Major stood up in the staff meeting and said, "Welcome the new Staff Sergeant to the team, she will be working in Bravo Company." As he turned to the new Staff Sergeant he said, "Don't let these guys fool you. They may bust your chops at first, but all in all, they are a very talented bunch, and we are very much a tight-knit family here. Come to the front and tell us a few things about yourself."

The new Staff Sergeant made her way to the front of the room. She seemed a little sheepish or intimidated at first, but quickly settled in. "My name is Staff Sergeant Carmen Dejesus, I am from Philadelphia, and I look forward to working with everyone and getting to know all of you." Carmen Dejesus stood about five foot one on her best day, and maybe weighed a hundred pounds soaking wet. She looked like she would be more successful as a swimsuit model than she would be as a Marine. The grumblings in the room started to get louder as everyone started to tune out her life story and started to complain that others in the room would most likely have to carry her weight. The other Staff Non-Commissioned Officers in the meeting from Bravo Company doled out a heavy dose of rolled eyes and dirty looks as the new Staff Sergeant continued to tell her story. But the room couldn't have been more wrong about this one. As the months and years went on, Staff Sergeant Carmen "Mickie" Dejesus not only proved everyone wrong about first impressions, but also blew most of the male Marines out of the water with her abilities. She held the highest score on the rifle range of all shooters male and female on base; she ran marathons, triathlons, and was a two-time Iron Man on her own time. Meaning, she did that stuff as a hobby, not because she had to. Most Marines' hobbies consisted of going home and drinking beer. But not her—she was a certified badass.

Many called her Mickie, but only a chosen few actually knew where that name came from. She was a Puerto Rican girl from Philly, and people started calling her M.C. Dejesus. The M.C. stood for "Muy Caliente." Translated to English it meant "Very Hot," and she was. It started as a joke, a term someone would say when they saw her out at the club or on base at the Enlisted bar, but never at work. At work it would be M.C. or Staff Sergeant M.C. Well, after being called M.C. for a few months, maybe a year, the nickname turned into Marines calling her Mick, which sounded too masculine, so it wasn't long before Mick morphed into Mickie, which stuck. Most didn't know Mickie's real name, as she introduced herself as Mickie and she actually signed her name as Mickie Dejesus also. Most of her junior Marines also called her Staff Sergeant Mickie.

She was small in stature, but huge in heart, determination, and ability. She was probably one of the top-ten most badass Marines Sherman had ever served with, but top three regarding his favorite Marines he had served with. She took everyone's excuses away, she was that tough. You were having a bad day on the obstacle course? Try being 5'1" and having to do it. Your feet hurt while you're hiking with the sixty-pound pack? Try doing it while only weighing a hundred pounds. There was no challenge too great, no mountain to high; nothing was impossible, and she made the Marines around her better. Her drive and determination was infectious, and Sherman learned a great deal from her. They became close friends throughout the years they were stationed together. But as the years passed, duty stations changed, and so did friends, email addresses, phone numbers, and physical addresses. As happens with most Marines, the distance and lack of communication often had Marines wondering what happen to one another but never having the means or ability to actually stay in touch. This was the case with Sherman and Mickie.

Sherman couldn't think of a better person to ask for help. Actually, she was probably only one of a few Marines he knew from Philly, but he knew if he could find her, there was no doubt she would help. She would not only be able to help him out, but would also be willing to keep his secret (or secrets). He knew she was in Philly, or at least knew she was from Philly. How many Carmen Dejesus' could there be in this city? That was a pretty specific name. Not like Rodriguez, or Sanchez. Still, Sherman didn't know if she had married and changed her name, stayed in the Marine Corps, or got out of the Marine Corps and possibly went to another state. He had no idea, but he was going to find out, because he needed her.

The plan was to go back to the library, attempt to research her name on the internet, then cross reference that name into a military database of past served service members, go to a local Veterans of Foreign Wars or American Legion to see if maybe they had some kind of list of service members from the area. Sherman still had to be careful with the amount of people he introduced himself to or what kind of information he provided people, because he didn't want to raise any red flags or have people start asking questions about him, such as why he would be looking for service members, or give anyone a reason to call the cops on him for looking or acting too suspicious.

As he made his way back to the library, he wasn't feeling too confident on his plan to find Mickie. A great deal of things would need to fall into place without anyone really noticing him snooping around. He started to get concerned that maybe he would just have to take this one on head-on, and alone. As he entered the library, he could see the computers were available, but something was just telling him that it might not be such a good idea for him to take a seat. He had been here now a number of times, and there would just be that one little mistake that caused this entire thing to come crashing down on him. Would this be the one step in all of this that he regretted doing? Everything in his body told him to turn around, walk out, and find another way, or just do it without the help. But completing the mission without the help would be much harder than if he had her assistance.

If he left the library right now, he wouldn't be able to come back in. It would look too suspicious for him to walk in, stand there for five minutes, walk out, stand outside, and then walk back in. He made his way to the computers, but instead of stopping, he continued to walk by. He wondered if maybe the information was stored somewhere in the library; did libraries have phone books? Or some kind of microfiche database of service members, maybe newspaper articles from when high school kids go off to the military? Sometimes they put a little blurb in the local paper about the person being shipped off to boot camp.

First, the phone book. Sherman made his way to the back counter of the library and asked the girl behind the counter, "Do you guys have a phone book?"

The girl looked at him like he had three heads. "A phone book?" she repeated. He said "Yes, a phone book." The girl said that they didn't, but was looking under the counter, moving small boxes around, looking under some papers. Sherman didn't actually mean *do you have it under the counter,* he meant more, *does the library store phone books.* As soon as he saw the girl fumbling around for a phone book, he realized what a dumb question it was. With the technology of the internet, people really didn't use phone books any more. Once the girl seemed to have completed her search, she looked up at Sherman and said, "Do we have phone books?" He looked behind him, as she clearly could not have been asking him the same question he asked her, when a voice from behind Sherman said, "Like the yellow pages? I think we might." A young kid made his way behind the counter and started on the same search that the girl just completed. The two continued their search for the phone book while Sherman patiently waited. "We have this." The young kid said to Sherman holding up a book. It was a smaller version of the yellow pages, but it was the yellow pages, although it was for businesses, not personal phone numbers. What he was looking for was the white pages.

But before Sherman could voice his disappointment, the kid said, "And this, and this," as he lifted up more books. Some were brochures of the city with maps and hotel numbers, and one of the books was the white pages. Smaller and thinner than Sherman remembered using when he was a kid, but it would hopefully work just as well.

"Could I use this to look something up?" Sherman motioned the book towards a table sitting near the counter. He thought saying "something" instead of "someone" was a genius idea. As if the cops ever came to question these clerks, they would say, "He came in and looked SOMETHING up in the phone book, not SOMEONE" and the cops would just shrug their shoulders with a disappointing snap of their fingers. "Dang, Something? Not Someone? I thought we might have been onto something, but with that bit of information, it is back to square one."

"Sure, no problem."

He took the book over to the table and quickly thumbed to the "D" section. Davis, Dean, Dejames, Dejesus—there it was, Dejesus. There was a long list of Dejesus': Ann, Barbara, Brian, and Carmen—not one, not two, but three Carmens. He quickly pulled out a napkin and jotted down all three addresses. He returned the book to the counter with a quick head nod and smile, picked up one of the tourist maps of the city, and made his way out of the library.

He stopped at the first bus stop bench and sat, took out the napkin, and started looking for the different addresses on the map. Two of them were within the city, and one was far away—well, not far away, but a great deal farther than the other two, but still within the city limits. He decided he was going to start at the nearest one, and work his way to the farthest. The nearest one was just off of Broad Street in the heart of the city. He figured it was about a twenty-minute walk.

Sherman headed to the address. The hustle and bustle filled the city, the streets were packed with traffic as were the sidewalks. An entire city moving in unison, but at the same time filled with millions of individuals following their own paths. It took Sherman about twenty minutes just as predicted. The address was an apartment building right off of the main avenue. It was five or six floors high, and blended into the city above the storefronts of a sandwich shop and sporting goods store. The building was just a door in between these two locations. If you didn't know it was there, you would probably walk by it without even knowing it was the entrance to where a few hundred people lived.

Sherman tried the door, but it was locked. *I guess a good old-fashioned stake out is in order,* he said to himself. He sat there for a few hours and watched people walk past the building. In the few hours he was there, he saw an old lady leave the building to walk a few dogs and a man with a child go in. This wasn't the kind of place where you could follow someone in. The people coming in or out were so random that they would know if someone was trying to follow them in. Sherman went to the door again and tried the handle, but it was still locked. He saw next to the door there was an intercom system with a speaker, names of the tenants, and buttons to ring the individual apartments. *Apartment 3F C. Dejesus.* So, he was in the right place. Part of him just wanted to ring the bell, ask for her, and if it was her, it was. If not, then he'd move on to the next one. But stealth and as little information and the fewer people he came across, the better. He would just wait it out.

Sherman figured that unless someone was on vacation, or at a sleepover, sooner or later, everyone that lived in this building would have to either come in or go out. So he decided to wait. Person after person, hour after hour, and none of these people seemed to be Carmen Dejesus; or were they? Maybe Carmen already came and went, but it wasn't his Carmen. Not the one he was looking for, anyway. It was getting late and dark, and Sherman was tired. He contemplated not going back to the basement, but knew that was the best shelter he had, so he decided it would be in his best interest to stay there for another night until he came up with a better option.

The following morning, Sherman was up and in front of the apartment building. He was pretty confident that if this person lived here and wasn't someone who went to work at three in the morning, he would see just about everyone who lived in this building come in or out within the next twelve hours or so. He was relatively well hidden; people crowded the street in front of the building, and traffic moved at a steady pace, so no one would feel that Sherman was loitering or probably even notice that he was standing there, sitting at the bus stop, or leaning up against the corner light post. Once again, people came and left from the building. Most seemed to leave right around morning work time, and saw the old lady with the dogs again. He saw that as a sign that the regulars had come and gone, as if the walking of the dogs was a shift change or a morning, afternoon, and evening ritual. This morning's dog walking shift had been completed.

As the old lady with the dogs was going back into the building, a younger looking lady was coming out. She was dressed in a dark business suit with a skirt and sneakers. She fit the age of what Mickie would now be; this lady looked older, but not old. She looked ten years younger than she should, but so did Mickie. Mickie looked like she was fifteen when she was a Staff Sergeant. While the rest of the Staff Sergeants were in their late twenties or early thirties and looked like they were in their early forties, Mickie looked like she was fifteen. And that fit the bill for this lady. It would be worth following this one.

She had a leather bag and looked very professional. She was short, like Mickie, slim, like Mickie. This could be her. Sherman was getting more and more convinced it was her. He didn't want to bring attention to himself near her building, just in case she took offense and started screaming or something crazy. He followed her up the main avenue, across a few traffic lights, and up a few more blocks, where she stopped in front of a tremendous skyscraper. She was talking on her phone, and as Sherman got closer, he knew it was her. She looked young and vibrant, but more of a lady, more established, she had matured. He found it hard to truly express, but he was sure it was her.

As she hung up the phone Sherman walked up to her and said, "Mickie?"

She turned and looked at him. "What?" she said.

Sherman locked eyes with her and said again, "Mickie? It's me, Tank."

Her gazed softened as she got a small smirk on her face and said, "Tank? You're lucky, you almost got your ass kicked. You really need to work on your tracking skills. I saw you standing outside my building since 0400."

Tank smiled back and said, "I need help, but I need to be discreet."

"Discreet?" she replied. "Meet me across the street at the parking garage. 1700, on the fourth floor on the ramp going down." And with that, she leaned against the light pole, pulled off her sneakers one at a time, replaced them with high heels, turned, and walked into the building.

* * *

"Everything I am about to tell you is going to sound nuts, but I am not nuts—I am crystal clear, and have never been more clear about anything before in my entire life." Sherman stood just inches in front of her. He spoke in a low monotone voice to ensure no one in the parking garage would be able to hear, even from just a few feet away. Anyone walking by would just assume it was a boyfriend and girlfriend talking, maybe a married couple, but they were standing far too close to assume they were coworkers or strangers.

"Tank, there is nothing you can tell me that would sway me from helping you. Once a Marine, always a Marine, and all of that. But what kind of help are we talking about? Is it the 'I need money and I have borrowed from everyone I can and now you're next on the list,' help? Or the 'I robbed a store and now the cops are after me and I need a place to hide out,' kind of help? Or are we talking, 'Meet me at this latitude and longitude with a shovel and a bag of lye,' type of help?"

Without hesitation, Sherman responded, "The latter."

Her eyes widened. She reached out and lightly placed her hand onto Sherman's arm, and asked, "Are you okay?"

"I am okay," Sherman responded. "I need to tell you everything, but we can't do it here. We need to go somewhere that we are sure there are no cameras and no one listening."

Before he could finish his sentence, she said, "There are eight public places in this city without cameras, and this is one of them. I have this entire city scoped out, and that is specifically the reason I picked this place for us to meet.

There are a few others, but if you really want to be unseen, the best course of action is to stay still for as long as possible. So, let's hang out here, you can tell me what you need to tell me, and we can go from there."

"That is the exact reason I knew I could come to you—you always know everything about your surroundings, and you have always been so well-prepared." They moved to a dark corner of the parking garage. Here, they were far enough away from vehicles to not look suspicious, but still close enough to the parked cars that it made them look like they were just sitting on a curb having a conversation, but doing it out of sight of people passing by.

He told her about the Police Chief, and how he too was a former Marine who wanted Sherman's help. He didn't go into great detail, but told her little odds and ends about what he had been doing for the last few months and how things had come to the place they were now. He didn't tell her about the killings, but rather told her that the NYPD was looking for him and why he needed to be hidden. He did tell her about the delivery boy and why he did what he did, but mainly he stuck to telling her about the task at hand, and how he felt that this person needed to be eradicated.

Surprisingly to Sherman, she was fully on board. Looking back on the conversation, Sherman wasn't 100% sure that he told her his plan was to kill the pimp—he may have just told her or hinted to her that they were going to catch him in the act, rough him up a little bit, and maybe hold him for the police to come. Actually, Sherman wasn't even sure if the plan was to kill the pimp or not. He assumed it was because the Chief told him the pimp was in and out of the legal system so much that they couldn't pin anything on him. So, the plan was probably to kill him. He just didn't tell Mickie that yet.

Sherman knew that Mickie was no-nonsense—she didn't mess around at all, she was all business. She was a great person, but did not hesitate to put someone in their place if they were doing wrong or out of line. It worried Sherman that at any point he might have decided to tell her everything, and her high level of integrity and honesty may kick in, and could spell disaster for him. He decided to let things remain the way they were, and as time went by, if more information needed to be provided to her, he would give it to her. And if worse comes to worst, he would skip town, and hopefully he could run to somewhere where no one would come looking for him.

Mickie had a great deal of detail on how she wanted to be used in apprehending this pimp. Knowing that they would be able to get his information from the police, she wanted to stake out his house, take notes on his daily activities, log his comings and goings from place to place, and interview people he came across. But Sherman just needed her to be a decoy, and continuously had to talk her off the ledge to keep this thing from getting too out of hand or involved. He truly just needed her to be in the area that this guy frequented, look pretty and weak, and hopefully this guy would strike at a moment in time that they would be able to apprehend him and either give him the basement treatment or find another way to get the deed done. He envisioned there being a moment in time in between the apprehension of the rapist, and them "turning him over to the police" where Sherman would be able to tell her, "Okay, I got it from here, thanks for the help. See you later, you can leave now." But he knew that would probably be unlikely. But he still hoped, in a perfect situation, that was the way it would take place.

They spoke for hours. They agreed that she wouldn't be able to come to his basement, because he didn't want people to see her coming and going with him or around the area, as well as him not going to her apartment, as they also didn't want to be seen in that area together. If for some reason they caught one, they wouldn't be able to catch the other. That was the plan, and they were going to work on ensuring they did everything they could to make sure that happened. For now, they would meet at the garage, and every time they left they would make a predetermined time for the next time they met with a clear understanding as to what information or planning materials they were going to bring at the next meeting.

Sherman was going to get the personal details from the Police Chief. He was going to research the crime scene locations, plot which ones were closest to the rapist's house, and try to determine where he would be most likely to strike again if provided the opportunity. As for Mickie, he said, "Get some skimpy clothes, and look cute." Mickie hated that idea, she actually seemed to want to punch Sherman in the face for even suggesting it. She wanted to do more, she wanted to be more involved, but she knew at this point in time that was really all that was needed for her to do. So, she agreed. Sherman said, "Seventy-two hours from now, we will meet back here. We will discuss what is next, and we will go from there. Any questions? No? Good. Go forth and do great things." That was the phrase that Mickie used to use to close out her meetings with her Marines and Sherman knew it. He always believed it was a great way to close out a meeting. It had a certain level of expectation, but at the same time, was a challenge to continue to forge forward. He thought it was an appropriate way to end this conversation.

Mickie looked at him with a half smirk and said, "Don't be stealing my shit. Seventy-two hours, and don't fucking be late, Marine." She walked down the ramp, and Sherman walked down the stairs. *There's work to be done*, he thought to himself. The sense of worth and need was back, and he was starting to feel good again. He needed to have this talk, he needed for someone to validate his mental status, he needed to know that what he was doing was okay. Although he didn't give Mickie all of the details, he gave her enough of them to have an idea of what kind of life he has been living, and he still felt like it was enough for him to feel better. He felt like he and his efforts were validated, and validated by someone he had great respect for. The planning stage had begun, and there was no turning back now. The list had officially just gotten one person longer.

* * *

Sherman knew it was the Chief as soon as he heard the door squeak open and not slam shut. Many people came in and out of the basement at all hours of the day, but very few caught the door before letting it close softly. It had only happened one other time at this hour of the night, and the last time it was the Chief, so Sherman just assumed like before that it was the Chief again, and he was right.

The Chief made his way down the hallway and into the darkness. He reached for his flashlight and turned it on. "No flashlight. Turn it off," Sherman said as he sat in the darkness. "What do you got for me, Chief?"

"Okay, here is the deal Sherman. We know exactly where this guy's track is and where he runs his girls. He makes appearances there a couple times a night. Usually twice, once when he puts the girls out there, and then again at the end to collect money from them. On occasion he will show up a couple of other times if there is a problem. So, if we can get a decoy to stand out there and blend in, maybe we have a shot of getting her to infiltrate his operation. Maybe become part of his stable, get an inside look at things, and then we can strike."

"That sounds like a decent plan, but pretty basic," Sherman replied.

"I tried to make it as basic as possible so we can get into the inner workings of it all, and then we can go into more detail as to how we want to handle getting rid of him. Do you have a better idea?"

Sherman knew he did, but it too was basic and filled with opportunities to be seen or get caught. "How about we drive up, throw him in the trunk of a car, take him out to the water, shoot him, and dump him?"

The Chief seemed unsure if he was joking or not, but instead of confirming it, he just moved on. "Okay, girl goes on the street, waits for him to come around, sees if she can get in with the girls, hopefully comes across him, and then sees what she can do from there. We can scope it out from a rooftop or car nearby within visual to ensure all goes well, and then once we have all the details, we will meet up again and brainstorm. Do you have someone in mind that can play the role as the girl?"

"Yeah, me" Sherman said. The Chief once again wasn't sure if he was joking or not. They were in the pitch blackness, so he was unable to read his face, and didn't hear him chuckle or snicker, so he wasn't exactly sure if he was serious or not.

"Are you serious?"

"Of course I am not serious. But I have it handled. Don't worry about it. Let's set it up for Friday at 2000. That's 8:00 pm, it's been a while since you were a Marine, Chief. I would hate for you to show up at the wrong time because you forgot how to tell military time."

"Whatever," the Chief responded. He got up, reached for Sherman's hand in the dark to shake it, and realized he wasn't anywhere near him. "I guess I will see you later," the Chief spoke into the darkness. Sherman's voice was no longer in the same place it was when he responded, "Okay, the plan is set. I will see you there." With that, the Chief walked back out of the darkness, down the hallway and out the door. The door squeaked and slammed behind him.

"You get all of that?" Sherman asked into the dark.

"Yup. Got it all. Not the greatest of plans, but nothing that I can't handle," Mickie responded from across the room. "We will be on the adjacent rooftop. We will have eyes on you at all times. Be careful. If things go bad, put your hands together like you are praying and put them in the center of your chest. That will be the sign if something is going wrong, or if you just need to get out of there."

"That will work. Hopefully I don't have to use it, but it is good to know we have something just in case."

"It might take a few minutes for us to get to you. We will be at the rooftop, and will need some time to get down the stairs and across the street. Don't get in any cars if you can help it, and price yourself really high so no one takes you up on your offers."

"No shit, really Tank? I was planning on banging out a few johns in my spare time as I gathered information."

"I'm sorry, I know you have every ability to do this, I'm just nervous and want to make sure every detail is covered. I don't want to miss anything."

"We won't miss anything. 1700 at the parking garage, Monday 1700." He could hear her voice getting further away as she made her way out of the darkness and down the hallway. "Go forth and do great things, Tank." Squeaky door,   slam.

Chapter 13

It was 1930, and Sherman started making his way to the building. He didn't want to sneak around the back and climb a fire escape or be super stealthy, because he thought in this circumstance it would make him more noticeable than if he just walked into the building like normal, up through the stairs, and up onto the roof as if he lived there or was supposed to be going up there. The building roofs here weren't like normal building roofs. These building roofs were a place that people came and hung out. There was lawn furniture in some areas, and some areas even had barbecues. It was a wide-open space, but since these buildings didn't have balconies, many people used the roof as their backyards. To sunbathe, barbecue, hang out, and just look around at the vast amounts of other buildings in the area.

This looked to Sherman like a place where people would come at night with a glass of wine and look at the stars. He made his way across the roof and passed a large cage that housed about twenty pigeons. He assumed right away that they must be homing pigeons, and thought to himself *That must be a cool hobby. Especially in this setting. You can really see the birds up close in flight.* He continued across the building and squatted down until he could see the street corner where Mickie was going to be, and could also see all four corners. It wasn't more than about ten minutes before he saw the Chief making his way across the rooftop and squat down next to him. "Anyone see you?" Sherman asked.

"I don't think so. I came across the back and up the fire escape." Sherman shook his head slightly and thought to himself, *Rookie.* The sun was starting to set, and it was still dusk. The streetlights had just come on and Sherman was glad they did, because it was getting dark enough that it was starting to get difficult to make out people on the corners. The girls were hanging out on two of the four corners. Several cars pulled up and picked up some of the girls after stopping for a minute or so, while other cars would pull up as girls got out of the cars and made their way back onto their respective street corners. At one point Sherman and the Chief were startled by the pigeons flapping and making a ruckus. There was a young man who came up to feed and let the birds out for to fly around a little bit. The man didn't look like what Sherman assumed the man with the pigeons would look like. Sherman had pictured in his mind an old Italian man who would come up and talk to the birds as they flew around him. This man was much younger. He wore a white tank top and blue jeans, and there wasn't anything out of the ordinary that stuck out about him. Just the fact that he was under sixty years old and probably in his late twenties or early thirties was enough to change the whole scenario in his head about what those birds were used for. *Do people really sell drugs using homing pigeons like I remember seeing in a movie one time long ago? Because if they do . . . this fits directly into that scenario,* Sherman thought to himself.

"There she is." Sherman nudged the Chief with his elbow and head nodded towards the street.

* * *

Mickie tried her best to be as sexy and loose as possible while walking over to the corner. She took great pride in her posture while in meetings and throughout her life. Especially while she was a Marine. In this situation, she wanted to portray the opposite of that. Maybe someone a little weaker, a little more able to be taken advantage of. A little more shy, but street smart, and street savvy. She wanted to come out in tight clothes that were trashy but not too over the top. When she scoped out the place she realized that she was going to have to go way over the top. Most of these girls were half naked. Mickie searched her closet for something she could cut or tailor into the proper outfit for the job. The only thing that she could find was an old lingerie set that an ex-boyfriend gave her as a valentines gift. She remembered thinking at the time that it was more of a gift for him than it was for her and wasn't sure how she felt about that. It was cheap and trashy, but she knew it was perfect for the task at hand. It consisted of a lace teddy that was discreetly covered in all of the important areas and there was a sheer robe that went over it that tied at the waist. The other girls were dressed in the same fashion and very intimidating. Mickie at one point came to the realization that if things started going sideways, she would be in a great deal of trouble. She wasn't worried on a one-on-one basis, and maybe not even on a one-on-two basis, but anything more than that and things could get out of hand. She was tough, but some of these street-battered women might be tougher. Surely an unfair fight of a group of them could be very bad.

She took solace in the fact that she would easily be able to outrun any of them if she needed to, and that helped to keep her nerves in check. There were a number of girls out this evening, and at any time there could be five to ten of them intermingled throughout the night. Many girls didn't stay on the corner long. It seemed like within fifteen minutes, they were back in another car and off they drove. A steady stream of cars drove by. Some would honk and keep driving, while others would stop, inquire about services, and then pull away without a girl, in disgust about the prices or maybe that the girl didn't feel comfortable with leaving with that customer for fear they were a cop, dirty, or just unkempt enough to be turned away by a prostitute. It was nonstop.

Mickie quietly made her way through the girls and went to a part of the corner that had one girl waiting under a street light. "Hey girl," Mickie said in a soft tone with a little bit of "What a night it has been already" attitude in the greeting.

The girl responded, "Hey, slow night for some?"

"Yeah, I'm not trying to just be with everyone tonight, I ain't feeling so good. Just out here cause I gotta be."

"I hear you girl," the other responded. "Them hoes over there are the dollar girls. That's why they are like a revolving door. I am trying to make some money, not trying to get broke and can't work. That shit's nasty."

"Really girl, who you telling? How much you getting tonight?" Mickie asked this question more to understand what the going rate was, rather than because of her general interest. "Depends. Around the world is going to cost them tonight. Probably four bills, maybe a few dimes less if I am feeling generous. But most of these johns are just bullshit anyway. They want them to tell you how manly they are while you jerk them off. But you know the regular stuff, you can make some good money out here if you just give them what they want and keep them happy. Tell them a sob story and they always will tip you more. They are so dumb." She paused and looked at Mickie. "I ain't never seen you out here before, you new?"

"New? No, I'm not 'new'—I'm old, but new to the area. I met up with Milky Smooth a few months ago and was working the badlands up North before him bringing me down here."

A white Cadillac pulled up in front of the girls. The windows were tinted so dark they looked black. Mickie stepped forward and leaned towards the passenger side window as it slowly went down. The other girl tried to nonchalantly put her arm in front of Mickie, trying to get her not to approach the car. "Girl, no, don't," she said, but it was too late. The window went down and Mickie was face to face with the pimp.

"Who the fuck is you?" he said, in disbelief that she had just walked up to his car and stuck her face in the window. Before she was able to get a word out, he reached across the passenger side of the car and mushed her face out of his car with such force it knocked her backwards and off her feet and onto her butt. She sat there for a second as he looked down at her, propped up in his seat so he could make eye contact with her. "Bitch, I don't know who brought you here, but they better un-bring your ass here. Ain't no one cleared you with me. You let them know they got property tax to pay and they better come see me." The car sped off, spinning its wheels and kicking dirt and debris towards the girls as it fishtailed back into the street and up the road. All of the girls stopped in their tracks and just looked at her and the other girl. Some of them made little remarks. "Girl, you dumb," said one. "This hoe must got a death wish," chuckled another.

Mickie knew this wasn't going as planned, and there wasn't any information to gather from this night. While still sitting on her butt, she clasped her hands together in a praying motion and put them in the middle of her chest. "You better be praying that he don't come back and see you here again," the other girl said as she helped Mickie to her feet and helped dust off her butt for her. "You need to get your orders straight and get your man to straighten it out with him before you come back. He doesn't play around with his property. But it was nice meeting you, girl." Mickie appreciated the kind girl's gesture and felt bad for her, that she seemed so nice and cordial and for one reason or another had to resort to this lifestyle. Mickie started to walk back up the road, and as she got farther and farther away from the street corner, the more silly and stupid she felt for the way she was dressed. She could see people looking at her and commenting to each other. She felt terrible, and the more it happened, the angrier she was at Tank and the Chief for coming up with such a dumb idea. She had a time and a place to meet Tank for the debrief, and she couldn't wait to be there in the parking garage to give him a piece of her mind. Tonight was a bust, and she felt stupid about it.

* * *

Mickie was dressed in what looked from the rooftop like lingerie. Sherman knew she couldn't have been out there in lingerie, but that is what it looked like. He instantly felt embarrassed for her. But she wore it well, and unfortunately it factored into the part she was playing. She was intermingling with one of the girls, and all seemed to go well. She was going to be out there for a while, so he knew they had to just settle in and wait.

As Mickie talked to the other girl, Sherman knew she was setting the trap or garnering information from her to help the cause. She wasn't out there for more than fifteen or twenty minutes when a white car with blackened windows pulled up. Sherman couldn't see who was driving and the car looked too nice to be a customer. He could see Mickie lean in the window, and almost as quickly as she leaned in, she fell back and landed on her butt with a crash. "Did he just fucking hit her?" Sherman jumped to his feet and looked down at the Chief. "Let's go."

"Slow down, it is too soon, not yet. Relax. Can you read the license plate number?" "Fuck a license plate number, let's go down there and drag whoever is in that car out and beat the shit out of them," Sherman barked.

"Slow down Sherman, don't be overcome by your emotions. She's fine, look, she is fine. Give it a second." The car sped off as a plume of dust billowed in the night air behind it. Mickie sat on the ground for a moment, gave the sign, stood up, dusted herself off with the help of the other girl and started making her way up the street. Sherman jumped to his feet and quickly walked across the roof, past the barbecue and outdoor lawn chairs, past the man and his pigeons, and pulled open the roof door and started running down the stairs. He was running so fast down the stairs that he was getting dizzy from running, around and around the flights of stairs. He busted through the front door of the building and then gathered himself as he made his way up the street. He could see Mickie way up ahead of him and across the street. She didn't look like she was in danger. She wasn't running or looking over her shoulder. She seemed, for now, to be okay.

He continued to follow her as she made her way out of the neighborhood and towards her own. Sherman wanted to run up to her, but also was worried that someone might be watching him or following her. He kept his distance and continued to follow her. At one point she went into a drugstore and was in there for a few minutes. When she came out, she was wearing a sweatshirt and a pair of sweatpants. She must have gotten tired of walking the streets in lingerie and decided to cover up. She was pretty smart. Sherman thought to himself, *I would have never thought of that.*

He followed her all the way to her apartment. He wished he could just go up to her and ask her if she was okay, but knew he couldn't do that. Just as she reached the front door of her apartment, she turned around, stepped off the front step, put both arms above her head in the air with her thumbs up, and walked to the street. When she got to the street, she turned back toward the building, put her arms down, walked back to the building, opened the door, and disappeared behind the door as it shut behind her. *She knew I was following her,* Sherman thought. *That was a message that she was okay. I feel better now. I will meet her at the garage, fourth floor on the ramp going down.*

Chapter 14

Sherman almost couldn't bring himself to enter the hospital room. He could see her through the glass of the door. She was a mess. Her face was swollen and cut up pretty bad. She had tubes running all over her that went into and out of her mouth and nose. Her eyes were swollen almost completely shut. He didn't know what stage of recovery she was in, other than what the nurse had told him on his way in. "She is not responsive right now," the nurse said, "and we aren't sure if she can hear you. Her brain is strong and did not receive any brain damage. She has broken bones and missed puncturing a lung from of her broken ribs by millimeters. It actually looks really bad, but she was lucky—no major damage to any vital organs and she still has strong brain function. It could have been greatly worse. Although she might not be able to communicate with you, treat her as if she can. Talk to her. Encourage her. Let her know you are there."

Sherman walked in the door and just stood there. He was truly in disbelief. She didn't even look like Mickie. He knew it was his fault. He could have and should have done more. He pulled the chair next to the bed and sat next to her.

"Hey, Mick." His voice was unsure, broken, and full of emotion. He tried to stay strong. Or at least sound strong. "Hey Mick, Jesus you look like shit." He knew if she could, she would smile to that comment. It made him smile a little bit and lightened his mood. After that, though, he wasn't sure what he should say. If he could say the perfect thing to get her better and healed and up and out of this bed, he would. He just knew that wasn't possible, but he wished it was.

There were no words that could be used that would explain his feelings. The hate and anger he was feeling, the love and sorrow, the remorse and confusion. There were no words that would truly put it all into a viable sentence. He sat there with his head down, trying to mask the oncoming wave of emotions. *Suck it up, push the emotions down. She would not want to see or hear you crying. Man the fuck up*, his inner voice demanded. Sherman wiped the forming tears from his eyes and took a few deep breathes. He regained his composure and reached out and took her hand in his, caressing the back of her hand with his thumb. Her hands were scratched and bruised, some of her nails were broken down to the quick, and others were ripped completely off down to the cuticle. "Hey, Mick. I hope you are not in pain . . . can you hear me? . . . If you can hear me, squeeze my hand."

He sat in the hospital room next to her bed and held her hand. The beating she must have endured had to be unimaginable. Her face was swollen and unrecognizable, her eyes were shut. He wasn't sure if it was from the swelling or because she had them shut. There were bruises and cuts, some deeper than others across her face, on her hands, legs, and arms; they seem to be everywhere. The bigger cuts and gashes were covered with bandages and tape. The entire scene was almost too much for him to take as he sat and just tried to be emotionally strong for her, as he didn't know if she could see him, hear him, or feel his presence. Her body occasionally twitched as if she was waking up from a nightmare, although she never made any sounds or woke up.

Sherman continued to hold her hand as it twitched ever so slightly. He tried to comfort her the best he could, but he knew that whatever happened to her, it was his fault. He was to blame, as it had been his idea to use her as a decoy. He now more than ever regretted his decision to include her. How could he be so stupid to think that something like this wouldn't have or couldn't have happened? He leaned into her, his face almost touching hers, his forehead to hers, and whispered to her, "I will find him, and I will kill him . . . I promise this to you. I will make this right. I am so sorry for letting this happen to you. I will find him. And I will kill him for what he did to you."

As he sat back up, Sherman thought that maybe he might have felt her squeeze his hand, but wasn't one hundred percent positive it was a squeeze and not just his emotions hoping that she may have possibly acknowledged his presence. He didn't rule out a slight squeeze, but since he didn't feel it again, he just assumed it was his adrenaline from being so emotional. He sat quietly, holding her hand to see if maybe it would happen again, but the longer he held her hand, the more he realized it must have been his imagination. Her hand continued to twitch, her fingers continued to tap and shake. He lifted up her hand, kissed the back of it, placed it back down on the bed, and left the hospital room.

* * *

Sherman was late. It wasn't like Tank to be late, but on top of all the other stuff she wanted to bust his chops about, being late wasn't going to help his cause. As each late minute passed, Mickie got more and more angry at him.

That was why she never saw him coming. He was stalking her, and she didn't even know it. He attacked her from behind, grabbed her hair, and violently pulled her backwards and to the ground as the back of her head smashed to onto the concrete floor with a thud. She saw a flash of light and then just felt the thud of her body being hit. It felt like she was getting hit by ten people. She was conscious, but unaware, and with a rush of adrenaline she snapped back to reality and saw her attacker pummeling her. Punch after punch, and when he got tired of punching her and banging her head against the ground, he stood up and kicked her. When he got tired from doing that, he threw and landed elbows to her face.

Mickie could taste her own blood starting to pool in the back of her throat and tried to spit it out, but the best she could do was gargle it. It was sticky, and thick, and choking her. She couldn't breathe. She lost vision in one of her eyes and could feel her other eye swelling as the blows continued to rain down on her. Her teeth chipped and broke and fell to the back of her throat, swimming in the pool of blood. She tried to roll to one side to clear her throat and escape, but her body wasn't responding the way she needed it to. *You can lay here and die if you want, or fucking do something,* her inner voice calmly said to her. *I choose to do something,* she barked back at herself.

As her attacker came down for another blow, she wrapped her arm in his and attempted to pull him as close as she could and hold on for dear life. If nothing else, her efforts would tie him up enough to get him to stop hitting her. She then wrapped her legs around his waist and smashed her assailant across the bridge of his nose with her forehead. She could feel the blood from his nose dripping onto her face. She knew she had caused some damage. She was fading in and out of consciousness.

"Listen up, ladies. The strongest part of a women's body is her forehead. I don't know if that is actually true or not, but it is a phenomenal weapon. Do you understand that?" the recruits sitting in a group around the drill instructor screamed, *"Ma'am yes ma'am!"* and rattled the sky with their volume level. The drill instructor continued. *"There are many ways to disable your opponent. It doesn't matter if they are bigger than you, or stronger than you. If you take them down in the right fashion, the biggest of opponents will crumble like a house of cards. You got that?"* *"Ma'am yes Ma'am!"* the thunderous response came. *"If it's a man, he got that wedding tackle, you understand? He got that soft spot. That will drop a man quicker than anything else. Aim well and hit hard, you understand that?"* *"Ma'am yes Ma'am."* *"All right ladies, get up and let's pick a partner and get back to training. Practice these moves. With practice comes proficiency, with proficiency comes speed, you understand that?"* *"Ma'am yes Ma'am."*

Her attacker was trying to bang her back against the ground in hopes that she would loosen her grip. She unwrapped her legs from his waist and used her leg to push his lower body off of her and up into the air as hard as she could. As his body lifted off of her and into the air, when his body started to fall back onto her, she aimed well and struck hard, and kicked him directly in the groin. As soon as her shin connected with his groin, she could feel the air release from his body and he let out a groan. His body went limp on top of her, and she positioned herself back to wrapping her legs around him and holding on for dear life. She could feel herself getting weaker, and she was afraid she was losing this battle. He was going to kill her. She could feel it.

She could feel that this wasn't a robbery or a rape. This was an attempt at taking her life. She wanted to fight, but was losing, and didn't have much left. He continued to strike at her and she felt him bite into her chest to try and get her to release her grip. As he banged her body and her head into the ground, she was slipping in and out of consciousness with each blow. She knew a few more of these blows, and she would not wake up. She had fought hard, but couldn't fight anymore, and she started to cry. It was all too much.

"You want a piece of this?" he teased her as he lightly swung weak slaps towards her head.

"Dad stop," she replied as she chased him around the yard.

"Get back here, you!" He was faster and bigger than her, but she was determined to catch him. He ducked and dodged her like a bull fighter rolling his body out of the way of a charging bull. Each time, her little arms and body reached for his waist. She finally caught him and he crumbled to the ground in a heap. "Aww, you got me, I give up."

"Too late pops, I got you now." She climbed on top of him and attempted to wrap his arm into an arm bar as she fell back onto the grass next to him. "Sweetheart, I am way too big and strong for you to arm bar me. You have to think smarter than that. Use my advantages against me. If my height is an advantage, take me to the ground. If my strength is an advantage, weaken me with softening blows. Go for the sensitive spots. Groin shots if it's a guy, the boobies if it's a girl. Isn't that a thing? Nipple twisters? The bridge of the nose, slap the ears with the palm of your hand attempting to rupture the ear drums. Trying to out-muscle me will not be the way to do it."

She shifted her focus and climbed back on top of her dad, this time pretending to headbutt him and rupture his eardrums with palm slaps with her hands. He laughed and chuckled as she was seriously trying. The more he laughed, the more frustrated and angry she was getting. "Don't get mad, get determined," he would tell her.

"I know, but everyone is bigger than me, everyone is stronger than me. I can't beat everyone."

"And I don't expect you to. There will always be someone bigger and stronger than you. There will always be someone trying to hurt you or even kill you." He sat up and rolled her off of him. "Listen to me. You must survive. That's what this is all about. Survival. If anyone brings harm to you, you are to make every effort to defuse the situation

with your words and your wit. But if they choose to bring harm to you, you make sure that they will regret that decision by any means necessary. Do you understand that?"
He caressed her chin with his hand. "Survival. There is no fairness in fighting. You gave them an opportunity to walk away. Once things get physical, all bets are off. Then it becomes survival, and you hurt them more than they can hurt you."

"But what if I can't?" the young girl asked.

"If you can't, and all else fails, my love, you make sure the last thing they will ever see is your face. You take their eyes. You dig your thumbs into their eyes as hard as you can, and you don't stop until they either run away, or until your last breath is their last vision."

As her head hit the pavement again, she could feel her hair sticking to the ground. The blows weren't as hard, and she thought this could be from the amount of blood or swollen flesh that was breaking the fall of her head. She shifted her hips and her attacker slipped slightly off her and to her side. She wrapped her arm that was holding him close to her off of his arm and around the back of his head. She swung her free hand around and jammed her thumb as hard as she could into his eye. She could feel her nail enter first and his eyeball move around each knuckle as it passed. Her thumb bent behind the eyeball and she could feel it suction against the absolute bottom of her thumb, almost touching the meat of her hand. He let out a bloodcurdling scream and stopped fighting her. He reached both of his hands to her wrist and started pulling on her arm to release her thumb from his eye. The suction of her thumb behind his eye was so great that she couldn't pull it out on her own, and was unsure with the amount of pressure he was using if he could either. He stood up, still holding her wrist, and continued to try to pull. Her shoulders were off the ground and he was trying to move away from her, pulling her arm, backing up, and at the same time dragging her body on the ground as he was on his feet but bent over at the waist. He was dragging her hard at this point as if he was trying to run away. He swung his head to the left and right, still pulling at her arm, resigned to the fact that he was probably going to have to pull his own eyeball out if he was to get her thumb out from behind it. He was now like a rabid dog, pulling swinging his head and dragging her. Her thumb let loose. She wasn't sure if the eye came with it or if it lost suction and slipped out. Her body crashed to the floor, and her head for the last time thudded and bounced off the ground, knocking her unconscious once again. This time she would not regain consciousness in this fight. The assault was over.

* * *

Sherman made his way down the street and onto the first floor of the parking garage. He could hear the sirens. As he stepped into the stairway, two police cars passed by at a high rate of speed, heading to the higher floors of the parking garage. He assumed it was just coincidence and continued to climb floor after floor until he was at the door of the fourth floor. He could see all of the hustle and bustle through the stairway window. There were police, paramedics, and people just standing by, those who'd on their way to their cars who stopped to see what happened. He wanted to crash open that door and run over there. He wasn't sure what to do.

He walked out of the staircase and onto the parking area, then towards the other staircase, and saw her laying there. Her shirt was cut open and the paramedics were working on her. One of her shoes was knocked off of her feet and she was covered in blood.

Sherman felt like he was going to throw up but pushed it down. Now was not a time to fall apart. What went wrong? What happened? Sherman had so many questions, but no answers. The one thing that he did know is that someone was onto her, or them. All of them? Maybe they were watching him right now. He wanted to run to the staircase and run all the way back to the basement and regroup, but he knew that would look suspicious. So he calmed his nerves and made his way to the other staircase and slowly opened the door. He had to fight every urge in his body to not run down the stairs and out the door. He calmly walked down the stairs while his mind raced about all the things that had led up this moment and how he was going fix it all, or at least figure out what to do next. He pushed the door open and spilled out onto the street. He didn't physically spill out onto the street, but more emotionally, he felt a sense of relief as he made it out. He turned up the road and headed back to the sanctity of the darkness of his basement.

* * *

Sherman returned to the room and held Mickie's hand again. This time, her hand no longer twitched, her body laid still, and the only sound in the room was from the breathing machines. He sat quietly next to her and just contemplated all the mistakes he had made. The first would have been getting her involved with this in the first place. What was he thinking? This had nothing to do with her, there was no reason to have even brought this up to her. If he had just tried to figure out a way on his own to find this guy, this would have never happened and she wouldn't be here in the hospital fighting for her life.

She squeezed his hand. At least, he thought she squeezed his hand. Maybe he was imagining it like he did the last time he was here visiting her. She squeezed it again. This time he was 100% positive it was a squeeze. He almost jumped for joy, and then he leaned into her and started talking to her. "I'm here, it's Tank, I am so sorry . . ." his words were interrupted by her hand twitching again. It twitched for a few moments, and then stopped just as quickly as it started. He worried that she might have brain damage and the twitches and squeezes may be involuntary. But then they started again. A squeeze followed by the twitching.

"Are you trying to tell me something? Are you trying to communicate with me?" His inner voice responded to him as if talking to a five-year-old. *Of course she is trying to communicate with you, pay attention.*

Okay, he thought, *but how?* He grabbed a pen and a small notepad that was on the end table next to her bed, then started counting the pulses of her fingers and waited for a pause. The pulses were sporadic, and didn't seem to have any rhythm or consistency. The first burst of pulses came for 10, and then he thought he felt a pause. He wrote down the number ten. Then they came at 14, then 7, then 21, then 5. The pulses stopped. He always believed that she could hear him while he was in the room, so she must be happy with the information she was providing and that was why the pulses stopped. She must have been able to get the message across to him. So now more than ever, he was convinced that it was a code. He matched the numbers up with the alphabet; 14 = N, 7 = G, 21 = U, 5 = E. *Okay, we have four letters that can be mixed around to form some sort of clue?* he asked himself. He started mixing the letters around; NGUE is the order in which he received them. Was that a name? And if so, how would she have known her attacker's name? Probably not a name. He knew where she was attacked, so it was most likely not an address, street name, or location, because that wouldn't move the information forward; they already had that information. Maybe there were letters missing? Did he not receive the entire code?

He started adding letters to see if anything made sense. He added a letter in the front, then in the back, he mixed the letters around, he wrote them backwards and in every and any form he could, but they just never made sense. He went back to the bed and held her hand. "Mickie, I am so sorry, I don't know what you are trying to tell me. I need more help. I need more. I am so sorry that I can't figure this out for you." He leaned his forehead down onto the back of her hand and slowly started to cry. And then it started again, but this time it was different. They were more sporadic, they were more frantic, they were more pronounced. The twitches and pulses were coming at a pace and strength to almost say to Sherman, "How dumb do you have to be? I am clearly showing you what I need, smarten up dumb dumb." It was a manner that only Mickie could get across, in a loving but yet firm way.

"It's a code, Mick, I get it. But what code? There are a million codes, literally a million. Wars were protected, won, and lost on the strength of codes. What fucking code is it, Mick?" The anger in his voice was stern but filled with emotion. His eyes welled with tears as the frustration started to overwhelm him. "There are literally millions of codes, there is Morse code, there is—" *HOLY FUCK, it is Morse code you idiot,* his inner voice screamed at him. He was still holding her hand, and as if a fog had cleared, it was as clear as a blue sky. These weren't pulses and twitches, these were dots and dashes. It hit him so clearly that he was almost embarrassed when he thought about it. *Morse code. She is trying to speak to me through Morse code.*

Twitch, twitch twitch twitch, twitch, pulse twitch, pulse pulse pulse, pulse twitch pulse pulse. The pulses and twitches were coming so rapidly that Sherman was having a hard time catching up, but he was so determined that he couldn't hide his level of excitement. He knew she was communicating, he knew she was telling him something, and he couldn't wait to crack the code. The code seemed to continue to repeat itself with a few minor variations in the same letters. E, S, E, N, O, Y. over and over again. ESENOYESENOYESENOY. YES NOE? Was it in another language? Maybe Spanish? Mickie was Puerto Rican, so maybe she was speaking in Spanish?

ESE. Doesn't that mean, Man, or dude, or something like that in Spanish? his inner voice asked him. He responded out loud, but in a low whisper, "I think it means man, or something like that, but we know it was a man. We just don't know WHICH man. That can't be it." He wrote the letters down, once again he wrote them forward, he wrote them backwards, he mixed them up. By this time,

Mickie had stopped communicating and laid still, with the room silent other than the breathing machine whooshing up and down in the background. YEN, NOSE, YES, NO, SEY, NOY, EYES, SNO, YO, ESE, NOEY. He wrote down every combination of letters he could until the notepad was full of jumbled up variations. He kept coming back to wondering if they were Spanish words, but he didn't know Spanish, and he knew Mickie knew he didn't know Spanish. It had to be English.

NOSE, YES, NO, EYES. Those were the only English words in the code. He looked down at the paper again of the original coded letters. He said out loud to himself, "He has a nose, the word yes in the code doesn't really make any sense, no eye, NO EYES, does he not have any eyes? That is the only possibility. She blinded him. SHE BLINDED HIM!" Sherman jumped to his feet, placed his hands on the back of his head, elbows out wide. "You fucking blinded him, you animal. Oh my god, you are great." He finished rejoicing and placed her hand in his. He leaned forward and placed his lips almost touching her ear. "Mick, I pray that you can hear me. You blinded him. You gave me something to go off of, you gave me a clue. You are incredible. I have one more question. Did you get one eye or both? Squeeze my hand once for one, and twice for both." Nothing. No squeeze, no twitch, no pulse, nothing. "It's okay Mick, I will figure it out. How hard can it be to find a recently blinded man? Or one-eyed man?" He leaned forward and kissed her on the forehead. He then stood up, still holding her hand. He lowered her hand back onto the bed, and she squeezed his hand. One solid, hard squeeze. He leaned down, gave her another kiss on the forehead, turned, and walked out the door.

* * *

She could scream at the top of her lungs, but no one could hear her. She knew his face, she screamed his description. She saw Sherman come in the room. She needed to let him know her attacker was hurt. "I thumbed his eye, he is blind, Tank, I literally removed his entire eye," she said in a boastful way. But he just sat at the edge of the bed and apologized. She continued to scream to let him know what she knew. He wasn't listening, he couldn't hear her. She felt as if the veins in her neck were going to burst with the force with which she screamed. *Grab him, shake him, tell him what he did.* She couldn't move; with every ounce of everything she had in her body, she couldn't move.

He held her hand. She couldn't feel her hand inside of his, but she could see it. Focus. *Focus. Squeeze his hand . . . squeeze with all of your might.* She felt as if tears should be running down her cheeks with the sheer force and effort she was putting into moving. As if she was on mile 25 of a 26-mile marathon. She was mentally and emotionally exhausted with the effort.

263

At last, it moved. Her hand moved, or at least her finger moved. *Do it again. Harder. And again.* It was one of the most difficult physical activities she had ever undertaken, but she did it.

She wanted to lay back and just rest, but she knew she had to soldier on and get him some sort of message, somehow, some way. Morse code. That's how. But with every movement, it was like trying to lift a truck off of a little old lady. It took every ounce of strength she had, and would leave her weak after each attempt of the message. *What is the least amount of words I can use to let him know who did this and how to find him?* She thought about it for a while, and then looked down at her hand and started moving mountains, charging hills, and lifting trucks off of old ladies. She was determined for Sherman to receive this message. One way or another.

Chapter 15

Sherman didn't sleep well. He kept dreaming about Mickie and what this animal had done to her. He would wake up sweating and angry. He had to do something, but wasn't sure what to do, or who to do it to. He tried to fall back asleep, but this time was awoken by a banging and thumping sound. It was coming from down the hall, and he decided to investigate the noise.

He quickly realized it was coming from the laundry room. He entered the laundry room, but it was empty. No one was there, but something was rattling around and making a crazy banging sound. It was one of the dryers. Someone had washed and was drying shoes. Sherman walked over to the dryer and opened the door.

Not only were they drying shoes, but they were drying what seemed to be about ten pairs of shoes. It was actually only three pairs, but with the amount of banging and rattling around it was doing, it sounded more like ten pairs. Sherman half-thought to just leave the dryer with the door slightly opened so he could get a little more sleep and peace and quiet. Then he wondered if maybe any of these shoes would fit him. He pulled out a couple of the shoes to check their sizes. There was a women's size 7 running shoe, and a man's size 13 running shoe. Sherman wore a size 12, but figured he could make the size 13 work. He threw the women's shoe back in the dryer and fished around for the other men's size 13. After finding the matching shoes and putting them on, he also fished out a pair of shorts from the drier and decided he would go for a run. Maybe that would clear his mind.

When Sherman was in the Marine Corps, he would often go running to clear his mind or reduce some stress. There was something about running in the crisp morning air that Sherman enjoyed. It was like a resetting of his inner clock. It gave him the opportunity to think through his problems with a clear mind. And this time it was no different. He needed a distraction to clear his mind and make sense of all of the issues and problems that he had swimming around in his mind.

He briskly walked out of the laundry room, out the door, and started jogging up the ramp and out onto the sidewalk. The more his mind filled with stress and anxiety, the less he paid attention to his running. Normally he could hear his breathing or feel the motion of his knees and ankles, which reminded him of how much he didn't enjoy running. But this time was different. This time his mind was clearly focused on Mickie.

He racked his brain on who would have known she was meeting him in the garage. Or was it just a random attack? It couldn't have been a random attack. It couldn't just be a coincidence that right after she met up with Sherman and plotted against this pimp, she was attacked. There had to be more to it, but Sherman couldn't figure out the angle.

The miles were flying by. He must have run six miles through the city as he turned into the park. He wasn't the least bit tired; he probably would have been if he really thought about it, but while he was trying to sort all of the details out, his mind was preoccupied on everything that was going on. He could return to the street corner, maybe, and wait for the pimp or his henchmen to return to see if any of them were injured. He could have the Chief check with the hospitals in the area to see if maybe someone had been admitted with an eye injury.

Sherman normally would have enjoyed running in the park. The wide walking and running paths, the long park benches that bent and flowed with the walking paths, the green grass, and the animal life that made the park their home. Sherman especially liked the squirrels; he always seemed to get along with squirrels, and they seemed to like him also. Often he would sit in a park and throw acorns or whatever he could find to the squirrels, and they would store them in their cheeks and run away. One time he was able to get a squirrel to come right up to him and eat an acorn right out of his hand. The park was pretty quiet today. It wasn't overly early, but the weather wasn't great, so there wasn't the average group of women pushing baby strollers, or older people out for a walk. Sherman did cross paths with few runners. They would pass each other and greet each other with a quick head nod.

Around mile seven or eight, Sherman started thinking that he should start heading back to the basement before he ran all the energy out of his body. He was starting to tire, and his legs were starting to get a little fatigued. As he came around the bend he saw two men, one sitting on the park bench with his arms spread out to his sides, resting on the back of the park bench. Another man was standing in front of him with his back to Sherman. As Sherman got closer, he thought to himself that the man sitting on the bench looked familiar but couldn't place his face. As he got closer, the face got more familiar. He wasn't injured, and seemed to have both of his eyes, so maybe he was just a guy he knew from the streets. Maybe one of his homeless acquaintances. And then it dawned on him that he knew exactly who that guy was. It was the pigeon guy from the roof.

Just as he was realizing who it was, he was passing right behind the man with his back turned towards Sherman. The man turned his head to watch Sherman run by. The man was wearing an eye patch, and had a bunch of cuts and bruises on his face. Sherman knew right away it was the pimp. Sherman almost turned right around and attacked him, but instead turned into the woods about a hundred yards up ahead of the two. Then he started running through the trees back towards the men. His adrenaline was growing, his heart was racing, and he could feel his blood coursing through his temples. He ran faster, and faster. He was now running so fast that he wouldn't have been surprised if someone saw him and said he was running on all fours, foaming from the mouth and kicking up dirt behind him like a rabid dog.

Sherman broke out of the trees directly behind the pigeon man sitting on the bench. He looked right into the face of the pimp, and saw his eye was covered with a bandaged patch. Sherman partially smiled to himself as he got closer and saw the damage Mickie had caused to his face. His face was deeply cut and scratched. His unbandaged eye looked swollen and bruised, as if she had been trying to get both eyes. *And it would have been worse, motherfucker, if you hadn't attacked her from behind and came at her face to face.* Sherman might have screamed this out loud. His adrenaline was pumping so hard, he was unsure what he was or wasn't doing, and his instincts just took over. His wild animal, bloodthirsty, war machine animal instincts.

In full stride, Sherman reached down and scooped up a rock about the size of a softball; the rock was heavy and dense. He jumped over the bench, and as he did so, he swung that rock with both hands and smashed it into the head of the pimp while still in midair. The pimp's body crashed to the ground in a heap, as if he had been knocked out from the blow.

Sherman then turned towards the pigeon man. It happened so quickly that the pigeon man was still registering what happened, and was just bringing his arms off of the bench when Sherman threw the softball-sized rock with all of his might into the pigeons man's chest. It landed with a solid thud, and the man let out a rush of air that gave the impression to Sherman that something in his chest had broken. He was gasping for air and wheezing. He brought his hands to his chest and started to fall forward, and as his head was falling towards the ground in front of him, Sherman kicked him right in the face, then lifted the pigeon man's body back onto the bench and knocked him unconscious.

Sherman turned his attention back to the pimp. He retrieved his rock, and everything seemed to slow down. Sherman had an ability that he didn't often realize he had until it was already happening, when it happened, it always came in handy. In the most stressful times of his life, everything slowed down, and he became hyper-focused and super sensitive to everything around him. As everyone around him seemed to move in normal speed, it was if Sherman moved fast but saw things happening in slow motion. The pimp was on his knees and trying to clear his head when Sherman hit him in the head with the rock again.

Blood squirted out of his head and started running down his face. The pimp fell onto his back with his legs still folded underneath him. Sherman jumped on his chest with both feet and started landing naked-handed punches with one hand and solid blows to his face with the rock in his other hand. From an outside point of view, Sherman looked like a chimpanzee that has wildly jumping on someone's chest as he rained down sideways punches and wild blows from every direction.

Sherman wasn't trying to kill the guy, but he wasn't trying to not kill him either. The blood started pooling around them, and soon they were both covered in blood. At no time was Sherman worried about the pigeon man. He was focused at the task at hand, and when his right arm got tired of hitting the pimp with the rock, he switched to his left. When that arm tired, he dropped the rock and searched for a stick that was big enough to do damage, but light enough for him to swing with his tired arms. The pimp was trying to crawl away, but wasn't able to get too far. One of his arms didn't seem to work and he was unable to keep his head up as he dragged himself about ten feet. Sherman reared back with the stick and hit him squarely on the side of his head. His head went limp, and Sherman jumped on the back of his head with both feet. He jumped again, but landed on the man's back on his knees. Sherman reached around the man's head from behind and hooked his finger in his mouth from each side of his head, and with all of his might, started pulling the pimp's mouth towards his ears until he could feel the man's face flesh tearing. The more it tore, the harder Sherman pulled. He continued to pull until his hands were at each one of the man's ears.

Sherman stood up and started kicking the man. He kicked his head, his ribs, his legs, his back, and back to his head. He retrieved the rock for the final time. He knelt next to the pimp and said, "This is for Mickie, you fucking piece of shit." Sherman stood up and held the rock over his head with both hands, and with all of his might, he swung the rock down towards the back of the man's head and let it go. Sherman's feet came off the ground like he was swinging a sledge hammer at one of those carnival games to try and make the piece go all the way to the top and ring the bell. The rock crashed into the back of the pimps head, but instead of bouncing off or ricocheting, the rock cratered in the back of his head and remained in the crater. Sherman stood up, heavily breathing and covered in blood. He looked around at what he had done and the slow motion of the moment stopped and everything went back to normal speed.

Run! his inner voice said, calm but firm. This time Sherman took the advice. Sherman didn't look back. He ran through the park and headed straight for the lake. He hit the lake almost in full stride. He wasn't sure if he wanted to dive in or run in due to his speed, so he got caught in between as the water hit him towards the middle of his thighs, and he was propelled forward and shot into the water. With a loud splash, he started to swim. He swam while at the same time trying to use a free hand at times to rub his arm on his body, trying to get some of the blood out of his clothes. He came to the other side of the lake after about five minutes of swimming. It wasn't a large lake, but it was big enough to do the job Sherman needed it to do, and that was to get most of the blood off of him. He popped out of the water on the other side and started running again. He ran all the way back to the basement. He didn't stop to rest, he didn't stop for traffic, he didn't stop at all. He didn't even remember breathing while he was doing it, and wouldn't be surprised if someone told him he ran back the entire way holding his breath. He was scared, but euphoric. He got him.

WE FUCKING GOT HIM! his inner voice cheered. He knew people had to have seen him. He knew that it wouldn't be long before they came for him. He knew there had to be cameras. This one was bad. He didn't regret doing it, but he also knew he might be in a lot of trouble, and wasn't sure if him being in trouble meant others were in trouble also. He ran down the ramp, squeak, slam, down the hallway, and into the darkness.

* * *

Sherman sat in the darkness overcome with emotion. He wasn't sure if he was crying out of fear, sadness, or joy. His emotions and nerves were shot, and he wasn't sure if his thoughts were still in the realm of reality or if he was truly losing his mind. His actions were ones he knew he was capable of doing, but never truly believed he would ever have to use. It was almost like an out-of-body experience.

Sherman changed out of the bloody clothes and neatly folded them up, then placed the bloody running shoes on top of them next to the concrete pillar in the dark. He put his own shoes and pants back on and walked to the laundry room. There, he stood in front of the deep sink shirtless and washed whatever remnants of blood or dirt he could find off of him that the water from the lake didn't remove. He heard someone walk down the ramp and into the hallway. The outside door was propped open today, so there was no squeaking and banging of the door.

The person walked in, and instead of turning towards the laundry room immediately turned towards the dark hallway. Sherman peeked out of the laundry room down the hallway to see the Chief walking into the darkness. *Oh shit,* Sherman thought.

"I'm down here, in the laundry room," he called out. The Chief turned around and quickly made his way into the laundry room. He got real close to Sherman, and in a low but stern excited whisper he said, "They got him. They got him and one of his guys in the park."

"Who got who?" Sherman responded.

"The pimp. Some vagrant got the pimp and one of his buddies in the park. It must have happened a few days ago and the animals must have gotten to the bodies overnight, because it was a gruesome scene. There was blood everywhere. And I mean *everywhere*. It looked like the animals dragged the pimp's body all over that park. It was on the branches and leaves, had to be 10-15 feet up in the trees. The concrete and grass were saturated with blood. It was quite a scene. There was damn near nothing left of those guys." The Chief started to get more giddy and excited as he explained the scene. "The pimp literally had the back of his skull bashed in. I bet the vagrant was on PCP or something. The shit looked like a savage or a werewolf attacked these guys. That's the type of strength drugs will give you. I don't think I have ever seen a more gruesome scene in all of my years of police work," the Chief boasted.

"What vagrant? What are you talking about?" Sherman inquired.

"The vagrant that they found at the scene. The guy was covered in blood. Well, he wasn't at the scene. He was near it, and he was covered in blood, so it's the guy."

Sherman couldn't comprehend completely what the Chief was saying. Was he saying that someone else was caught, and they were saying a homeless guy or vagrant was responsible for the murders? Or was he saying that there was a vagrant there who knew Sherman did it? He was so confused. "Wait a second, was the vagrant a witness?" said Sherman. "No, he was the guy. He's the perp. They have him down at the station. He isn't doing much talking, but they say he is the guy."

"Chief, none of this makes sense, that can't be the guy."

"The hell it can't. He was near the crime scene, covered in blood. That's the guy. Sherman, don't make more of this than there has to be. He's the guy."

"I'm the guy!" Sherman shot back.

"You're what guy?" the Chief said with a look of puzzlement on his face.

"I'm the one that killed the pimp. And it didn't happen a few days ago, and there were no animals. It happened a few hours ago and that was all me. I did it all myself. I was the werewolf, I was the vagrant, I was the guy on PCP. Except I wasn't on PCP, just full of rage and hate. I was running in the park and saw him. I went into a blind rage and it was me. I did it. I killed the pimp. Oh, and guess what. His buddy in the park—"

"Yeah, he's dead too." The Chief interjected.

"Yeah. I didn't mean to kill him also, but he was the guy we saw up on the roof."

"What guy?" the Chief asked.

"The pigeon guy. The guy exercising the birds. It was him. He's the one I saw first in the park, and I couldn't figure out where I knew or had seen him before, and then it dawned on me. It was the pigeon guy. And now it all makes sense. The pigeon guy must have seen us on the roof. How stupid could we have been? You are the fucking Chief of Police. Of course he would know who you are right on sight. He must have seen you on the roof and put two and two together, and told the pimp." He suddenly realized that the Chief didn't know about Mickie and the beating that she took at the hands of the pimp. But he didn't want to tell him anymore, because he didn't want to have Mickie dragged into this any more than she had already been.

Sherman stood there staring into space, thinking about how it all now added up. It all made sense. The pimp had most likely realized that Mickie was part of the sting operation, or what he might have thought was a sting operation, and decided to try and kill Mickie to send a message to the Chief of police. *But why not just come for me or the Chief? Why the girl? He must have known that if we wanted him before, after hurting or killing Mickie, we would be after him even more.*

That part didn't make sense to Sherman, but all the rest added up and all made him feel responsible for what happened to Mickie. If he had just planned it out better, really dove into the details, maybe this wouldn't have happened. Maybe he could have kept Mickie from being hurt, but he couldn't dwell on that right now. He had to get to the bottom of how someone else got arrested for what he did.

"So an innocent man is sitting in a jail cell because of something I did? You need to get him out," Sherman barked at the Chief while putting his shirt back on.

"Get him out? Get him out of where? I'm not getting him out of anywhere. I can't just get a double murder suspect out of jail just because I feel like it. Let the justice system do its thing. They will soon realize he isn't the guy, and they will have to release him."

"You are the fucking Chief of Police. If you can't get him out, who can? Let the justice system do its thing?" Sherman shot back in a sarcastic retort. "I don't like that idea at all. Every second that man sits in jail is a second he doesn't have his freedom because of me. That isn't why we're doing this. Don't lose focus of what the main purpose of doing all of this from the beginning was. It was to rid the world of bad people, not put innocent people in jail for bad things that we did."

"Okay, slow down, breathe. Listen. You're off the hook. They have no idea it was you. I can run some interference so they never look towards you and you're off scot-free. Onto the next one, right? This isn't a bad thing Sherman. This isn't a bad thing by a long shot. Think this through for a minute.

This keeps you out here, able to still focus on the main goal. You are no good to us in jail," the Chief reasoned.

"Good to us? None of this is supposed to be good to us. It's about being good for them. All of them. Everybody except us. I need to turn myself in." Sherman said the words with such conviction that the Chief knew he was more than serious; he was determined, and the Chief didn't like that. At all.

"Holy Shit Sherman, Turn yourself in? For some fucking bum who is probably going to have a better life in jail than he would on the street? Think about what you are saying. It doesn't make any sense, Sherman. I can't let you do that."

"Let me do that? You aren't letting me do anything. An innocent man is not going to sit in jail because of me, and that is that. If you aren't going to help me, I will do it on my own. Believe me when I tell you, I am turning myself in in twenty-four hours if that man is not released from prison. With or without your help."

"Okay. Wait, let me see what I can do. Don't do anything until you talk to me again. I promise you we can make this work. I just need to figure a few things out. And I may need a little more time. Don't do anything stupid."

"Twenty-four hours. That's all the time I have for that man to sit in jail. Twenty-four hours. Do whatever you feel you can do, but if you aren't able to have him released, I'm going to turn myself in so he can be released." This time Sherman left the basement first. He walked out of the laundry room, through the open outside door, and up the ramp.

The Chief stood in the laundry room with his hands on his hips, contemplating his next move. "God Damn it, Sherman," he said out loud. He stood there thinking for a few minutes and then made his way out of the basement. He wasn't sure what he was going to do, but knew that something had to be done if he was going to be able to salvage this situation.

Chapter 16

Sherman caressed Mickie's head and hair with one hand and held her hand with the other. "I kept my promise Mick. I got him," he said to her, as if he knew she was listening. "But I screwed up this time and it all went wrong. I got him, but someone else is getting blamed for it, and I'm not sure what to do. On the one hand I know that what I did was right. But on the other hand, I feel bad that someone else is taking the fall. What do I do? I wish you could tell me what I should do. I wish you could give me advice. I am lost and need help. How do I get the innocent man off the hook without giving myself up? Or is that even possible? Do I just turn myself in and let the chips fall where they may? Or do I run? Run far and never look back? I'm so torn on what is the right answer." He held her hand in his. *Please squeeze my hand, give me a sign, give me a Morse code. Yes or No. Please give me something.*

Sherman sat in the silence. Hoping, waiting for Mickie to give him a sign. But nothing came. Not a twitch, not a tap, not a pulse. It was just silent, other than the sounds of the machines in the room. "They say you are going to make a full recovery one day. The road will be rough, but someday this will all be behind us." Sherman knew that Mickie could hear him. And he knew that she wasn't giving him a sign or message on purpose. Her silence was deafening. She was giving him a message without giving him a message, and he knew it. He knew deep down in his heart what the right thing to do was, and this visit solidified it for him and he was at peace with it. His decision was made, his mind was made up.

"Thanks Mick, you always were a great listener." He brushed the hair from the side of her face and gave her a kiss on her cheek. *Thank you Mick, I love you. And I am sorry.* Sherman stood up and stood over her for another minute, then he slowly let go of her hand and left the room. He knew he wouldn't be seeing Mickie for a very long time, and the final time that he let go of her hand would stick with him for a long time. But he was at peace with it. He was tired. He needed a rest from all the worry and stress. He needed to tell his story. He had to take responsibility for his actions. He was ready to make a very hard decision. Now it was time to go and let the Chief know of his plan.

* * *

They seemed to meet more in the laundry room now than they did in the dark hallway. This was far too important to not be able to look each other in the face while decisions were being made. The Chief looked visually flustered and started speaking although he was tongue tied and having trouble finding the words to get his point across. "Listen, I can say whatever I can to change your mind... or tell you why a thousand times, whatever your decision is... why that is a bad idea. It's just a bad idea, Sherman." What the Chief was saying didn't make any sense, but Sherman understood the basic point the Chief was trying to get across to him. The Chief didn't want Sherman to make a bad decision, but knew his mind was made up, and there wasn't much he was going to be able to say or do to change his mind.

"Okay, you go back to the station and stay in your office. I will come in, ask for you, and tell you I have some information about a crime, and ask if I could come to your office to discuss it. You will say that I can, and we will go to your office where I will tell you everything I know about the delivery boy, the pimp, and the pigeon guy. Of course, leaving out any involvement of yours or our prostitute friend."

The Chief lowered his head and shook it in disappointment. He hoped it wasn't going to come to this but was prepared if it did. "I knew you were going to make that decision, and I told you that I would take care of you, so I will. I called on all my friends, every favor that I can. I didn't tell them why yet, but they are willing to help me anywhere they can. I have powerful friends. They are not just friends, but Marine friends. Powerful Marine friends in high places."

"I appreciate that Chief, but I just want this over with, and I want the innocent guy out as soon as possible.

Anything you can do for me once he is out would be greatly appreciated, but I am not expecting anything. You don't owe me anything. We helped each other out where we could, and whatever happens now, happens. Go back to your office. I will see you in about an hour."

The Chief leaned into Sherman and embraced him in a hug. "You are a good man, Sherman. We need more men like you in this world. I promise you I will do everything in my power to help you. You are doing important work." The Chief patted Sherman on the back and left the laundry room.

* * *

The Chief sat at his desk as he watched through the front of his glass-walled office as Sherman walked into the precinct. Sherman stood at the desk and talked to the officer at the desk for a few moments. The desk officer turned and started walking to the Chief's office. "Hey Chief, there is a guy to see you about some information he has on a crime."

"Okay, send him over."

The desk officer walked out of the office and motioned his arm to Sherman. "All right, come over here." Sherman walked through the desks of the office and stood outside the glass door.

The desk officer said, "Put your hands up real quick, and let me just make sure you don't have any weapons," as he felt Sherman's waist and over his chest. "Okay, he's clean."

Sherman's inner voice jumped into the conversation. *Okay, hold up. You didn't admit to anything yet. You can still leave. If you walk in there and spill the beans, it is over. The second you start talking, it is over for us. Are we 100% sure we want to do this?* Sherman didn't even respond this time and walked into the office. "I have some information about a crime. It seems that you have someone in custody for a crime that I committed."

"You committed the crime?" the Chief said. "What crime?"

"There was an assault in the park that lead to the death of two individuals. I am responsible for their deaths, and I believe that you have an innocent man in custody that had no part in the assaults."

The Chief stood up and said to Sherman, "Put your hands behind your back. You are not under arrest, you are just being detained until we can figure out what is going on." The Chief handcuffed Sherman and asked him to sit on the chair in front of his desk. "Okay, tell me what you know."

Sherman told him everything. He started with the delivery boy. He figured that was a good place to start, because anything before that wouldn't be in the Chief's jurisdiction, so that information would have to be saved for another time. He went into great detail about every crime he'd committed. How he lured the delivery boy to the basement, and how he found the pimp. He explained that the pigeon guy was just at the wrong place at the wrong time, and must have seen him on the roof, and that was why the pimp was trying to harm Sherman. He figured he had to get to the pimp before the pimp got to him.

He told him about the bloody clothes and where they were in the basement. He left out all parts about the Chief or Mickie, and filled them in with what he thought were believable tidbits of information that seemed to fit into place.

At times, the desk officer who was acting as the witness in this confession would chime in and ask Sherman questions, as if he was a fan of his work. "So you were only killing bad people?" he asked, and he would nod in agreement as Sherman responded. At one point he said, "So a retired Marine kills a pedophile and a pimp? I would hate to have to be on that jury. I'm not sure I could convict no matter how much evidence there was."

"That's enough!" the Chief snapped at the desk officer. "I want you to take him downtown and put him in cell 36. Do you understand that, Sergeant?"

"Yes Sir, cell 36."

"Okay, let's go." He motioned to Sherman to get on his feet and start walking towards the door.

As Sherman sat in the back of the police car, a calmness rushed over him. He felt good about what he did. He knew the road was going to be rough, but he was okay with that. He saved one more life—the life of the innocent man being blamed for his actions. The desk officer escorted Sherman through the cell block and stopped him at cell 36. "Open 36!" the guard shouted into the air. The steel door of the cell started sliding open as if the guard was using some kind of magic and had screamed "open sesame" instead of "open 36."

Sherman entered the cell and stood there. It was tiny. The cell door slid closed behind him with an eerie scraping of metal on metal as it closed and locked. "Back up to the bars," The guard directed of Sherman. Sherman backed up and put his hands through the bars so the guard could remove Sherman's handcuffs. "Welcome home," the guard said, and then walked down the catwalk and out of sight.

Sherman turned around and thought again about how small the cell was. He could probably stretch out his arms and touch both walls. There was an older man sitting on the bottom bunk; he seemed disheveled and dirty. He didn't come across as threatening or intimidating to Sherman, but in this circumstance he wasn't going to take any chances. He wasn't sure what he should say in this moment. "Hey, what's up? How are you doing?" seemed a little weird. "How's life?' also seemed somewhat inappropriate. He went with, "Hi, my name is Sherman."

The man responded with, "Hi Sherman. I'm George." The man stood up and nodded towards Sherman.

"It is nice to meet you, George."

"And the same to you, Sherman." It all seemed very nice and cordial. Almost too cordial. Sherman looked around the cell for a place to sit, and the only place was the bottom bunk or the top bunk. "So I guess the only places to sit are on our beds?"

"Yeah, but it's cool if you want to sit here without having to climb up on your bunk. It's okay." The man gestured to the foot of his bed.

Sherman nodded to the man to show his appreciation. "Thank you," he said, and sat on the foot of the bed. "How long you here for?" Sherman asked the man.

"Probably forever."

"Same here," Sherman replied as both men got a good chuckle from it. The men sat there for hours discussing each other's lives, where they grew up, and the people in their lives. Turns out his cellmate had a couple off adult kids he hadn't seen in a while, but had fond memories of times that they were all together. They discussed their times in the military, Sherman in the Marines, and his cellmate in the Air Force. They joked and jabbed at each other and their respective services.

"Are you like all the rest in here? I mean, are you innocent also?" George asked.

Sherman chuckled a little bit and responded, "Nope, I am guilty as they come. I am free from my chains, but unfortunately now I'm stuck behind these bars. What about you? You guilty too?"

"If I was, I think I would say so, but I truly am not. I was in the wrong place at the wrong time, and I knew as soon as I did what I did that it was a mistake. I tried to check the pockets of some badly beaten-up guys and I got blood on my hands and clothes. Next thing I know, I am the prime suspect in a double homicide."

The hair on the back of Sherman's neck stood up. "In the park? The other day?"

"Yes sir, that's the one."

"Well, I have some good news for you, my new friend George. Now, don't freak out on me when I tell you, but that is the crime that I am guilty of. I just confessed to those murders. I promise you I'm not a bad person, but that day I was, and I will pay for my crimes as I will one day pay for all of my crimes."

George wasn't sure what he was hearing. He wasn't sure if Sherman was being genuine or if he was pulling a jailhouse prank on him. "You did it? Did you tell them that I was blamed for it?"

"I didn't know who you were. I didn't know you would be in this cell. I will tell them whatever I need to tell them to get you released." The guard came to the cell door and

Sherman shouted to him, "I did it, it was me, George is innocent."

The guard responded, "Whatever, tell it to the judge, get out of the way. George, step forward, cuff up, you are being released." Sherman turned to George, smiling from ear to ear and excitedly pacing around the cell. "Oh God, George I am so happy for you." Sherman quickly calmed down, as he knew he only had a few seconds to be with George. "Listen George, it isn't too late to turn your life around. Go find those kids, make a difference in your life. Use this time of solitude to your advantage. This was a sign for you. Don't let it go to waste." Sherman was still speaking as George was being led away, Sherman's voice getting louder the further George got down the catwalk. "Don't let this second chance get away. Don't let it get away, George!"

* * *

The killings were all over the news. They were on the front pages of all the major newspapers and all over the internet. Most of the headlines still had the old information, as it didn't seem to get out yet that the vagrant they had in custody was released and that Sherman had confessed to the killings. There wasn't any mention of the delivery boy being included in the murders or that there was a person on the street who was killing multiple people. Sherman wasn't concerned about what people would think about him and his actions, but he did have some curiosity on how people would take it. Would they paint him as a monster who was savagely killing people, or would they see his vision and the entire goal that he was trying to achieve? Neither truly mattered to him; he was just curious on the direction it would go.

Sherman was reading one of the newspapers about the killings. *Two Men Killed In Park* was the headline. *The two men were both fathers and left behind small children. They were pillars of the community who did a great deal for those around them.* Sherman didn't like how they were portraying these guys in the newspaper as good people. He knew that they weren't and that they were horrible people. They were horrible to women and they were horrible to children. They both had long records of violence and sex offenses. Sherman wasn't sure why the paper would paint them in such a positive light. They had quotes from people in the neighborhood that stated they would be missed, and how they always did nice things for others and the person responsible for their death should get the death penalty.

That was the first time the death penalty occurred to Sherman. He could actually get the death penalty for his actions. The thought of that scared the hell out of him, but he felt rather confident that given his time in court he would be able to get the truth about these men across to the judge; to explain that although what he did was wrong, what happened to those guys was deserved and not death penalty-worthy. The paper still mentioned that they had a homeless man in custody as the suspect in the deaths. Reading this made Sherman smile; the whole thing was a disaster, but Sherman took solace in the small positives that came out of it all.

Sherman spent most of his days in his cell. He was allowed one hour a day to go out in the yard, which was made up of a chain-link fenced cage about twenty five yards long and ten yards wide. It had a basketball hoop, and in one end of the exercise area was a solid concrete wall. Sherman spent most of his time reading books in his cell. He would stay in there twenty-four hours a day if they would let him, but he had to spend one hour outside a day, so he did. He was still the only person in his cell since George left, and although he didn't get much interaction with other inmates other than when he was in the yard, he didn't crave or yearn for human contact like many of the other prisoners. Sherman enjoyed being alone, and although this was an extreme version of it, he was able to find peace in his surroundings.

As the weeks and months passed by, word started to get out on who Sherman was and what his overall goal had been. He would mainly get visits from his lawyers before his many court dates and occasionally they would bring him down to the visiting room to meet with people wanting to interview him. He didn't mind, and gave most of them whatever information they wanted. He quickly realized that there were many people who supported what he was doing, and that was evident in the amount of mail he received. People would write him handwritten letters stating their support. People would send him cards with words of encouragement and to "Stay strong." Sherman enjoyed the fan mail, but found it a little odd. What Sherman enjoyed most was the mail he received from Marines and other service members. They were proud of him, appreciative of him, and envious of the decisions that he'd made. Those too were filled with words of encouragement and invitations for when he got out that the first round of beer was on them. Or if he needed a place to stay, he could stay with them.

One letter from a Marine stated that Sherman should let him know when he gets out if he needed a sidekick to help him continue his vision. People wanted to visit Sherman and just be around him, ask him questions, show him support. In the beginning there were a lot of visitors, but as time went on, the visitations dwindled. They would pick up every so often after someone came and interviewed Sherman and put a follow-up story in the paper or in a magazine, but for the most part the visitations were at a minimum, and Sherman was fine with that. The only time Sherman really left the jail at all was for his court dates.

His court dates were pretty cut and dry. Sherman admitted to what he had done and pleaded guilty to all charges. Sherman was never in trouble before, and had a long military record of honorable service. Those things helped in his favor. Sherman's lawyers had a psychiatrist come in and say that Sherman suffered from post-traumatic stress disorder from his time in the military, as well as some other psychological ailments which seemed to trend in Sherman's favor. Sherman felt that the judge was strict but fair. He received twenty years for each killing in the park and a ten-year sentence for the delivery boy.

Sherman felt like it could have been a lot worse. He didn't get the death penalty, and he was relieved about that, but felt that in a sense he did get the death penalty; it was just a slower version of it, because a fifty-year prison sentence assured that there was a good chance Sherman was going to die in prison.

The reality of a caged life started to settle in as Sherman realized that this was now his life, and would be for a very long time. It had now been over a year, and all of his appeals had been heard and denied. One day, a guard came to his cell and announced, "You have a visitor."

A visitor? Sherman thought to himself. They placed the handcuffs on him through the cell door and then released him from the cell. They walked him down the hall and stood him outside a solid door. Sherman hadn't had any visitors in months. And the ones he had before that were mostly lawyers and newspaper people who wanted to know his story and write articles about it. The door opened up, and Sherman was overcome with emotion as he saw Mickie sitting at a table across the room.

His cheeks started to get warm and his eyes began to fill up with tears. This was the first time he had seen her since she was in the hospital. She looked the same, but she also looked different. Like she had makeup covering scars on her face. She looked a little more hardened, a little less innocent. A little less like Mickie. Sherman knew he was the reason for that and he felt terrible about it. He sat across the table from her and put his handcuffed hands on the table. She slipped her hands under his and just held his hands in hers.

"You look like shit, Tank," she said as she smiled and raised one of her hands to wipe the single tears that were running down his face.

"I am so sorry, Mick."

She placed her finger over his mouth in a shushing gesture. "There is no reason to be sorry. What is done is done. I'm okay, and I wouldn't have changed anything. Are you okay?"

"Physically, I am okay; mentally, I'm not so sure. I guess I'm fine. Just remorseful," Sherman sheepishly admitted.

Mickie made sure to quickly get her next point across and said it with a certain amount of firmness. "Don't be remorseful. You are good man, Sherman, and you did good things for good people. You will be okay. You will be fine. Stay strong." She placed his hands in hers again and just looked into Sherman's eyes. He felt like he could see into her soul. He could see her goodness shining through her eyes, and it made him feel good and really believe that he was going to be okay. That was when he felt it. Her finger was stretched out under his hands and lightly tapping on the underside of his wrist. *Tap. Nothing. Tap, Tap, Tap. Nothing. Long Press, Tap, Long Press, Tap. Nothing. A, P, E . . .* Morse Code again. He looked directly into her eyes as she continued to tap and press on his wrist with a slight smirk and a smile. They both sat in silence. The message was clear: *E.S.C.A.P.E.*

"I would like to come see you more often, Tank. Stay strong. I got you. Keep your head up." She stood up, leaned forward, and kissed him on his forehead. "Wipe those tears before you go in there so they don't beat your ass," she joked as she stood up, and with the assistance of a cane, walked towards the door on the other side of the room "Go forth and do great . . ." Sherman started to say from the other side of the room.

"Don't fucking do it, Tank. Stop stealing my shit."

Sherman sat at the table alone, staring into space thinking about the possibility. *Escape? Are you insane* his inner voice inquired. "Insane? Yeah, probably" Sherman responded out loud. His inner voice quickly followed it up with, *cool, whatever, I'm in.*

Sherman was escorted back to his cell. He laid in his bed, contemplating escaping. He wasn't sure how they were going to plan it or what it entailed. The thought of all of the possibilities flooded his mind, and he found himself swarmed with all of the details. *Maybe Mickie was planning out the details right now. Maybe she was involving others to help, like the Chief? He surely would have information about the prison. If anyone was able to get her the information she needed, it would be him.* Sherman liked the prospect of that. It made him feel alive, it gave him purpose. It gave him something to look forward to and something to strive for.

The commotion of the cell block was starting to pick up, as it was now lunchtime and the guards were making their way down the tier with the squeaky food carts. It was one of the busiest times of the day and the loudest. The clanging of trays hitting the bars, the sounds of cups being placed on the cell shelves, and the banter of conversation back and forth from the guards and prisoners. For the prisoners that were in single cells, this was the only time they got to interact with other human beings, and they took as much opportunity as they could to converse with the guards. Some guards would banter back and provide sports scores or just talk about everyday life in general, while other guards were strictly business and just gave the inmates the food tray and their drinks and moved on to the next cell. The guard stepped in front of Sherman's cell, turned, and handed him his tray through the bars. As he did this, his half-rolled-up sleeve rode up his forearm to reveal a huge tattoo of an Eagle, Globe, and Anchor, the unmistakable emblem of The United States Marines.

Sherman held the tray a little tighter in a manner that got the guard's attention "Marine?" he asked.

"Yeah, 2003-2007," the guard responded.

"Iraq?" Sherman inquired.

"Yup, Battle of Fallujah 2004."

"Me too, small world. Semper fi."

"They don't usually house military in this wing," the guard said.

"I am a special breed," Sherman responded.

"Of course you are." The guard grinned. Sherman turned and placed his tray on the table in his cell. He was surprised when he turned around and saw that the guard was still standing there. The guards would usually hand him his tray and be on their way to the next cell. Sherman turned back towards the guard, but the guard was just standing there. Sherman stepped up to the cell door again. The guard stuck out his hand to shake Sherman's. Sherman knew that this wasn't allowed. Prisoners weren't allowed to touch guards, and guards were not allowed to touch prisoners. But he was a Marine, so Sherman reached his hand out of the cell door window and grasp the guard's hand in a firm shake. The guard tilted their hands so the back of the Sherman's hand was facing upwards. From below, Sherman could feel a tapping and pulsing on his wrist from the guard's outstretched finger. He was so surprised by the gesture, and it all happened so fast that he couldn't comprehend what the message was, but he had a good idea. *E.S.C.A.P.E.*

The guard released Sherman from the handshake and said, "We sure are a special breed, a bond that cannot be broken. We are Marines."